Born in Anderson, Indiana, Gary Lee Edward Kreigh graduated with an accounting degree from Ball State University. He also studied at the University of Indianapolis for Computer Technology and the Gonzaga University for Organizational Development.

Gary uses his thirty-five years in the fields of forensic accounting, fraud examination, and internal auditing to write about corporate and social issues, and experiences that affect ordinary people in extraordinary situations. His experience spans the banking, retail, finance, education, and medical industries. He now juggles his time and residence between New Orleans and Gulf Shores, Alabama.

WHY BIRDS FALL

AIA PUBLISHING

Gary L. Kreigh

To Tanna. Always.

CHAPTER ONE

Callan Morrow sat in his car and let the rain patter against the windshield. He contemplated what he was going to say when his best friend answered his phone.

The call went directly to voicemail, however, so he said simply, "Hey, Red, it's me. Gimme a call when you get a chance."

That wasn't enough. His heart knew it wasn't. He pressed the number again. "Red, it's me. Look, I just wanted to tell you, um, well, I wanted to say I'm sorry."

That wasn't enough, either, but it was going to have to do until Red returned his call—that is, *if* he returned his call, and *if* he was still his best friend.

The phone dropped into Callan's lap. He laid his head back and closed his eyes, listening to the rain continue its relentless pattering. He deserved the rain. He deserved every bit of the agonizing torment the rain symbolized.

He'd let Red down.

What's more, he'd let himself down as well.

He didn't know which was worse. Both caused the same pangs of disappointment in his gut.

He opened his eyes with a start. He didn't remember dozing off, and he certainly hadn't intended to do so, but he must have. He checked his watch; thirty minutes had passed without any recollection of the time going by. He started the car and pulled out of the parking lot.

The drive from downtown Indianapolis to Castleton on the northeast side was cold, slow, and miserable—typical for late October—so he welcomed the warmth of his home. A television in the corner of the family room showed the news. He heard his wife, Terese, in the kitchen, and the sound and smell of bacon sizzling in a skillet permeated his senses—awakening his melancholy spirit for a fleeting moment.

Glad to be home, he called for his wife and listened for her response.

None came.

He glanced toward the television. A reporter gave a news update at the international airport. The urgency of her voice and the anguish on her face—a strange mix of agitation tempered with reverence—drew him in, compelling him to stay watching, but he hadn't embraced his wife yet, and he really needed her hug this evening.

Callan moved undetected through the doorway and approached Terese quietly where she stood at the stove. She sensed his approach and turned her left cheek his way. He kissed it.

"I didn't hear you come in," she said.

"Yeah." He reached into the salad bowl and popped an arugula leaf into his mouth. "You're home early tonight."

A crossword puzzle sat on the counter. Terese must have been working on it while she prepared the meal. He didn't understand how deciphering puzzles could help her wind down after a long day at the physicians' office. And he had no idea how she could renew herself by immersing herself in vocabulary. His idea of mentally detoxing was to flop into his favorite chair and to flip from channel to channel with the remote, staring blindly at a screen of celebrities he recognized, but didn't know by name.

"I didn't get home that much earlier than you," she finally said.

"Where are the boys?"

"Where do you think?"

Their two teenage sons were fairly predictable with their evening schedules. He surmised that Brandon was sitting in the living room of his girlfriend's home, watching television as she finished her homework. Gil, on the other hand, would be with his friend, walking through the woods to the fort they'd built with his tools—tools they never returned to his toolbox.

"I figured you could use a good meal tonight," Terese said thoughtfully.

Callan turned and looked out the large kitchen-nook window as if his doing so had a purpose more important than their conversation.

"So how did it go?" she asked reluctantly.

He didn't answer.

She walked toward him and gently wrapped her arms around his midsection. "I'm sure he's fine," she whispered softly. "I know Red. He understands."

"No, Terese; he can't be fine. There's no way he can be fine. Not this time."

"That can't be true."

"You don't know him like I do. He's been my best bud since grade school. I let him down." Terese tried to interject, but he added quickly, "No, really, I let him down for good this time. There's no getting our relationship back like it was before."

"Cal, that's not true."

"What do you mean it's not true? I betrayed him, Terese. I reneged on a promise that was going to be our livelihood. He lined up a big client for us to meet in Chicago tomorrow, and I backed out on him at the last minute. That's unforgiveable."

Terese stepped back. "Now that's where you're wrong, Cal."

"How?"

"It's wrong to think of this business venture as our livelihood. Our livelihood is what you have at the bank. Resigning your position as an audit executive to go into business with your *best bud* when your sons are about to enter college is not what I call livelihood."

"You didn't let us give it a chance."

"Oh, don't make this out to be my fault, Callan."

"I didn't say it was."

"But it was implied."

"No, I'm just stating a fact. You never really considered it. You said okay at the beginning and then at the last minute changed your mind."

"Because of our livelihood."

"It's called betrayal, Terese."

She turned abruptly and walked back to her skillet.

"Don't give me the cold shoulder, please."

"Then don't use a word like betrayal in front of me," she said without looking back. "It's hurtful enough to hear you say it regarding your best friend, but it's inexcusable to think that I don't feel betrayal as well."

Anger welled in Callan's chest. He wanted desperately to say, "It's not what I did to you, Terese; it's what we did together," but the words would be ignored—or, worse yet, retaliated with more hateful rhetoric.

Besides, her back was turned.

4

The conversation was over.

Callan unraveled the knot in his tie and returned to the family room. He arrived in time to watch an on-the-scene reporter interview a member of the Indianapolis Public Schools' Board of Directors on additional budget cuts. He must have missed the commotion he saw earlier. Not interested in a budget cut story, he picked up the evening newspaper and settled into his recliner to read. He'd barely started reading when the anchor team reappeared. Callan listened and lifted his eyes from the black and white print.

"Back to our lead story this evening from the Indiana State Police post in Lowell, a Midland Airlines commuter originating out of Indianapolis International Airport to Chicago O'Hare has been confirmed down north of the town of Monon. The twin-engine LAN-27 Air Titan dropped from radar screens at O'Hare shortly after four p.m. Central Standard Time. It appears the plane disintegrated upon impact in a bean field south of the Kankakee River and all sixty-four passengers and four crew members were killed. The crash site is located in a rural portion of northwestern Indiana, half a mile from the nearest road. The condition of the soybean field is hampering recovery efforts at this hour. No cause of the crash has been determined, but it is suspected that inclement weather in the Chicago area played a significant role. Authorities have made no further comments, but we will interrupt our regular scheduled programming to bring you additional information as it becomes available. Again, Indiana State Police has confirmed that a Midland Airlines flight, originating out of Indianapolis, is confirmed down with no survivors."

Stunned, Callan sat silently for a moment before collapsing the newspaper into his lap. "Hon, I think Red went to Chicago this afternoon."

"What for?"

"To meet that client I told you about."

"I thought that was tomorrow."

"It is, but he mentioned something about going up tonight when I bailed out on him."

"Well, I'm glad. He'll be better prepared and rested that way. By tomorrow morning, you'll both be back to being bosom buddies again."

"I don't know, Terese. I'm not so sure. Some commuter plane crashed up north this evening with about sixty people on board. I don't feel good about it."

"What airline was it?"

"I dunno. I think it was, no, wait, it was a commuter. Midland."

"That's not him," Terese said convincingly. "He always flies on one of the major airlines, remember? He's a large man. He'd never fit in a commuter, and you know how much he needs his leg room."

"Yeah," Callan replied, wanting to believe. "Just to be sure, I'll give him a call after a bit."

Callan didn't wait.

He hoped he was wrong about Red flying to Chicago. There was only one way to find out. He rose from his brown recliner, went to the phone, and nervously punched in the digits of Red's home phone number. Immediately he received a voice mail recording, asking him to leave a message after the beep. He left a half-panicked request for Red to return his call as soon as he could. No call came, so he called the number again.

That evening, he called four more times with the same results. At three o'clock in the morning, Red's father called to tell him that Red was one of the passengers confirmed on board the ill-fated flight.

By the next morning, reporters and investigators of *The Indianapolis Star* had begun a comprehensive fact-gathering mission of the crash and put faces to the names of the victims.

Callan paced the floor like a hunted animal in search of anything that would relieve his pain. Sometimes, he sat emotionless, staring into the darkness, trying to make sense of a tragedy that made no sense at all.

Following memorial services for the flight crew and passengers at Saints Peter and Paul Cathedral, Callan stood on the curb along Meridian Street and cried for the first time. Terese could barely sustain him. His friend, Larry Southard, ran to them to physically support them both. Callan's unexpected breakdown along the city's main north-south thoroughfare confused even him. He'd never dealt with such grief in his life—a relentless sorrow shrouded by remorse and regret.

Eventually, Callan engrossed himself in detail, putting his audit-examination skills to work for a personal goal. He was determined to peel through the layers of information he'd accumulated from public documents of the National Transportation Safety Board, the French Bureau Enquetes-Accidents, and the French Director General a l'Aviation Civile to get to the source of the accident.

As well as following their progress as best he could, he researched the structural design and engineering of the aircraft. His research into the accident concentrated on a variety of factors, including the information transmitted by the Chicago air-traffic controllers, the climate in the area, and the expertise and conduct of the flight crew during the flight.

He gathered names, as many as he could find of the airline executives, manufacturers, and government inspectors, and researched their backgrounds and any conflicts of interest they had that could've indirectly contributed to the crash.

"Have time for lunch?" Terese asked. "How about we find a place in Broad Ripple? Someplace quiet and simple, just the two of us."

Callan frowned at first, but took the hint. He'd been spending every Saturday like clockwork at the Central Library downtown.

He set his backpack by the door, made a bee-line for his wife, and wrapped his arms tightly around her waist. She accepted his affection warmly and leaned her head back so that his chin could rest against the side of it. For a brief moment, neither of them said anything.

Finally, Terese asked softly, "What's wrong?"

He shook his head.

"No, something's wrong. You haven't been yourself since the accident. These trips to the library seem to be more than a fact-finding mission."

"It's the library. It's not like I'm going to a bar every Saturday afternoon."

"I'm being serious, Cal."

"I'm sorry. I'm okay," he said unconvincingly.

"It's Red, isn't it? You don't have to feel guilty."

"I don't feel guilty."

"It wasn't your fault."

"I know that."

"Then what is it?"

"I don't understand in this day and age how an accident like that could've happened."

"It was ice. The de-icing mechanism failed. It was cold in Chicago that night and it failed. You know that."

"But why? What about the testing results?"

"What testing?"

"Exactly. Testing by the manufacturer. Testing about de-icing. Test results should have detected a problem with that type of aircraft."

"Maybe they did. Maybe something else went wrong or the mechanism on this one plane failed. Cal, sometimes we have to accept that bad things will happen for unknown reasons."

"Do we?"

Terese's gaze darted around the room as if she hoped to find the answer out of nowhere. "Well, I should think," she said, "or else we'd drive ourselves crazy, searching for answers that are so complex and beyond our comprehension that it would consume everything within us. Just like what's happening to you right now."

"So we don't try?"

"I didn't say we don't try. I'm saying that we should accept the facts as they are."

"Something seems wrong with that."

She gave her husband a long, hard look, one he tried to ignore. "And what's so wrong about that?"

"For one, not searching to find answers is a passive way of going through life. I mean, if we've been given the talent, the power, and the resources to seek answers to what we don't understand, it's wrong not to seek them."

"How, Callan? How could it be wrong?"

"By not preventing this sort of thing from happening again."

"That's it?"

"Isn't that enough?"

"Why you?"

"Why not me?"

"For starters, I don't remember you being an engineering expert on commuter jets. I'm thinking that's a good enough reason."

Callan lowered his head. He didn't have an answer to that objection.

Terese backed away, then stopped and regarded him with narrowed eyes. "It's something else, isn't it? It's more than just seeking answers. We've talked about this before."

Callan flinched.

"No, let's talk about it again. Tell me, Cal. It's about the guilt you have over the last conversation you ever had with Red, isn't it?"

"So what if it is?"

"The crash wasn't your fault. It happened. It happened whether you had that conversation with him or not. Don't you understand?"

"Yes, of course, I understand. This isn't an intellectual conflict I'm having. It's something inside, Terese. It's deep inside my gut, and I have to turn this bullshit of a crash into something positive, something better than it was before."

"Whether you know anything about jets or not, is that it?"

"Oh, my god, Terese, you don't understand."

"I'm trying to understand, Cal. I really am, but it's difficult. I'm the type of person who expects things to be right the first time all of the time. I don't want to unravel the mysteries of what is bad in the world and why it's bad. It should be good all of the time."

"Yes, it should, I agree."

"But sometimes it's not. A bird flies, a bird falls. A jet goes up, a jet comes down. That's life."

Callan bit down on his lower lip, then said, "I'll remember that the next time the garbage disposal jams."

"What? I don't see what that has to do with anything."

"It jams. That's life. We don't need to find out why. It happens, and we should accept it. From now on, I'll let it sit as it is—broken and jammed."

"Don't be immature. What's gotten into you? That's so totally different, and you know it."

Callan jerked his head and glared at his wife. "Why is it different, Terese? Because you depend on it? I get that. You depend on a garbage disposal working in our home so when it jams I should find out why and fix it, but Red kinda depended on that jet landing in Chicago, too. So tell me something, Terese. Who's going to fix that?"

CHAPTER TWO

"I'm going out," Callan said one night, grabbing his leather jacket and car keys. It was unseasonably cold.

"Where?" Terese asked. "I just asked the boys to come home to spend some time here for a change."

"I'm meeting, uh, Larry for a couple of drinks, maybe coffee."

"Larry who?"

"You know."

She shook her head.

"Southard."

No response.

"The airline pilot."

Her lower lip tightened with disapproval. "You're not going to talk about that Monon crash again, surely."

"I just have some questions about conduct in the cockpit."

"Callan, what more could you possibly find out? You've been to meetings, read reports and white papers, taken copious notes, and interviewed Larry until he's blue in the face. Where has it led you? You don't know, do you? Well, I'll tell you where. It has led you right back into the crater that damn plane dredged when it crashed."

Callan stammered for a rebuttal that Terese would accept without argument. "I'll be back," he said, ignoring her plea.

Terese disguised her anger by grasping a women's magazine she'd received in the afternoon post, acting as though she didn't care.

He reassured her that he wouldn't be long.

"Just go," she said.

He did.

Callan drove to Larry Southard's home off Dandy Trail through a chilly night and periodic encounters with sleet hitting his windshield.

Larry climbed into the car, rubbing his hands together for warmth. "I'm surprised you were able to get away," he said. "I thought Terese had had enough of this Monon stuff."

Callan kept his eye in the rearview mirror as he backed the car out of the drive. "She has," he said, reflecting back to the rejected look on Terese's face, "but it's not about Monon."

"Oh? So what's it about?"

"Nothing," Callan replied.

"Ah, nothing," Larry mocked. "Yeah, nothing seems to be the root of a lot of my married friends' problems."

"I meant nothing that's any of your business. It's between her and me, something she hasn't accepted yet."

"Then it's something serious."

Callan shrugged and blew the comment off. "We get by. I've learned to listen and to keep my mouth shut."

"Sounds like a healthy solution," Larry chided.

They said little more until they reached a favorite hangout, an open, casual restaurant and lounge overlooking the lake at Eagle Creek.

Callan trusted Larry's expertise and confidence. He always had. Through junior high and high school in St. Joseph, Callan looked up to his friend and admired the self-confidence, almost cockiness, of his abilities. As they grew older, however, Callan realized their friendship balanced each other. Larry's sandy brown hair, clean and smartly styled, bounced energetically around his face while Callan's hair, trimmed and closely cropped, accentuated his conservative banker appearance. Larry was spontaneous and spirit free, often leading the two into mischief; Callan was organized and spirit filled, often serious and professional. Larry was single with no children that he knew about; Callan had been married for years to his college sweetheart, with two children and anxious for grandchildren some day.

Through the years, the balances had served them well.

Callan looked up as their waitress approached their table.

"How you boys doing?" she asked.

"Just coffee, please." He was driving.

Larry ordered alcohol, but when his beer came, he didn't take a sip.

Callan had seen the look on Larry's face before. "Spit it out."

"I wasn't going to say anything."

"Yes, you were, Larry. You and Terese are two peas in a pod, I swear you are. I seem to get quite an earful for two people who never have anything to say, so spit it out then drink your damn beer."

"You gotta get it together, man. I'm telling you as a friend. Somehow you have to find some closure with this

Monon crash or it's going to eat you alive. It's going to ruin your marriage, your friendships, your career, and you."

"How can you talk to me like that? Doesn't it bother you, too? Didn't the crash have any affect on you? You grew up with Red, too, you know."

"Of course it bothers me, but I'm not going to let it control me. I'm going to do something positive with my life. I'm going to make changes for the future as I see fit. I'm not going to live in the past like you. No, Cal, I'm making a change. I'm heading for Chicago."

"Chicago?"

"That's what I said."

"What are you going to do up there?"

"Work my ass off for one thing."

Callan shook his head. "No, tell me."

Larry explained that he'd accepted a high-level position with an executive commuter airline.

"Commuter?"

"Not the same. Don't go there. It's an executive commuter. It's a good opportunity. I want to take it. I know I can make a difference."

Callan laughed. "Well, they say bad things happen to good people. I guess it can work both ways. What airline is it?"

"GrandAire. Heard of it?"

Callan shook his head. "No, I can't say that I have." He paused and thought for a moment. "Wait. Yes, I have. GrandAire, you say?"

"Did you read about them during your research?"

"Yeah, but I don't know why or remember where."

"Good."

"What do you mean good?"

15

"They're pretty much on the up and up—very ethical, interested in doing the right thing. They have exciting new plans. It's good that you don't remember. Keep it that way."

The more Larry talked about his opportunity, the more Callan recalled information associated with commuter airlines in general.

Larry saw the gears churning in his head. "I'm telling you, buddy. Don't be making a mountain out of a molehill. Concentrate on what I said earlier. Get your life back together. GrandAire is one investigation you don't have to sink your teeth into."

"But I think I'll look over some of my material just in case."

"No," Larry said sternly. "I'm moving on. You do the same. Keep your research to yourself. I don't want to hear about it."

CHAPTER THREE

The next month, Callan went to Chicago—not to see Larry, but to attend a four-day public hearing and conference of the National Transportation Safety Board, a large affair held in one of the city's prominent downtown hotels.

Terese surprised Callan by asking to come along. "Not to go to the hearing," she'd said lightheartedly, "but to Chicago. I wouldn't mind going up there—with you, that is."

They met for coffee in the hotel café early in the morning on the last day of the hearing.

"You haven't been bored?" he asked.

She smiled coyly. "I found plenty to do along the Miracle Mile, and when the stores started to bore me, I did my crosswords. Speaking of which, what's a word for an *otismobile*?"

"I don't know."

"I was hoping you would."

"Does elevator fit?"

"It might. Yes, I think it does. I didn't know what an otismobile was."

"The manufacturer. Otis."

"Oh, that would've been good to know."

"I hear you. That's why being here for the hearing and conference has been so helpful. I learned a great deal about manufacturers, vendors, and names associated with the crash. I hope I haven't neglected you."

"No, you've been fine, Callan. I understand why you're here. When I invited myself, I knew what I'd be up against. All I wanted was a free ride. What are you doing later, though? Do you have time for lunch?"

"I was going to catch the keynote session, but how about at the afternoon break, say about two thirty? Does that work? I can meet you here."

Terese agreed. She gave him a light kiss on his forehead and pulled her sunglasses over her eyes before trotting toward the door and the enchantment that awaited her.

Callan watched through the front window as she scurried on the sidewalk. He could tell she was in her element the past four days. The trip had done her good. In spite of his concern that the meetings, panel discussions, and workshops would cut into their free time, she seemed to take it all in stride.

While thinking about his wife, he nearly missed the approach of a middle-aged man to his table. "Please," the man said as Callan reached for his coffee. "Don't let me disturb you. May I have a seat?"

Callan motioned with indifference for him to do so as he took a sip. The coffee was still very hot and not to be wasted.

"Your name is Callan Morrow, is it not?" the man asked.

Callan didn't acknowledge one way or the other.

"My name is Murray Thompson. I'm an acquaintance of your friend, Larry Southard, at GrandAire Airlines."

"Ah!" Callan replied. "Larry must be making quite a mark in town for someone who works with him to seek me out."

"I don't work with him, Mr. Morrow."

"But—"

"I used to, but no longer. I don't want to give you the wrong idea. I'm not a colleague or a friend of Mr. Southard. I've been with him in meetings he's attended, but I doubt he knew I was there."

"And why is that?"

"I'm no longer associated with GrandAire, but I was there long enough to know your name was mentioned in various conversations within the company."

"Whatever for?"

"That will become clear very soon. You're right in one regard. I sought you out. I looked into you. I knew from my inquiry of you that I needed to meet and talk with you."

"I don't understand."

"Don't be alarmed. We're on the same track."

"Look, Mr. ..."

"Thompson."

"Whatever. I'm not sure where this is going or what my friend, Larry Southard, has said or implied, but I'm not comfortable continuing our conversation."

"Fair enough. Then let me give you something to read, and I'll be on my way." At that, the man removed a manila folder from his satchel and slid it across the table.

"What's this?" Callan asked.

"Information you can use, that I hope you will use."

Callan tried to slide the folder back toward his unwanted guest, but the man placed his hand on top of the folder to stop its progress. "If you don't take it, Mr. Morrow, I caution you that hundreds, maybe thousands of lives will be at stake. I don't believe you're the type of man that would want that to happen."

Callan frowned. "What's in the folder?"

"It'll be self-explanatory when you read its contents. Not at first, mind you, but you'll find it extremely helpful and interesting as you progress in your investigation."

"How do you know that I've been investigating anything?"

"Haven't you? If not, you seem to spend an exhorbitant amount of time and energy on an air crash in a remote part of Indiana that would otherwise be overlooked by experts."

"This hearing and conference proves you wrong on that. I've gleaned a lot of information these past four days. I can't think of one sound reason why I should take this folder. You're not being forthcoming with me, and I have no reason to trust you."

"That's correct; you don't, but you will."

Callan shook his head.

"I believe you will, Mr. Morrow. I don't believe for one minute that you'd let your friend, Red, die in vain."

Callan felt the blood rush from his face.

"Do me a favor, Mr. Morrow. Take the folder. Do what you want with it, but keep it confidential. Give it to no one. Trust no one with it. If you decide to dispose of the folder without reading its contents all I ask is that you destroy the information by shredding it completely."

Callan stared at the man, but didn't say anything.

"Good," Thompson said. "There's one other thing. I suspect very strongly that they will be offering you a position."

"Who will be?"

"The executives at GrandAire."

"Whatever for?"

"For reasons I won't discuss with you here. In a nutshell, however, you've made a name for yourself through your friend, and with the questions you've asked in these conference discussions."

"I don't see how my random comments here and there would be cause to take notice."

Thompson shrugged. "You sell yourself short, I'm afraid." He stood to go.

"With what you've just told me and gave me, why should I consider a proposal from GrandAire?" Callan asked.

"Because, Mr. Morrow, you are a man of integrity. Most of all, you're a man of pride, and I don't believe your pride can take another professional mistake. What I'm saying is that if you don't take my folder of information, and if you turn down any offer that GrandAire extends to you, it will be the biggest mistake of your life." Thompson leaned so close to Callan that Callan could smell stale coffee on his breath. "Yes, even bigger than the mistake you made with your friend, Red, on the day he died, and even bigger than the mistake you made with your wife. Do I make myself clear? I do hope so for your sake, Mr. Morrow. I do hope so."

Callan tried not to look too anxious when Thompson left his table, but beads of perspiration formed rapidly and slid down his temple.

Mistake with Red? Mistake with my wife? How could he possibly know?

Callan wanted to fling the mysterious folder open and read its contents immediately, but he didn't want to appear too eager in the event that the mysterious Mr. Thompson was watching from a distance.

He took a deep breath and decided he'd had enough of the hearings. Enough of the conference sessions and workshops. Enough pontificating and analyzing. Suddenly, before his very eyes sat the hope of tangible evidence he'd sought with his months of research and toil.

Callan moved aside the other documents on the table and placed the folder squarely in front of him. He wondered who was watching and who had as much interest in the contents of the folder as he did. He opened the folder slowly and read an introductory note that Thompson had written. It didn't say anything substantive, so he turned it over and began to read.

The morning conference sessions started, but Callan didn't go. In fact, he missed the keynote speaker he'd wanted to listen to. When Terese returned from her day's adventure, Callan was still reading.

She plopped a sack of purchases onto a chair beside him. "You haven't moved, have you?" she said, teasing lightly.

Callan lifted his head. "What time is it?"

"Two thirty, silly. Have you really been sitting here all this time?"

"No, of course not," he jested, trying to hide the fact that her observation was correct.

"Is there one more session this afternoon?" she asked.

"Yes, I believe so, then we can head back to Indy if you like."

"That's fine, whatever works for you. I'm in no hurry. Do you have time for a cup of coffee with me?"

He closed the folder and hid it in between two other folders. "Plenty of time." Callan stood to get the coffee for them.

"Sit still," she said. "I wouldn't want to peel your moltened butt from your chair. My treat. I'll be back in a jif. Oh, and if you're in a good mood, I wouldn't look in the store sacks while I'm gone if I were you." She left for the café counter.

Callan smiled, but he didn't have time to look into the sacks anyway. Another man walked to his table, pulled out a chair, and sat down.

Callan felt more alarmed this time than the last. This man had a darker demeanor about him than the Thompson fellow. Callan presumed he was younger than the gray hair made him appear. The creases across his forehead and around the edges of his mouth made him look haggard and unpleasant.

"I'll make this brief," the man said. "You're a very interesting man, Mr. Morrow, and I'm interested in interesting people. You've asked some very poignant questions these past few days. They've been spot on, I've observed. I suspect members of the National Transportation Safety Board have taken notice as well."

"It wasn't my intention to get noticed."

"And that's what's interesting about you."

"How so?"

"Why go to such extremes to get noticed if that wasn't your intention?"

Callan frowned. "Who are you?"

The man extended his hand.

Callan didn't take it. "Just tell me who you are. That's all the niceties I want."

"My name is Alan Cavanaugh. I'm Senior Vice President of Operations at GrandAire Airlines here in Chicago. That should explain who I am. I work with your friend, Larry Southard."

"Work with him how?"

"He reports to me directly."

"I see. Now that I know who you are, what do you want?"

Cavanaugh grinned. "I like this. This is nice. No bullshit; straight to the point."

"Then I'd appreciate if you got there. What do you want?"

Callan looked up and saw Terese approaching cautiously with the coffees. He shook his head subtly to let her know not to come near. It wasn't a good time.

She got the hint, set the coffees on an adjacent table, and sat down, then she uncapped the plastic lid on her cup, her gaze fixed on her husband and the ominous-looking man.

"What I want, Mr. Morrow, is information."

"You'll have to explain. What? Why?"

"I'm a busy man," he said. "All properties and facilities report to me. I'm not just talking about our main operations at O'Hare. I'm talking about the facilities we have in Minnesota, too. I manage the facilities at Gary, Midway, Milwaukee, Detroit Metro, and Lambert. That includes airport gates, ticket counters, office space, and maintenance facilities. On top of that, I've got to prepare and review professional service and lease agreements and maintenance contracts. I have to ensure that the terms of those contracts and agreements are being administered properly. While this is going on, I'll have something to resolve with at least one or two of those facilities at any single point in time. In a nutshell, Mr. Morrow, my job is a freaking hell in a handbasket. So you see, information is very valuable to me. That's why I want information, Mr. Morrow."

"Are you offering me a job, Mr. Cavanaugh?" Callan asked bluntly.

The COO stared into Callan's face. A brief moment of silence passed before he said, "I hear you're a banker."

"Yes, sir."

"And you're asking if I'm going to offer you a job to help me make sense of all this? A banker?"

Callan hesitated before delivering a candid statement of truth. "Probably not anything you can't do for yourself."

"If I can do it myself, then why do I need you? Why would I offer you a job?"

"Are you going to do it yourself?"

"Hell, no. I just told you the helluva mess I'm in."

"That's why you need me."

Cavanaugh smiled.

"I'll admit," Callan continued, "I've never worked for an airline, never flown a plane, and never fixed a jet engine. Don't want to and never will, but I have reviewed contracts and maintenance agreements for problems. If I'm unsure of what I'm looking at, I'll find the resources and references to learn. At the very least, I can give you enough comfort so you can sleep at night."

"I hate when auditors say that. I've never read an auditor's report that helped me sleep at night. You people don't write them that way, so why do you keep saying that? It's nothing but a cliché. It's bullshit. Let me tell you this. If I'm sleeping soundly at night, I can assure you it's not because of an audit report."

Callan sat back in his chair and looked at the COO with distrust.

"Tell you what," Cavanaugh said. "We can talk about the job, Mr. Morrow, but what I'm offering you is cash for some information you have."

"Information?"

"Don't be coy and stupid. You were given a folder this morning. I suspect very highly that the folder contained intellectual property that belongs to GrandAire Airlines. We take the security of our intellectual property very seriously and prosecute to the fullest extent of the law those who mishandle or take that property without authorization. Have I made myself clear?"

"Very, and I wish I could help you, but the folder was returned to the person who gave it to me."

"I doubt that very seriously. You barely went to the bathroom since this morning, Mr. Morrow. I don't see when that transfer of information could have occurred."

"Did you check the bathroom after I left?"

Alan Cavanaugh didn't respond.

"It's probably no longer there," Callan said, "but I read its contents, and I determined that it meant very little to me. I texted the person who gave it to me, and I told that person where the folder could be retrieved. The bathroom, Mr. Cavanaugh. I said it could be found in the bathroom. I wouldn't worry about its contents. There was very little intellectual property in the folder, if you ask me. I do know intellectual property when I see it, Mr. Cavanaugh."

"And I know a bullshit lie when I hear it, Mr. Morrow. I'll leave you now. I wouldn't take this conversation lightly. It would be a mistake."

This time, it was Callan who grinned.

When he left, Terese picked up the coffees and walked quickly to Callan, who sat taking deep breaths and wiping beads of sweat from his brow.

"Who the hell was that?" she asked.

"Terese, I'm going to tell you honestly that he was no one of any concern to us. He was someone interested in what I learned at this hearing and conference because I asked a lot of questions and took a lot of notes, but I told him I didn't know any more than what he heard himself."

Terese watched her husband with narrowed eyes, as if trying to process what he'd said.

"What's the matter?" he asked.

She shook her head.

"Terese," he said curtly, wanting an answer.

"He scared me, Callan. I couldn't hear what you two talked about, but his disheveled look, the way he peered at you, that laugh he had. I didn't like any of it. He scared me."

"That's it?"

"Isn't that enough?"

"Not when I believe there is more you want to say."

She didn't respond.

"Terese, tell me. What else is the matter?"

She looked sternly at her husband. "I'm not sure I believe your story."

CHAPTER FOUR

The midday sun broke through the branches of the trees surrounding the Morrows' home. Callan and his sons spent the majority of the morning cleaning debris from the backyard caused by a recent outbreak of violent storms.

Terese sipped coffee with two of her co-workers, enjoying the sun's warmth streaming through the windows as they watched the guys work. She grimaced as her husband placed goggles over his eyes and lowered a chainsaw into the lifeless limb of a sycamore damaged by the torment.

"So what were we talking about?" Ellen prompted.

"I don't remember," Terese replied, mentally moving her sons away from the grinding power of the saw.

"Something about the church," Candice said. "Mission work, I think. So you're going to do mission work, Terese?"

"What? Heavens, no. What made you say that?"

It was a fair question given the amount of time Terese devoted to talking about doing something charitable with her life—that is, before she got sidetracked by her husband's chainsaw.

"What I think Candice is saying, Terese," Ellen said, "is if the mission field interests you, you should give it a try someday."

"Oh, well, I don't know; I guess maybe someday. To be honest, I haven't given it much thought." Terese glanced through the window. The boys had nearly finished stacking the pile of wood.

The phone rang, and Terese excused herself to answer it. Callan's friend, Larry Southard, wanted to talk to Callan. "Just a minute," Terese said. "Don't hang up, Larry. He'll be here shortly." She hurried to the back door to usher Callan in from his lumberjacking. "And, boys, you better come in, too."

Callan entered through the back, dusted his hands on his pants, and motioned that he'd take Larry's call in the den. Terese left him to it and returned to her friends.

Callan picked up the phone in the den and answered with his usual greeting, "Hey." He settled into the chair behind the desk.

"Hey, man. Remember when I said I was coming to Chicago to work harder than I've ever worked? It's true, man. I don't think I've worked so hard in my life, but I love it."

Callan smiled, glad to hear his friend was happy and doing well.

"I want you to come up here."

"I will. We'll take a weekend and be up for a visit soon."

"No, man, I mean I want you to come up here. There's a guy I want you to meet."

"Who? Where? At GrandAire?"

"Yeah, I told him about you and what you do."

"I may have met him."

"When was that?"

"The Safety Board meetings in Chicago. Is his name Cavanaugh?"

"What? You met Cavanaugh? That's my boss."

"Yeah, I know. Nice guy you work for. Is it him you want me to meet?"

"No, I was talking about Burris. Tony Burris, the CFO. He needs to hire an internal auditor. He told the board of directors that they'd started the process of trying to find someone, but they hadn't. He's in a bind. Besides, I told them you knew something about the airline industry, and he said he could use someone like you."

"Larry, I don't know jack about the airline industry."

"Well, technically, you do. You know more than most people through your research on the Monon crash. I told them your research was quite impressive."

Callan reflected back on his conversations in Chicago with Cavanaugh and the man who gave him the folder. "You may have said too much, Lare."

"Just bits of info here and there. Hey, look, as much as I've blown you shit about your research in the past, I kinda used some of it to impress them. I owe you a beer for it, by the way. They're interested in hearing more."

Cal shook his head. He didn't consider amateur sleuthing into the cause of a plane crash as experience that would impress a potential employer. He also didn't think his conversation with Alan Cavanaugh was a good first impression for a job interview. "Look, I appreciate it, Lare, but, well, I'm pretty good at the bank here, and I don't know about moving my family, just, well, just because someone I don't know is in a bind."

"I know, I know," Larry conceded. "I understand, but the situation's not like that, not all of it. Just get up here and meet the guy and see what he has to say. If all goes well, they'll make it worth your effort. I promise you. He's interested in meeting you and talking about what you know."

The conversation ended, and Cal sank into the back of his office chair, thinking of Chicago. He liked Chicago. Terese liked Chicago, but he couldn't see how the thought of moving would appeal to her. After all, there was more to living in Chicago than the Miracle Mile.

The idea of talking to the people at GrandAire did interest him, though, if for no other reason than to see why they cornered him at the Safety Board hearing. The conversation with Cavanaugh, while creepy and threatening in one way, was also flattering and intriguing in another. Perhaps he could use the experience to his advantage.

He was tempted to accept Larry's invitation.

Callan pulled open the lower right-hand drawer of his desk and pulled a folder, identified lightly in pencil with the word *Monon* from the bottom of the pile—the folder Mr. Thompson had handed him at the hearing. He'd lied to Alan Cavanaugh, hadn't told Thompson to retrieve the folder from the bathroom because it had no value. On the contrary, the folder contained an immense array of facts and details Callan hadn't previously considered. He hadn't acted upon the information, though. So far, he'd only had time to review it in depth, outlining what he would do when he had the chance to make a serious move against the names listed in the folder.

Perhaps GrandAire was that chance.

He tucked the folder back behind the personal documents and closed the drawer, leaving the folder in its safe haven while he decided what to do.

CHAPTER FIVE

"It suits you, I'll grant you that," Terese said of the job in Chicago as they prepared for bed two nights later.

Callan had told her about the job opportunity that afternoon, but she'd responded then with silence. He didn't want to talk about it now, though. Callan didn't like talking about life-changing topics right before bed. He wasn't like his wife, who liked to get what was on her mind off her chest before climbing under the sheets. Callan yawned, and tried to sneak to the bathroom, hoping Terese would catch the hint.

She patted her hand on the mattress. "Wait, Cal. Come here. Sit down for a second."

He did so reluctantly.

"If you decide you'd like to interview up in Chicago, I think you should."

Callan struggled for words, surprised by the announcement.

"Don't get me wrong," she added. "I don't like it—I really don't—but I know you'll always wonder about it if you don't interview at least."

"What if it goes like before?"

"Before what?"

"You know, Terese. Like other ventures. What if it goes wrong, and I lose the job. What if we lose money? How are you going to handle that?"

"This is different."

"Not by much."

"Yes, it is. My problem isn't that you'll take this job if it's offered and it turns out bad. My problem is that your motive for wanting this job is wrong."

Callan rose from the bed and finished his path to the bathroom. "There's no motive, Terese. It's an opportunity, and it may be a good fit, just as you say."

A noise, like a snap of a twig or branch, came from below their bedroom window.

Callan peaked around the bathroom's doorway with a foamy toothbrush in his mouth and repeated, "There's no motive, hon."

Terese stood facing the window, though she addressed her husband. "But I feel there's something you're not telling me."

"Like what?"

"Like your conversation with that man I saw talking with you in Chicago. It was an odd encounter. I couldn't hear very much, but I could see everything. I saw every expression he made and every reaction on your face. I didn't like it, and if one of the reasons you're going to Chicago is because he threatened you in some way, you need to reconsider, Cal."

"Threatened me? Oh, Terese, your imagination is astonishing sometimes."

"Don't berate how I feel, Callan. You're not telling me all the facts. What is my imagination supposed to do without facts? I have to know if you're being honest with me. That's why I'm so angry about our past. You weren't honest with me at all that the business wasn't going well, and when it happened, when it collapsed, I was in total shock. Well, I can tell you one thing, Callan Morrow, I saw the look on that man's face, and I don't plan to be in total shock about that."

"Okay, okay, I get it." He unbuttoned his Dockers, let them drop to the floor and slid between the sheets before realizing that he should fold his pants neatly and place them on an adjacent chair if he wanted his wife to believe that he understood her comments.

"You have to give me something, Cal."

Callan did the required folding, then climbed back into bed, rumpling the covers on top of him. He plopped his head on the pillow and stared at the ceiling, hoping the conversation was at an end. The panging memories of the past and the haunting premonitions of the future grew too much. Sleep was his only escape now.

The two said little more as Terese finished her nightly routine and climbed into bed beside him. She draped her arm over his body and nestled her head on his chest. He pulled her close.

"Is the back door locked?" she asked.

"Mhmm."

He woke sometime later to Terese poking him in the side and whispering his name. Her head still rested upon his chest.

He didn't respond.

"Cal," she whispered again, this time louder, poking harder.

He opened his eyes and tried to focus in the darkness, but had trouble doing so. Very little light shone through the window.

"Do you hear something?" Terese whispered. "It's downstairs."

"What?" he asked, shaking out the cobwebs from his confused brain. He did detect a noise, but wasn't sure what it was.

"Downstairs," she repeated.

Callan removed the covers and slipped out of bed, grabbing the pants he'd folded on the chair.

"Call the police," he whispered as he left the room. "Wake the boys and hide."

Callan crept on the balls of his feet down the hallway toward the stairs, feeling the muscles in his legs tense. The wind blew gently through the shrubs, causing their branches to hit the side of the house and add to the confusing conglomeration of noises. By the time he reached the stairs and peered down into the foyer below, Callan couldn't hear anything unusual. No ominous shadows lurked in doorways or cast themselves upon the walls. He stopped to listen, hoping that the weather explained what he and Terese had heard from the bedroom.

The rustling of papers and the opening of what sounded like a cabinet drawer in the den confirmed his fears, however. An intruder had entered their home. But what could he do with his empty hands? He had no weapon, nothing to act as a club. His bare feet were useless as a defense against an intruder. Callan turned back towards the bedrooms to find something of use. The shadowy silhouette of a figure in the middle of the hallway startled him.

"I'm coming with you," the shadow whispered in his oldest son, Brandon's, voice.

"No," Callan mouthed emphatically. "Get back with your mother, and make sure she and your brother are safe. I mean it."

Callan sensed his son taking a deep breath. "Then take this." He held something long and solid in front of him.

Callan grabbed the object, a *Louisville Slugger.* Empowered now, he turned toward the stairway. The noise from the ransacking of his office heightened. It unnerved Callan to think the intruder cared little about being detected. He couldn't imagine what the burglar was after—money, investment certificates, bonds, what? He and Terese kept nothing like that in the house, and if they did, he wouldn't keep them in the den because it was such an obvious location for burglars to invade.

He gripped the bat tighter and descended the last steps on the stairway. Suddenly, the noises stopped completely.

Callan stopped also.

Silence.

No sound came from the den.

The sudden stillness confused him. Did the man sense he'd been detected and now waited patiently for Callan to come to him? Or had he located what he was looking for and was making a plan of escape?

Where're the police?

He thought of Terese and the boys and made the sign of the cross across his chest as he took another step toward the landing. At the bottom of the stairs, Callan raised his bat in preparation for a fight, but he still couldn't hear anything coming from the room, and he wondered how he could defend himself when he could hardly see a thing. The house was virtually void of light.

He turned the corner.

Umpf!

Callan bumped head on with a figure bolting through the doorway. The man bashed Callan against the wall as he maneuvered his way through the darkness to find a way out. Callan fell onto the steps, but jumped quickly to his feet, fueled by the adrenalin in his veins. He raised the bat to meet his nemesis and swung just as the large-framed man kicked him squarely in the gut, catapulting him backward against the wall.

The man lunged for an open space, but Callan, ignoring the pain, rebounded off the wall, and wielding his bat, struck the man squarely on his back, forcing a vulgar expletive from the intruder's throat. The blow threw the man against a table, knocking everything on it to the floor.

A small end table flew past Callan, barely missing him. He reeled back in shock. The man lunged, wrapped his large hands around Callan's neck and squeezed as they crashed against the opposite wall. A picture fell from its hook and shattered against an adjacent lamp. The hands released, and Callan fell to the floor, gasping for air. Footsteps faded toward the back of the house. A door opened and closed and suddenly the house was silent once again.

Callan rose to a sitting position and took several deep breaths, relieved the man had gone. Exhaustion overwhelmed him. He wasn't sure he could stand. He reached his hand up and touched his head, feeling a sore spot, a bruise he didn't remember receiving. The skirmish was a blur. Too much had happened too quickly to fully understand what had happened. Confusion took hold. He didn't know what to do. It didn't matter, though.

The intruder had gone.

They were alive.

~

Two days later, the afternoon sun shone brightly through the windows of the front room, and three full suitcases lay near the door. They all belonged to Terese.

Ellen Holloway had offered the family a place to stay as a sanctuary until they could finish the repairs to the house and gather their bearings. Terese and the boys had accepted immediately.

She finished cleaning the kitchen before she left, wiping down the countertops with soft-scrub soap and water. A plastic bag of used paper towels and other cleaning items lay to her left. She lifted an edge of the bag and threw the towel in with the rest. A rush of sadness filled her, memories that could not be suppressed. She took a deep breath and closed the bag.

She didn't want to feel sad.

She didn't want to feel regret.

She just wanted out.

Ellen's invitation was a godsend. Terese had made up her mind the minute the police left the house that she was going to leave. It angered her that someone had the audacity to enter their home and encroach upon their personal belongings. It frightened her, though, that nothing in the home had been taken. She feared the intruder might return to look for what he came to get the first time, but didn't find.

Terese knew Callan was sitting in the middle of the living room, waiting for orders from her that it was time to load the car. She was glad he'd decided not to make the temporary move with them to Ellen's, because she was angry at him, too. She'd told him that his decision to accept an interview at GrandAire immediately following the break-in was hasty and lacked sensitivity and compassion. Even though Callan touted the job as a great financial opportunity for the family, the decision provided little solace to her and left her with more questions than answers.

Before loading the car, Terese tried to avoid a final word with her husband. She maintained a safe distance emotionally, but tried to listen to him just the same. She didn't listen long, however. Terese had heard everything he had to say before—that in spite of outward appearances, his love for her was the reason he needed to do what he needed to do.

She didn't confirm his words. She wanted to believe them, but couldn't. All she said was, "I suppose you want me to say something hopeful like this isn't a big deal, and we'll make it through somehow. I can't, though, Cal, and I won't." When he didn't say anything, she added, "Yes, well, I better get going." She turned to leave, then suddenly turned back to face him, determined and angry. "I just want you to know one thing. I'm not the one who's following some will to accomplish something that seems to be better left undone. I'm not the one who has to make a choice, so watching me go isn't about me, Callan. I want you to know that."

He placed his index finger on her lips so she wouldn't say anything more and let her go.

After Terese and the boys had left, Callan entered the empty house and meandered to the den where he eyed the mayhem of his once-orderly domain. All this destruction, and the burglar took nothing. Callan must have thwarted the attempt, the police said. He walked to his desk, stepping over piles of papers and office accessories that had once sat on its surface. He pulled his chair upright from the floor and sat uncomfortably amidst the chaos, then he opened the lower right-hand drawer and looked inside.

He drew a deep breath. The police were wrong. Callan hadn't thwarted a theft at all. Terese was wrong, too. Whoever broke into their house would not be back. Despite everyone's original conclusions, the intruder had taken what he came to get.

Callan cursed and slammed the desk drawer shut. His folder, *Monon,* was missing.

CHAPTER SIX

Callan made his way through the crowded lounge of Viva, Larry's favorite restaurant in Chicago. He'd arranged for Callan to meet a member of GrandAire's senior management.

Callan sensed he had the look of a plowboy in the city, timid and awestruck minus the straw sticks stuck behind his ear. He smiled, though, as Larry approached, impressed by his pilot friend's tall, solid build and smart dark suit with a striped red tie. Expensive links clasped the French cuffs of a white tailored shirt. What goes around, comes around, Callan thought. Larry had often teased Callan about the bank's strict dress code to which he'd been forced to adhere. How ironic that Larry was now an exact replica of the target of his previous jokes.

The two hugged briefly and shook hands, relishing their friendship. Larry's glowing smile showed he was genuinely pleased that Callan had agreed to meet him.

Larry ordered a Seven and Seven for each of them, and they leaned against the granite top of the bar, careful not to crowd those occupying the stools along the front. He turned to Callan and said, "The guy you'll be meeting tonight at dinner is GrandAire's Chief Financial Officer."

"What's his name?"

"Merle Burris. Call him Tony. He doesn't go by his first name."

The bartender leaned over the bar and sat their drinks in front of them.

Callan lifted his glass and proposed a toast on Larry's behalf. He took a welcome sip and savored the bold taste. "What's he looking for, this Burris guy?"

Larry hesitated as if he didn't know the answer.

The couple seated on bar stools next to them headed off to their table for dinner, and Larry motioned for Callan to sit. "How's Terese with all this?" he asked, ignoring Callan's original question.

"She's fine."

"Just fine? I thought she'd be thrilled with the opportunity to live in Chicago."

Callan nodded and slowly stirred the ice cubes in his drink with a swivel stick. "Things are up in the air with us right now, Lare." He took a sip and set his glass on the bar.

"What does that mean?"

"Like I said, not going that well. My Monon research put a wedge between us."

"Monon did that? Really? Wasn't a wedge already there? I mean, with what happened with her father's money and all."

"Stop it," Callan implored. "Not here, not now. I don't need to hear that right now, okay? Not from Terese, not from you."

"Okay, okay, I'm just saying because I need to know. Are you up for this?"

"Up for what?"

"This move, this job."

Callan shrugged as if to ask why not.

42

"Because I want you up here to make a difference. I believe in this company and the service we're providing. I want to see it prosper and succeed. I want to see opportunities expand for the two of us that wouldn't have come otherwise. I believe you can help make it happen, buddy."

Callan winced. He needed another drink.

"What's the matter?"

"Nothing, it's just that, well, that's what Red said to me when he asked me to go into business with him. That didn't work out so well, did it? That's what I said to Terese when we took her dad's money, and I blew it. That didn't work out so well, either, did it? You get it now? I can't have it happen again."

"It won't. Listen, you can help this airline reach its objectives and make a name for yourself, but you gotta be in the game. You gotta have your head on straight."

"I'm okay."

"No, seriously, Cal. I want to know you're okay working for an airline."

Callan suddenly realized that his friend had the same concerns as Terese. Would his obsessive passion to get to the bottom of the LAN-27 crash at Monon hinder his ability to work successfully for the company?

Callan looked him in the eye and replied, "I'm okay. Working for an airline will give me an insight and understanding of the industry. Maybe I'll make a difference as a result of it, you never know. One never knows about these things, but one thing is for certain. You don't have to worry about me. You don't have to worry about Terese and me, either. We'll be fine in the long run. We'll be just fine."

Larry didn't have time for a response to Callan's adamant affirmation. He slid off his stool and gestured Callan to rise to meet the man with the olive face who approached the bar. "Mr. Burris," he said to the man, "I hope traffic wasn't too bad for you this evening. May I introduce you?"

The CFO extended his arm, shook Callan's hand firmly, and smiled broadly. "So this is the auditor you've been telling me about. It's my pleasure, Mr. Morrow. Tell me our table's ready, Larry."

"Yes, sir, right this way."

"Excellent. I'm eager to get started. We should have lots to talk about, Mr. Morrow, don't you think?"

Callan noticed a glisten in the executive's eye.

The trio enjoyed a delicious meal and conversation about GrandAire and Callan's career. Tony Burris asked pointed questions, and Callan responded professionally and honestly without embellishing.

"I think we accomplished a great deal, Callan," Burris concluded as they nursed their after-dinner drinks. "I'll be happy to forward my recommendation regarding hiring you to our CEO, Hamilton Perry, and others on the executive team."

Promptly at nine the next morning, Hamilton Perry's administrative assistant, Velma Hofmeyer, escorted Callan to the chief executive's office.

Hamilton Perry looked important sitting behind his mahogany desk deep within the confines of his leather chair. The man in his early sixties appeared to have made looking important his living. He formally introduced himself as he walked around the desk to shake Callan's hand. His voice resonated in a rich, low, masculine tone that exuberated confidence and poise. Even Mr. Perry's silvery gray hair gave him a distinguished and respected look.

"Please sit down," he said, pointing to an oval mahogany conference table topped with plate glass.

Callan placed a leather-bound notebook on the glass top and thanked his host.

"Mr. Burris talked very highly of you, young man," Hamilton said immediately. "You made quite an impression on him last night. I'm sure he's discussed with you why it's so important for us to maintain credibility with our investors and the business community. There are several important initiatives we want to pursue over the next few months. The establishment of an audit function will help us sustain them."

Hamilton's administrative assistant interrupted him briefly by entering the office with a tray of coffee, ice water, hot water, and Earl Grey tea bags. Velma picked a porcelain cup from the tray and set it in front of Callan. Without saying a word, she looked at him and waited patiently for him to respond with what he'd like.

"Coffee, please; cream."

Velma smiled politely, poured Callan's coffee and whitened the Columbian blend with Half and Half. Hamilton Perry didn't need to say anything. Of course, she'd know exactly how he preferred his coffee—black, a little sugar. She prepared it and left the room as she came—ceremoniously.

As if the performance of bringing in the coffee and tea was a preface to what he was about to say, Hamilton stirred his coffee gently with a silver spoon, but he had very little of substance to discuss. It appeared to Callan that Hamilton was more interested in small talk and emphasizing GrandAire's high integrity and ethical practices than he was about learning of Callan's professional expertise.

Was he not interested in what value Callan could bring to the company, or was his mind made up before the interview began and the discussion was moot? Callan couldn't tell.

What Callan did know was that he was glad to get out of Hamilton Perry's office. He took the elevator to the smartly decorated office suite of Carol Chambers. Although a member of the executive team, the senior vice president preferred her office to be with her employees of the Marketing and Public Relations Division rather than isolated from them like the executives on Mahogany Row. Chambers greeted Callan with the poise, politeness, and energy one would expect from a leader whose job was to promote and market the proper image of an executive travel airline. He liked her immediately.

Chambers joined Callan at the table situated in front of her desk where he'd taken a seat. She moved the floral centerpiece to one side, presumably so she could relate to him better and study his body language.

"I understand you've had a chance to meet the rest of our management team," she said pleasantly, opening a folder on the table containing his resume and credentials.

"Yes," Callan replied, "everyone but Mr. Cavanaugh."

Chambers jotted a couple of notes on Callan's resume before looking up to say, "Yes, but that won't be necessary today."

"Why is that?"

"I understand he's already met you."

Callan laughed. "That's true, but I would hardly consider our meeting an interview."

"Doesn't matter, really. He was impressed just the same."

A timid knock at the door interrupted their discussion. Velma Hofmeyer poked her head through the open crack.

Chambers acknowledged that it was okay for her to enter.

Velma didn't, though. "Excuse me, Ms. Chambers, but Mr. Perry was inquiring if Mr. Morrow would be available for a meeting at one thirty with Mr. Dunham, Chairman of the Board. It seems that Mr. Dunham is in the building, and Mr. Perry would like him to meet our candidate. May I tell them you're available, Mr. Morrow?"

"Absolutely," Callan said.

"Splendid."

Chambers watched the dutiful assistant close the door behind her. To Callan's surprise, Chambers' pleasant demeanor dissipated as she did so. Callan tried to read what was behind the glare.

Rather than saying anything, Chambers stood and moved away from the table and chair. She said coolly, "May I walk you to where you will meet Mr. Dunham?"

Based upon his opening comments, Zane Dunham—a stately gentleman, early sixties, with white hair—had a good knowledge of an audit function and its objectives. He told Callan that quarterly reporting to the audit committee and annual submission of a master audit plan were vital. The first meeting was scheduled for December. Additional meetings would be placed on the agenda as necessary, with advance notice to Velma Hofmeyer, who served as recorder for the meetings. Those were his basic expectations.

"Has management discussed staffing with you?" Dunham asked. "If not, then I'll get with Hamilton right away to make sure you're covered. I can't have you doing grunt work when there's so much to do from an executive level." He sat back in his seat and added, "I agree with Tony Burris' assessment. I talked with him about you earlier, and it looks as if you and GrandAire will make a good fit. I'll talk to Hamilton Perry by the end of the day. I expect you should be hearing something from human resources very soon. Sound fair enough?"

More than fair, Callan thought. He didn't expect the process to be this smooth and fast. It was as if his hiring had been pre-arranged and his presence today was just a formality.

CHAPTER SEVEN

Three days later, an offer from Celia Hart, GrandAire's Vice President of Human Resources, came by phone. Callan accepted the offer immediately for two reasons. First, the salary and bonus benefits were significantly more than the minimum he needed to make the move to Chicago worth his effort. In fact, they were extraordinarily more than he thought the position to be worth. Second, and more importantly, Terese refused to accept any of his telephone calls to her cell phone or to Ellen's home landline. She used Ellen and the boys as go-betweens. He didn't know what it meant, but he knew it wasn't good.

Brandon and Gil stopped by the house one evening when they heard about his new job. A warm southerly breeze moved through the trees where Callan and Brandon sat in lawn chairs. Brandon played catch with his cell phone by pitching it into the air in spite of his father's warning that if he dropped it, the cost of replacement would be his to bear.

Gil stayed inside, remaining quiet and reserved. He turned on the television and lay on the couch, removing himself from any conversation between his older brother and father.

Callan tried twice to interrupt Brandon's conversation about visiting Chicago so he could go into the house to talk with Gil, but his attempt to leave was cut short when Brandon mentioned his mother.

"I don't know what's gotten into her, Dad. She doesn't want you here, but she doesn't want you to go, either. What's up with that?"

"I don't know. Is she doing okay?"

"I guess. Want me to ask her?"

"No," Callan replied curtly. "I was asking for your observation."

"So what are you going to do?"

"I'm going to give her some space. That's all I can do."

Brandon huffed and resumed pitching his cell phone into the air.

"What about Gil?" Callan asked.

"What about him?"

"How's he doing?"

The young man looked reflectively at the door leading into the living area where Gil flipped channels on the television. "He's having a tough time, I think."

"How long has he been like this?"

"Pretty much the whole time."

"The whole time what?"

Brandon looked puzzled.

"I'm sorry. Stupid question," Callan replied before his son could answer. "Hey, do you mind running over to that place in Nora to order a pizza so I can have a word with your brother? We'll consider it supper."

"Sure. He likes pepperoni, you know."

"Then get a large one with whatever else you think he'll eat."

Callan thanked his son and pulled out a couple of bills from his pocket to pay for the meal. He waited until he heard the engine of Brandon's car *vroom* down the street before attempting any conversation with his youngest son. It didn't seem to matter, however. Gil clearly wasn't in a mood for conversation.

"I need you to do something for me," Callan said.

Gil gave his father a fleeting glance, then returned his attention to the television to flip the channel once again.

"I was wondering if you'd like to come up to Chicago sometime to watch a Blackhawks game with me. You like hockey, don't you?" Callan thought he noticed Gil's head twitch slightly in agreement, but that wasn't enough of a response to satisfy him. He asked Gil to look at him. "I don't know how to say this so that you'll believe me, Gil, but I want you to know I'm going to be here. I'll always be here for you and your brother and mother. This job won't change that."

Gil arched his back as if he was going to straighten his posture to sit up and talk. Instead, he straightened just enough to reach for the remote control so that he could flip the channel button once again.

Callan's heart felt as if it dropped into his stomach when he realized his heartfelt message to his son was going to be ignored. He rose and rubbed the palms of his hands on the front of his pants' legs, waiting for a response. When none came, Callan walked to the front door and looked out, hoping Brandon would return with the pizza soon.

~

In the month since Callan presented his notice to the bank of his intent to resign, he made three trips to the western suburbs of Chicago to look for housing. Encouraged by Larry and Marlene, he chose a one-bedroom apartment in a building named the Wingate-Powers, though only the word Wingate was etched into the cement arch above the door. Peaceful and clean, the apartment was also conveniently located north of The Avenue Commercial District in Oak Park.

Though small by Indianapolis standards, the apartment was certainly adequate and desirable by those who canvassed apartments in the western suburbs. He happened to call the management of the building on the day number thirty-four became available. Mrs. Bernadette Powers answered the phone and seemed to take an immediate liking to Callan. He met her in casual business attire, hoping that his trimmed haircut and wire-rimmed reading glasses would make him appear distinguished and trustworthy.

She said she had a good mind for tenants, and that she could tell upon first sight that Callan Morrow was a good tenant.

He told her he'd take it, almost before she had a chance to finish her recital of the flat's amenities and working appliances.

"Oh, I'm so pleased," she said. "I'm glad to have a conservative, well-dressed individual occupying the apartment once again."

Callan surmised by this lecture that previous tenants did not meet her rigid standards and expectations.

"Ernest Hemingway was born in a home near here," she remarked casually when Callan asked about the parking situation along Putnam Street. Upon Callan's interested response to her mention of Hemingway, she added that she believed her family used to know the Hemingways at one time, or at least knew of them. Almost as if the next sentence perfectly transitioned into a meaningful conversation, she added, "I can usually count on everyone's rent precisely on the first of each month. I trust this won't be a problem?"

"It will not," Callan assured her. He was an accountant, and he paid his bills promptly.

"Yes, well, I happen to know a few cobblers whose children have no shoes. It never hurts to mention it just the same."

Callan liked the apartment very much, and Brandon spent a long weekend helping him move what belongings he had. What he didn't like about the apartment was more than compensated by what he liked about being in the village of Oak Park. The convenience of shopping, restaurants, culture and other activities helped take some of the edge off realizing that he'd come to Chicago without his family.

The fact that Larry and Marlene lived within walking distance of his apartment building helped ease the burden of being alone, although it was a hefty walk. The couple encouraged him to get acquainted with the area by taking in a myriad of community events.

When alone, however, Callan fancied going to Argos' on The Avenue across from Scoville Park. There he was able to relax with a beer at a table next to its expansive windows overlooking a world that hustled quickly amidst the rustling autumn leaves at their feet. Callan enjoyed watching people. Much of his job was about watching people and their reactions, looking for signs of mischief or wrongdoing. Inside Argos', either along Lake Street or Oak

Park Boulevard, Callan judged people's choice of dress, considered their lifestyle, guessed at their economic status, and reflected on their past.

It kept his mind off his own past. Sometimes he felt the past was all he had, but that had to change. As he sat one evening in Argos', he envisioned what he wanted his future to be.

That was the night he met Mrs. Argos.

The seventy-plus-year-old widow had married a Greek immigrant decades ago, and after all these years, she acted as though she were a Greek immigrant herself, though she was from Joliet, born and raised. Periodically, Callan would see her sitting in the restaurant at a table near the waiter's station, eating a light dinner and conversing with the staff. Callan later realized her son, George, Jr., tended the bar and managed the restaurant during the week.

She caught a glimpse of Callan looking in her direction and took it as an invitation to sit with him and talk. She stood and walked toward him. "I've seen you here before, young man. I should have introduced myself before now. I'm Wynetta Argos."

Callan introduced himself in return.

Mrs. Argos smiled and asked what he did for a living, where he was from, was he married, and if his mother was still alive. She told him about her son, George, Jr., and his father who died of heart failure eight years ago. This explanation of her life opened the door for Callan to talk about his immediate family and his situation with Terese and the boys.

Before he finished, his entrée arrived at the table. He ate and talked as Mrs. Argos listened about Terese, the boys, his work, the plane crash, Terese again, how he liked living in Chicago, and Terese again.

"So what are you doing here?" she asked bluntly. "Why aren't you at home, mending your relationship?"

He didn't know. No, that wasn't true. He knew why. He just didn't want to tell her what he was doing in Chicago. Callan sensed she wouldn't approve, and he didn't want to listen to her rebuttal.

CHAPTER EIGHT

The next morning, Callan caught the 6:45 Green Line elevated train at the Oak Park Boulevard station for downtown. He leaned his head on the train window and strained to see the city's skyline. It was incredible. As impressive as the skyline of many cities are, nothing compared to the view of Chicago. Coming from the west while the sun crept over Lake Michigan's horizon, the buildings awoke with electric lights and the lives of people fulfilling the wills of those who employed them.

The phone rang just after Callan arrived at his office. Tony Burris requested a meeting and gave Callan his first special project from management. Although eager to do something meaningful, Callan found Tony's assignment unimaginative—a review of management expense reimbursements.

The second part of the meeting was more interesting, however. Tony escorted Callan to a conspicuous corner office, overlooking the lake and adjacent office buildings. There, Callan was introduced to Kenneth Holloway, GrandAire's Legal Counsel, who had recently completed the transfer of his job and family from Minneapolis.

"You wouldn't happen to be the son of Ellen Holloway, would you?" Callan asked. "I think your mother works with my wife in Indianapolis."

The tall man with a dark complexion, handsome features, and a calm confident demeanor shook Callan's hand firmly and responded, "I know who you are. My mother has talked about you in great detail." A tinge of Texan influence peppered his Hoosier dialect, the result of years in Houston before moving to Minneapolis.

"But she never told me you worked for GrandAire," Callan said.

Ken smiled. "I'm sure she's told your wife. I'm surprised word didn't get to you. Their little secret, huh? As an auditor, you should have had a sixth sense about such things, eyes in the back of your head, that sort of thing. If you don't, you might need them. You have a mighty big job ahead of you here. While it will be challenging, it won't be without its rewards as we attempt to capture a lost market and build a grand fleet of aircraft right here in the Great Lakes."

Ken elaborated on his professional background. The greatest part of his career, he explained, was his litigation practice in Houston representing airlines, airline manufacturers, and aircraft component parts manufacturers. He defended the organizations from loss of life and injury claims as a result of aviation accidents.

Like a worn-out news anchor, Holloway rattled off the leading roles he'd played for the defense of major airlines. Several of the accident cases led to precedent-making changes in aviation law, many of which Callan could recall from his previous research.

One in particular captured Callan's attention immediately.

"Yes, I had the unfortunate opportunity to represent Midland Airlines in the crash of their twin turboprop commuter plane in Indiana," Ken said. "It was a damned case from the beginning, unfortunate because it was a no-win situation for both sides. Plaintiff attorneys were able to convince Midland and the manufacturers to admit to liability, but to our credit the verdict was almost a million dollars short of the three-and-a-half million the plaintiffs were asking. Fortunately, we were able to reduce the amount by another four hundred thousand."

"What made it so damned?" Callan asked cynically, curious about the mindset of a lawyer who would defend clients who knowingly and wrongfully caused the deaths of sixty-eight people.

"There were three individuals who opted to try their cases separately, hoping to hold out for bigger settlements."

"Did they?"

Ken nodded and paused to reflect.

Callan noticed a subtle change in the lawyer's facial expression. Flashing back to the case seemed to incense him.

"Yes, they did," he said, "especially the family of one of the flight attendants. They made out like bandits. I can still picture the mother around the mediation table. The whole thing was sensationalized by the fact that it was her daughter's first flight with the airline, and she had warned her daughter ahead of time not to go. It was the perfect making of a good fight."

Callan knew from his research the flight attendant to whom Holloway referred. Only one lawsuit was prompted by a mother angered by the airline's lack of responsiveness to compensate the victims for their loss.

"You can't blame her, really," Callan said coolly. "I doubt that Mrs. Holland or any one of the other plaintiffs felt as if they came out like bandits, considering the price they paid."

The lawyer didn't respond, but he eyed Callan differently now, less casually and with skepticm, apparently unaware that Callan was familiar with relevant names and details associated with the accident. He abruptly changed the subject. "So what do Tony Burris or Alan Cavanaugh have you doing to start the audit function within this company?"

"The review of management expense reports, for one thing."

"Expense reports? What for?"

"Probably to determine that only valid reimbursable travel and entertainment expenses were disbursed."

Holloway laughed. "Oh, God, I can see the fur flying in this company already. People around here aren't used to having their expense reports examined."

"I'm afraid they'll have to get used to it. I believe management wants me to audit them on a regular basis."

"Oh, I'm not saying it shouldn't be done. It'll be good for them. It'll be good for all of us, and it sounds reasonable, but in another way it's just lipstick on a pig, you know."

Callan smiled at the phrase Hoosiers often used. He sensed that the Hoosier in Holloway's sophisticated demeanor hadn't dissipated completely. "Why? Most companies do these audits," Callan reminded him.

"Yes, I know, but you don't do audits like that when there are major risk issues that need to be addressed. We need to be putting you to work identifying our risks and exposures, prioritizing them for resolution, and making each vice president accountable for mitigating those risks and exposures. That's what we need to be doing."

Silence followed until Callan gathered the courage to ask if he could say something off the record. "Why did this company hire me, Ken?"

"What do you mean?"

"Was I hired for cosmetic purposes or to genuinely fulfill a responsibility to investors with an audit function?"

"I don't know," Kenneth said, leaning forward to wipe some dust off a brass pen set. "I don't know any more, Callan, but I'll tell you this. You won't be spending your time bean counting. Zane Dunham will see to that. You won't be ticking and tying yourself into oblivion or reconciling bank statements for managers who have the responsibility for doing it themselves."

"Do I have the consensus of all executives on that?"

"Who are you thinking?"

"Alan Cavanaugh."

Kenneth Holloway sat back in his chair, but didn't answer.

CHAPTER NINE

Shortly after nine thirty the next morning, Callan received a call from Velma Hofmeyer, Hamilton Perry's assistant.

"I'm calling on behalf of Mr. Perry," she said. "He would like me to inform you that you may expect an individual to begin employment in your department tomorrow morning."

"Tomorrow?"

"Yes, sir. Her name is Aysha Marks. She's a member of our marketing team. Human resources will have the necessary paperwork for her transfer by the end of the day. Is this acceptable?"

"I'm sure it will be," he said skeptically.

"Is there something wrong?"

"No."

She detected the reluctance in his voice. "What is it?"

"I just didn't think it would happen this way."

"Pardon me?"

"You mean she's transferring?"

"Yes, sir."

"No interview? No acceptance or agreement by either one of us?"

"Orders by Mr. Dunham and Mr. Perry. She is to report to you tomorrow."

"I see. Thank you, Velma."

Just as Velma stated, the young Aysha Marks arrived at his office the next morning. Professional, both in appearance and demeanor, she arrived promptly and introduced herself.

"A-sha, is it?" Callan asked to be sure.

"Eye-sha," she corrected politely.

Aysha handed him a portfolio of her vitae and samples of her project work.

Callan accepted it and invited her to sit down across from him. He offered her coffee or water, which she refused. She placed a briefcase on the floor and crossed her legs, gently tugging her skirt to cover her knees.

Callan didn't open the portfolio right away although Aysha's expression indicated that she wanted him to focus on it. He wasn't interested in her portfolio, however. He was interested in Aysha Marks, the individual. Aysha Marks, the individual, not her portfolio, would get him what he needed as an auditor. "I appreciate your acceptance of this assignment," Callan said, but her lack of acknowledgement indicated no acceptance on her part. "Tell me about yourself," he asked earnestly.

Aysha raised her eyebrows in an expression indicating that she didn't understand why he would ask such a question when the portfolio under his nose would tell him all he needed to know. "Not much to tell, really, Mr. Morrow. I've been with the company a little over a year, all in marketing. I've had the opportunity to work on a variety of projects specifically aimed toward corporate imaging and branding within the business community."

She paused as if questioning whether Callan wanted to hear more.

He urged her to continue.

"Well, as a Chicago native involved in numerous civic organizations, particularly in the African-American community, I've been able to contribute significantly to the organization in that regard."

"Do you like marketing?"

"Very much. It was my undergraduate major at Champaign."

"How do you feel about the change of focus? This isn't marketing here."

"The correct answer is that being able to adapt to change is a virtue, but I'm of the belief that not all change is for the better. I'm sure you're aware of that at your age."

Callan noticed her emphasis on his age.

She caught herself. "I apologize. I meant to say your experience. Surely your experience has made you aware that not all change is for the better."

"Is that how you feel about this move to auditing?"

"Time will tell, won't it? I'm open to the change if you are."

Callan didn't reply. He wasn't sure how open he really was to the transfer. More importantly, he wasn't sure how open she was, either. "Who did you work for here at GrandAire?" he asked instead.

Aysha mentioned the name of Rob Abington, Director of Marketing and Public Relations.

Callan hadn't met him, although he'd heard his name mentioned in various meetings around the company. On the organization chart, he recalled that Rob reported directly to Carol Chambers.

Callan talked with Aysha about what she knew of the organization. Although lacking auditing or accounting experience, she maintained an aptitude for understanding operations. More importantly, she understood how a well-organized company should function and how a professionally developed marketing promotion can support activities to achieve results.

Poised. Confident. A little arrogant, perhaps, but that was okay. Direct and finite. Could she be objective? That, he wasn't so sure about. "Let's go back to an earlier question, though. Do you mind?" he asked.

"Not at all."

"How do you feel about transferring to internal audit now that we've had a chance to talk?"

Aysha shifted uncomfortably in her seat.

"I'm sure this is a difficult move for you," he added.

"Yes, it is difficult, Mr. Morrow. I'm not sure why I'm here exactly."

"It was not explained to you?"

"No, and I'm not sure what you're expecting of me. I'm not sure the value I'm going to be able to bring to you, so, you see, yes, this is rather difficult."

Callan shared her concern. When he'd raised the topic of staff with management, he'd fully expected to be given an open position through human resources to be able to hire a professional who met the qualifications needed for the job. Instead, someone had been assigned to him. He also wondered why management chose Aysha Marks to be that someone. Clearly her transfer had been hastily put together, and no aspect of it had been discussed with her in advance. Perhaps her former supervisor, Rob Abington, didn't even know.

"Let me see if I can ease both of our apprehensions, Aysha, because I, too, have asked the same question. What value can you add given your experience and education in marketing? I accepted this position at GrandAire believing it to be a good opportunity for myself, but I'm not naïve. This organization has never had an audit function. They haven't had to defend decisions and transactions that don't add value or are outside of established policies and procedures. That's where you come in. I know how to audit, Aysha, but someone like you with a marketing background can help me sell the function to management while we look into their closet of skeletons. Do you see what I'm getting at? It's a tough sell. We need a tough marketer. Maybe that's what Mr. Dunham and Mr. Perry had in mind when you were chosen."

Aysha visibly relaxed at Callan's explanation of the possible method to management's madness regarding her transfer.

When there was nothing more to say, he stood and asked, "Would you like to see your office?"

Aysha entered her office and thanked Callan for having a place where she could think in uninterrupted peace. He apologized that it didn't have any windows, and she said she didn't mind.

He watched as she sat behind the desk and rubbed her palms over its simulated wood-grain top. "They'll have your phone connected this afternoon, by the way," he said, interrupting her daydream.

Aysha picked up the receiver to see if it was, indeed, a dead line. "There's a dial tone. Seems to be working."

"Really? I guess someone's on the ball. I didn't realize they knew I'd need it."

She smiled as she stared at the phone, and Callan wondered who she wanted to call.

CHAPTER TEN

Early the next morning, Callan walked briskly toward GrandAire's office building to remove himself from the outdoor elements as soon as possible. The northwesterly wind impaled him more brutally than the cold. It howled between high-rise buildings in search of shivering victims, and his overcoat wasn't thick enough to keep him warm.

Callan swirled through the revolving door and into the company's foyer, gaining immediate relief. With his palms over his ears to warm them, he walked across the marble floor toward the elevators and almost missed Velma Hofmeyer's greeting as she passed nearby.

"Oh, I'm sorry, Velma; how rude of me. How are you this morning?"

Velma allowed the apology to pass, but her smile showed how much she enjoyed his attention. "I'm doing very well, Mr. Morrow. Thank you. You appear to be in deep concentration. I'm off to the main post office." She lifted the nondescript package tucked securely under her right arm, and moved it slightly to better conceal it, but not before Callan noticed Texas in the address.

"There you go," Callan replied, not knowing what else to say.

Velma glanced at the package she held like precious cargo, opened her mouth, then closed it again, as if she'd wanted to say something about it, but then had second thoughts and chose not to do so.

"Do hurry when you go outside," Callan said to fill the gap. "It's pretty cold out there."

She agreed, bid him good day, and exited the building, protecting the package with her arms.

Callan barely had time to get a cup of coffee from the break room and settle into his morning routine when Aysha appeared at his door. If she dreaded the thought of reporting to work as an audit professional, it didn't show on her face.

She entered his office with a fresh spark in her eye, sat comfortably in the chair by his desk, and placed a fresh pad of paper and a ballpoint pen on her lap.

"You seem eager," Callan said, shuffling papers to organize his thoughts.

"Yes," she replied. "I don't give up easily, Mr. Morrow."

Callan explained the review of management expense reports to her thoroughly. He saw by the glazed look in her eyes that much of the accounting aspects of his instruction went over her head. Her enthusiasm appeared to wane.

Cal tried to empathize with her. "I know it's not a great audit to start your career in auditing, but it is one of the fundamental things we do as auditors. Do you have any questions? I noticed you didn't take any notes. Anything you need me to repeat?"

Aysha shook her head.

Callan couldn't tell if she was too embarrassed to ask questions, didn't know what to ask, or just wanted to scream and run out of the office.

Aysha stood, thanked him, said she would get on the assignment right away and left his office.

Despite her calm exterior, she entered the accounts-payable department confused and uncertain. She'd never been inside the department, didn't know what they did, and didn't particularly care. She felt angry at Callan Morrow, Rob Abington, Carol Chambers, and every other member of management that had arranged her transfer to auditing, and that only added to her frustration.

The young receptionist inside the accounts-payable office, who remained nameless as far as Aysha was concerned, read Aysha's demeanor and responded with reverence. Aysha flipped through a stenographer pad of notes to find the name of the person who could pull the executive expense reports she needed. When she couldn't find a name, she blurted out a command to get the department manager.

The assistant retreated through an adjacent door, her long, dark hair flowing freely, and soon reappeared, leading a large, older woman in a plain, brown pant suit. The look on the woman's face indicated that she was not amused by Aysha's indignant intrusion into her area.

"Hello, I'm Marcia Downing, Department Manager for Accounts Payable," she said, extending her hand. "What can I do for you?"

Aysha introduced herself, relieved to recognize Marcia Downing as the name she'd written on her notepad. Aysha told her what documents she needed.

"We're rather busy," the manager replied as the receptionist slithered back to her desk.

Aysha felt taken aback by Downing's curtness. "But I'm here at the orders of Mr. Morrow. I need to do a review of these reports."

Downing didn't budge. "Then have Mr. Morrow, whoever Mr. Morrow is, email me, and we'll schedule a time for you to review these reports."

"Mr. Morrow is the new Vice President of Auditing," Aysha explained, hoping that would help.

It didn't.

Aysha dropped her shoulders and stood helplessly in front of the department manager. She didn't know what to say or what she should say. All she could mutter was "Oh, dear."

Downing sighed and said reluctantly, "Follow me." She led Aysha through a maze of beige cabinets and retractable filing shelves labeled A through Z. "People come in here all the time wanting this and that at a minute's notice without regard to our processes," the manager spouted. "Pay this, pay that. When can I have this? When can I have that? As if they don't realize that if they want something paid quickly, they need to realize we have procedures. We have strict procedures."

Downing took Aysha to a windowless office where a small table was buried under stacks of papers. She transferred the papers to the top of some filing cabinets as she talked. "It's no wonder your Mr. Morrow wants to look at these expenses. Velma Hofmeyer and I have been telling management for months that things have got to change around here."

"Ms. Hofmeyer?" Aysha asked.

"Yes. Senior management reports funnel through her for Mr. Perry's signature." Downing lifted the last stack of files and papers and held them in her hands. "It is senior management you want, isn't it?"

Aysha nodded. "I need their expense reports and credit card statements for the past year."

At that, Marcia Downing took the last stack of folders in her hands, and slapped them haphazardly on the other piles she had created. "Here," she said, pulling around a small, plastic chair that had been pushed off to one side of the table. "You sit here, and I'll have Tina get them for you."

Aysha sat motionless until Tina arrived about fifteen minutes later with the first batch of expense reports and statements.

Surprised she'd turned up so quickly, Aysha thanked her for working so hard and apologized for the abrupt way she'd treated her earlier. She picked up three folders, noted they were labeled by individual and month, then scrounged through the stack and determined that the same labeling held true for each of the other folders. She alphabetized them by last name:

Anthony Burris, Senior Vice President and Chief Financial Officer
Alan Cavanaugh, Senior Vice President and Chief Operating Officer
Carol Chambers, Senior Vice President of Marketing and Public Relations
Celia Hart, Vice President of Human Resources
Kenneth Holloway, Senior Vice President of Risk Management
Hamilton Perry, Chief Executive Officer
Mark Reasoner, Vice President of Facilities Operations
Lawrence Southard, Vice President of Commercial Operations
Murray Thompson

71

Even after double checking, Aysha could find only one folder with the name *Murray Thompson*. She determined there must be some mistake. The folder included one piece of paper with a simple sentence stating no expenses had been submitted for reimbursement by the executive.

"Who's Murray Thompson?" Aysha asked.

Tina shook her head. "I couldn't tell you. He may be someone before my time. I've only been here a few months. Want me to ask Ms. Downing about it?"

"No," Aysha said emphatically. "I've got enough to look at here. I only have time for the members of management still with us. Here. Put it back where it came from."

Aysha extended her arm to give Tina the folder. "And thank you," she added. "I mean it. Thanks a lot."

CHAPTER ELEVEN

"Hey, Miss Velma," Callan teased as he stepped into the doorway of the office of Hamilton Perry's executive assistant. He took the liberty of informality, knowing that Mr. Perry was out of the office for the next few days.

Velma Hofmeyer stopped typing and looked up from her computer screen. They exchanged a few words of greeting and niceties, including the time and weather.

"How is Aysha Marks working out for you?" she asked. "I'm pleased something worked out to accommodate your staffing situation."

Callan was grateful she'd brought up the subject. It gave him the opportunity to obtain some inside information without appearing to be prying. "I am, too. I hope it didn't put anyone out. Were Carol Chambers and Rob Abington okay with the move?"

"Oh, absolutely. In fact, Carol was in Mr. Perry's office with Alan Cavanaugh when it was decided. The rest is history."

"Is that so?" said Callan with interest.

She gave him a smile of acknowledgement.

He moved closer to her desk to talk more privately. He wanted to ask her about GrandAire and the personalities within the company, especially those within the management ranks, but the small switchboard on her phone interrupted their talk.

Velma looked at the caller identification display and turned to Callan with an apologetic expression. "I'm sorry, Mr. Morrow. I need to get this."

He understood and, tipping his hat symbolically, left her office. He wished he'd come earlier in the day to take full advantage of Hamilton Perry's absence.

The corridor along Mahogany Row was almost as wide as it was long. Just off the elevators on the top floor, the GrandAire atrium basked in the rays of the sun during the day and dazzled in the reflection of Chicago's skyscrapers at night through arched skylights that spanned the length and width of the room. Cherry paneling skirted the lower third of three sides of the atrium. Live palm trees and ferns bordered the room with dramatic flair. The fourth side sported floor-to-ceiling-length windows that faced east toward the cool blue waters of Lake Michigan.

"Callan," Alan Cavanaugh exclaimed from behind the palm trees, "a coincidence to see you."

Callan's intuition told him that coincidence had little to do with it.

"Perhaps you've seen the meeting notice my administrative assistant placed on your calender for this afternoon. Very important that you be there. We're going to need your service."

Callan responded that he'd be happy to attend.

"Good. You're not working on anything important that would interfere, are you?"

"Not at all. We're beginning reviews of management expenses. That's about it."

Alan's eyebrows lifted with interest. "Is that so?"

"Yes, sir, at Tony's request."

"Well, let me tell you what's on my mind. Keeping costs low and prices competitive are how we're going to make a go of this damn business. Financial numbers have been fluctuating. I'm not sure how to control the variances in our budget. I'm hearing through the grapevine that there are complaints about the budget constraints I imposed. I suspect they're bubbling up because I'm putting a kink in the misappropriation activities of my management team."

Callan stepped closer so Alan didn't have to speak so loudly. "Misappropriation? Are you talking about fraud? That's something very serious."

"I guess you did learn something from that bank you worked for. I'll explain later in the meeting. Management expenses, you say? If you're doing an audit of management expenses, I want to be the first to learn of your scope and findings. You understand?"

"Yes, sir, but I'm not sure how appropriate that would be considering you're one of the members of management I'm looking into."

Cavanaugh took a step toward Callan. "You didn't listen to me. I said I want to be the first. You'll report your scope and findings to me first. Is that understood?"

"Yes, sir."

"Good. I'll see you this afternoon."

Callan left the atrium a little unnerved and entered the hallway of his office. It was unusually quiet. He reached Aysha's office, but the door was closed. *She must still be in accounts payable.* He gave the knob a quick twist to make sure the door was locked securely. He'd taken two steps toward his own office when the door popped open behind him. Frowning, he walked back to her office and peeked into the dark room. A dim blue light emanated from her computer terminal. A few papers lay on her desk, but as far as Callan could tell nothing confidential had been left exposed. He reached behind the door knob, clicked the push-buttoned lock, and closed the door soundly. He'd remind her about locking her door.

Callan found his own door unlocked as well. He frowned. Though certain he never would've left it unlocked, he couldn't specifically remember locking it, so perhaps he had neglected to do so. He cast his eye around his office, but everything was just the way he'd left it—undisturbed. A shiver crept up his spine, however. He'd thought nothing had been missing at his home after the break-in, but something had disappeared from a desk drawer in the den. Were his workpapers undisturbed in his office now? The thought of someone breaking into his office as they had his home made him cringe.

He composed himself and arrived promptly at Alan Cavanaugh's meeting, only to find it already in progress. He took a seat across from Alan beside his friend, Larry Southard.

"There're a lot of factors contributing to the low numbers, Alan," the head of accounting said.

"Like what?" The glare of the COO stilled the accountant before he could reply. "I'll tell you like what," Alan Cavanaugh continued. "It's like mismanagement by my staff, that's what." He went on to dissect the issues facing the operations group one by one and the shortcomings befalling their team that were leading the organization to a less-than-stellar bottom line. "Maintenance contracts," he blurted. "Inspection records, waste, productivity, expenses. How about job safety and injuries? Do any of these topics ring a bell with you people that something isn't right in our division?" He looked into the eyes of those attending. "May I ask what the hell you people are doing with your time?"

Celia Hart, Senior Vice President of Human Resources, squirmed in her chair.

Alan caught her uneasiness and turned upon her. "I don't know, Celia, but do any of my people's job descriptions say anything about screwing up the company?"

Celia didn't answer.

Cavanaugh looked across the table at Callan and said, "Morrow, you're the auditor. What do you have to say about this mess my people have made of our bottom line?"

Callan shook his head. "I'm not sure I see it as a mess, Alan. There's a bigger issue in front of you."

"Such as?"

"Such as the systemic lack of internal controls and formalized policies and procedures throughout the enterprise. I've only been here a short while, but what I've seen so far is inadequate. When a weak infrastructure is compounded by a lack of sound internal controls, it stands to reason that there are going to be problems that no one division can resolve on its own."

"Really?" Alan said unenthusiastically. "That's not what you told me a bit ago when we met in the atrium."

Callan frowned. "What?"

"I received a totally different impression from you about individual accountability. You told me there were people in my division circumventing controls that you now say are nonexistent. Which is it, Morrow?"

Callan remembered no such conversation. "Alan, I don't know what you're trying to pull here, but—"

"I'm going to make this short and quick for you, Morrow. Celia Hart of Human Resources is here at my request because I want her to hear what I have to say. There is reason for me to believe that certain controls have been circumvented to facilitate personal means over the success of the organization."

"Are you talking fraud?" Larry asked.

"That's exactly what I'm talking about, Southard."

"That's insane!"

"It's a domino. One breakdown in controls causes another. It's not how we do business at GrandAire."

Celia Hart shifted uncomfortably before saying, "Alan, if you suspect improprieties within your division, we have policies and procedures to deal with such behavior. This is the first I've heard of such problems."

"Well, then, listen and listen good because I'm going to spell it out for you. You, too, Southard. This affects you and one of your employees directly."

"My employee?"

"Isn't that what I said?"

"Which one?"

"Cliff Pierceman."

"Pierceman? What about him?"

"He will no longer be working for us. You'll find that he authorized an expense reimbursement that was outside of his authority. I want the termination paperwork filed immediately after this meeting, and I want you, Southard, to make sure Pierceman's sorry ass is out of the building within the hour."

Celia Hart slammed the palm of her hand down hard on the surface of the conference table. The force of the impact startled those around the table.

Callan's heart jumped into his throat. He glanced toward Larry for his reaction, but if he was shocked, he didn't show it. Perhaps the surprise announcement left him unable to speak in defense of his employee.

"Alan, I've met Cliff Pierceman," Callan said. "Cliff is one of the most highly regarded individuals in the organization."

"All the more reason to nip this in the bud, Morrow."

"I assume you have adequate documentation to prove this allegation."

"It's not an allegation; it's a fact. I'm not a dumbass. Yes, I have proof, but I'll be damned if it's turned over to you. The investigation is over. It belongs to HR now."

Celia Hart shook her head. "This entire calamity is out of order, Alan. Callan's involvement is crucial before I file any paperwork on your behalf. I want your proof validated."

"I'll remind you, Hart, that as Senior Vice President I have authority to run my division as I see fit."

"Save it. I'll remind you that I report directly to Hamilton Perry, not to you, and thank God I do."

Larry, apparently unable to stand any more, rose from the table and walked toward the door, leaving his belongings behind him.

"I haven't adjourned, Southard!"

Larry kept walking.

Callan stood to follow his friend.

A grin spread across Cavanaugh's face. "Let him go, Morrow. You stay."

Callan left the meeting anyway. He wasn't after Larry. He went in search of Aysha. She wasn't in her office, so he searched through her workpapers of management expenses, but couldn't find anything to support the allegation that Cliff had filed any recent expense-reimbursement reports.

He left and headed for Larry's office, only to find the chair behind Larry's desk vacant. Callan combed the area, but found no one who'd seen him. He entered Mahogany Row and walked toward the office of Velma Hofmeyer. As expected, Hamilton Perry's assistant typed dutifully on a keyboard, her reading glasses tilted slightly on the bridge of her nose.

"Excuse me, Velma, but is Larry Southard in with Mr. Perry?"

"No, of course not," she answered with surprise. "Mr. Perry is out of town. May I help you with something?"

"If you see Mr. Southard, tell him to get a hold of me right away. I need to talk with him."

"Certainly."

Callan started to go, but pulled himself back into the doorway.

Velma didn't budge from her inquisitive pose. She waited patiently for him to collect his thoughts as if she knew what he was going to say. She removed her glasses and pointed toward Alan Cavanaugh's office. The raised voices of Alan and a woman penetrated the walls. Although the words were inaudible, clearly the two individuals were arguing. "Ms. Hart is in with Mr. Cavanaugh right now," she stated.

Callan turned and walked determinedly into the middle of a tumultuous conversation in Alan's office. He stood in solidarity next to the Human Resources executive.

Celia placed her hands on her hips and said, "We were set up, Callan."

"I figured as much."

"For Pete's sake, you two," Alan spewed. "I'm in charge of making sure operations are functioning in accordance with the board of directors' wishes. My personnel are not performing to the goals and standards established for them. All I did was invite our human resources and our internal-control experts to witness what needed to be done to make sure we get back on track."

"But you've just made the organization vulnerable to a lawsuit by this action. You had no right to do what you did in a staff meeting."

Alan Cavanaugh turned and reciprocated her angry stance with a venomous glare. "Don't you dare tell me anything about being right," he blurted. "I did you a favor, Hart. I did your whole statistical reporting of our corporate demographics to the Feds a huge, big-ass favor. He's a white male. He has no rights. So get the hell out of here, and hire me a replacement before I have Perry fire *you* for insubordination."

Celia and Callan remained where they stood in the middle of the executive's office.

"Go on!" Alan yelled. "I said get out!"

At that, the two did as they were told, stopping to regain their composure in the sterile confines of Mahagony Row.

"I can't believe it," she said, shaking her head.

"It's not the belief I can't fathom, Celia, it's the why. Why is this happening? What's going on that we don't know about?"

"I don't know. It makes me wonder, though." Celia looked at her watch. "Oh, God, I'm late for my own departmental staff meeting. Let me know if you need anything, Callan. We may never be able to find the answer to that question, but I want to help you figure it out if I can."

Callan smiled. "Keep your cool. Don't fire anyone."

Celia returned the smile graciously.

Callan rushed into Aysha's office with such a fury that she pushed her work aside to accommodate his impending request. He stipulated succinctly each procedure he wanted her to follow and each document he needed her to obtain.

She didn't ask why or for what reason. The expression on his face told her something was materially wrong and urgent. As soon as her boss had gone, Aysha hurried to accounts payable and told Marcia's assistant, Tina Stratman, that Callan requested pulling the most recent management expense reports for Cliff Pierceman.

Tina indicated it would take just a few minutes to do so.

Aysha waited nervously in the small room where she'd worked previously. It took only a few minutes, just as Tina said, but there was nothing in her hands when she returned.

"That can't be," Aysha said. "Mr. Morrow specifically stated that the unauthorized transaction had to do with management expenses."

"I'm sorry," Tina replied, "but I didn't find anything. There's nothing in the general ledger related to an expense for Cliff Pierceman for the entire year."

"That doesn't make sense."

"Are you sure it was an expense reimbursement?"

"What do you mean?"

"It could be a normal accounts-payable invoice."

"But Mr. Morrow said specifically it was an expense."

"Just a thought. Maybe it was a requisition to pay an invoice."

Aysha considered Tina's alternative. What could it hurt to look? "Sure. Let's give it a shot. How long will it take to find out?"

CHAPTER TWELVE

When Callan arrived for their late afternoon meeting, he found Chief Financial Officer Tony Burris standing behind his desk reading a management report. Burris repeatedly ran his hands through his thick, dark hair in agitation. Clearly, the contents of the document disturbed him.

"I'll be with you in a moment, Cal."

Callan took a seat.

"New accounting guidance," he explained. "Are you linked in to receive these reports?"

"Yes, sir."

"I suppose you would be. So how are *you* doing? You look a little beat today."

Callan shrugged as if it was all in a day's work. Obviously, Tony had been occupied within the confines of his office or else he would have heard the buzz about Cliff Pierceman's firing.

"So what have you got for me?" Tony asked.

"First of all, I appreciate the strings you pulled to get Aysha Marks on board." Callan presented the comment and waited for a response. Burris' blank stare was his answer. Clearly the executive didn't know anything about the selection of the new auditing staff member. "She's been a big help in the review of management expense reports you requested. I have some results on that audit whenever you're ready to hear about them."

Tony shook his head as if Callan didn't need to bother. "I know about it already."

Callan looked at him skeptically. "Really? I didn't realize that Aysha had met with you to present her findings."

"Who?"

"Aysha Marks," Callan annunciated slowly, "my new staff person."

Tony drew in a short gasp of air. "Aysha. Yes, well, but it wasn't her. It was one of my managers, I believe. Does it matter, really?"

"No, not in the scheme of things, I guess, but it's very curious."

"Very well," Tony said, nodding his head as if Callan was free to go.

Callan wanted to stay, but took the cue.

He entered the dark atrium, the result of the sun setting behind the skyline, and took the elevator to his office floor. The floor was quiet, but rather than welcoming him with peace and tranquility, the solitude emitted a sense of paranoia, uneasiness, and conjecture. He unlocked the door to his office and turned on the light. Everything appeared to be as he'd left it. He set Tony's agenda items on his desk and walked toward his chair, eyeing each paper clip, every piece of scrap paper, each scribbled note, and every desk accessory as if any one of them would reveal if mischief had occurred while he was gone.

He sat placidly in his chair and gave the desktop a final glance before convincing his skeptical mind that no one had entered his office in his absence. Did Tony really know what was in the results of Aysha's expense audit or was he bluffing to get him out of his office? Was Tony weary of hearing about GrandAire's poor financial control system? If he did know, the news hadn't come from Aysha. Callan was even more doubtful that the news came from one of Tony's managers.

No, if Tony knew the results of the audit in advance, he obtained the results directly from Aysha's workpapers that were supposedly secured in her office.

The telephone rang. He jumped with a start. The caller identification revealed a Chicago metro-area code, but the number was unfamiliar to him.

He took the call.

An unexpected voice said, "Cal, this is Aysha."

"Yeah," he said curtly, sounding weary and doubtful even to his own ears.

"You okay? You don't sound well."

"Caffeine-deprived. What's up?"

"I went down to accounts payable. Marcia Downing, the director, was out, but her assistant, Tina Stratman, helped me pull the management expense reports for Cliff Pierceman like you asked. But, Cal, there was nothing in the expense reports."

"I don't understand."

"What you were looking for wasn't in management expenses. Instead, Tina pulled all invoices that Cliff approved. She found one item that might be the one in question."

"You mean Cliff approved an invoice he wasn't authorized to approve?"

"Yes, by quite a large amount. It was to an individual. Someone by the name of, oh, shoot, I don't see it. The person's name is in my other folder, I'm afraid. I'm sorry."

"That's okay. I'm sure that invoice was the straw that broke the camel's back for Alan."

"What happened today? May I ask?"

"Cliff was let go during an operations staff meeting."

"For this invoice?"

"Apparently."

Aysha fell silent.

"What's the matter? What's on your mind?" he prompted.

"Well, Tina was surprised that the invoice made it through the system under Cliff's signature. Marcia's a stickler for following proper approvals."

"What are you saying? That someone forged the invoice and processed it without Downing's knowledge?"

"That's what it looks like. I'm just telling you what Tina confided to me."

Callan thanked Aysha for her diligence and willingness to go beyond what he'd requested. After bidding her good night, he imagined the aroma of a cup of hot, strong coffee. Caffeine deprivation was starting to wear on his ability to concentrate. He would accept even stale, burnt coffee if it had caffeine.

Callan walked toward the the kitchenette. A minimal amount of coffee sat at the bottom of the pot. He lifted the carafe gently from the burner, emptied the black syrupy contents, swished fresh tap water around the bottom, and refilled the brew machine with distilled spring water from the cooler. Overhead, where the coffee packets were stored, he found a half packet of coffee open. *What good fortune.* With this half pack and another full pack, Callan would have fresh, strong coffee to his liking.

Now all that was left to do was wait.

Callan stood in the break room and watched the coffee drip into the glass carafe. Funny how the stillness of an otherwise-hectic office building heightened the sounds and smells, he thought. The sound of coffee gurgling as it brewed and the first whiffs of its aroma were some of his favorite sounds and smells, but he missed them in the chaotic routine of the day. Funny, too, how the office floor was almost pleasant, somewhat enjoyable in the reflection of stillness at night.

A click sounded, as if a door latched in place.

He listened intently, but the sound didn't repeat. It couldn't have been anything else but a door latching. He looked through the doorway of the break room and turned toward the sound that was now only in his memory.

Did I imagine it?

The smell of the ground Columbian grew stronger. The light on the machine signified that the coffee had finished brewing. Callan reached for the cabinet that held the creamer packets. The last time he'd looked for cream, the box had been almost empty. *Please let there be some.* Ahhh, there they were—packets of delectable powdered cream hidden under the pink and white box of Sweet and Low. Cal emptied a packet into a white Styrofoam cup and watched the contents dissolve into a bronze mud color as he poured in the liquid life.

Click.

The sound again, only louder. Definitely a door latching shut.

Callan perked his head and listened. He replaced the carafe on the burner, turned toward the door, and set his hot cup of coffee on the edge of the microwave stand, its steam rolling over his fingers and into the air. Then he crept to the doorway and stood patiently, turning his head left to right for a full view of the hallway. Adrenalin welled inside his chest, the same sensation he'd felt not long ago on the stairway of his home, waiting for a shadow to emerge from his den. He knew it then. He knew it now. Someone was nearby, waiting and watching.

Crash!

The sound of glass smashing into hundreds of tiny pieces around his feet made him jump. The piercing sting of scalding liquid on the back of his left calf stunned him. He looked toward the floor then to the coffee maker. In his haste to listen for the source of the clicking sounds, he'd neglected to set the carafe squarely on the burner. Gravity prevailed, and it'd crashed to the floor.

He took a deep breath and shook his pant leg. The mess, the tragedy of a broken carafe and wasted coffee was secondary to his sense of danger. Callan moved cautiously down the hall, checking each door along the way to see if it was locked. Finishing one side, he moved across the corridor and made his way down the other.

He stopped at the storeroom. The door opened easily. He looked into the dark room and called out a hello, hoping that whoever was in the storeroom was as scared and unsure of the situation as he was. No one answered back.

Callan flipped on a light switch, illuminating a storeroom filled with steel shelves of office supplies and boxes of documents requiring retention. Although he'd been in the storeroom many times, he never took the time to study the room's layout and look at its contents in depth.

It was an odd-shaped room for storage—a square layout for the most part except for a few jutted wall alcoves for hidden pipes and vents. The layout of the cabinets and storage shelves was particularly odd—a maze to facilitate mobility versus functionality. Another door he'd not noticed before stood on the other side of the room.

He walked to a small metal-basket cart on wheels positioned in front of the door and moved it to one side so he could open the door. The door was locked. After replacing the cart back in its original place, Callan took one last glance around, exited the storage room and walked briskly down the hallway toward his office, remembering he'd left his own office door wide open with all the contents vulnerable in his absence.

Nothing appered to have been disturbed. Callan reached over his desk, picked up the receiver and dialed the number of the Safety and Security Department. Max Dennison, a burly, solid family man, answered the phone. Callan began to talk before Max finished his standard greeting.

"Yeah, Max, this is Callan Morrow up in auditing. Is it possible to know who has come in or out of the building within the past fifteen minutes or so?"

"You mean right now?"

"Yes, it's important."

"We have monitors and surveillance cameras at the entrance, sir. Is that what you want?"

"Did you see anyone leave?"

"Leave, sir?"

"Yes, within the past fifteen minutes or so."

"I'm sorry, sir, it's hard to say. I mean, a lot of people work late. People come and go all the time."

"Oh, yes, of course. It's all right," Callan conceded.

"Are you sure? Do you want to see any tapes or images?"

Callan thought for a moment. "No, it could be a lot of looking for nothing, Max. Thanks, anyway, man."

"Anyone you're looking for in particular, sir? Can I help?"

Callan didn't know how to answer. It could be anyone, or it could be no one. He only felt a presence; he didn't see one.

"Sir?" the security guard prompted.

"No, thank you, Max. I appreciate it, though."

"Anytime, sir."

Callan hung up the phone and decided to leave the office building. On the L train heading west toward Oak Park, he studied the faces of passengers riding with him. Every face became a suspect, though their expressions revealed individuals too tired and weary from the work day to care about invading his office space. He slumped in his seat. The ride passed smoothly and uneventful. He even found the walk from the L station toward the Wingate-Powers apartment building casual and pleasant, and the crisp December air, though cold, wasn't bone-chilling.

He entered his warm apartment and removed his outer garments, draping them across the chair closest to the entry. It, too, was quiet. After years of listening to the rough-housing and antagonistic teasing of two sons and a wife that yelled unmercifully at their play, Callan hadn't gotten use to the serene apartment that was now his home. He meandered toward the refrigerator to grab a longneck off the bottom shelf and enjoyed the mellow taste as he swallowed.

With the after-taste of beer lingering on his palate, Callan reached for his cell phone and punched in the numbers to Larry's phone.

Come on, Larry, pick up.

Disappointingly, the call went straight to voicemail. After the message spiel, Callan said simply, "It's me again. Give me a call."

The lights outside the window caught his eye. He walked over to the panes of glass and peered onto Putnam Street below. The scene was as still and serene as the ride home. He waited a few minutes for signs of life on the streets, then turned away when he decided there were none.

CHAPTER THIRTEEN

The next morning dawned gray and brisk due to an atmospheric low that spit dry, stinging snowflakes from Lake Michigan. Icy pellets darted toward the ground as Callan made his way into the city, clutching his coat. He entered the building and strode down the hall toward his office.

Brrrr.

Chicagoans took the harsh extremes of winter in their stride and chastised the rest of the world for being weather wimps. This morning, Callan admitted he *was* a weather wimp. He'd rather be warm than accepted.

The only thing that kept his mind off his tingling nose was the thought of talking to Aysha. He had questions concerning the recent work she'd performed and the security of her workpapers. He knocked two times on her office door, but met only silence. After unloading his overcoat on a hook behind his own door, he looked around and satisfied himself that all was how he'd left it the night before, then he made his way to the office across the hall. It belonged to Mary DeFrantz, one of Tony's accountants.

"Good morning," he said, smiling while rubbing the palms of his hands together to create additional warmth.

Mary looked up and returned his smile. "Looking for something to burn? You look cold! You should be used to this. Indiana's not exactly a tropical paradise, you know."

"I don't know what it is, Mary, but it's different up here. It really is. It must be the lake."

"Save it." She laughed. "I do understand. We're getting a spin from the north. When the wind starts to shift and moisture off the lake collides with a clipper, we all complain, even Chicagoans."

Callan looked down the hall. "Hey, I have a question for you. Do you know who has the keys to the storeroom?"

"Should be just you, me, and some of the people on our staff."

"Does any other department store their stuff in the room?"

Mary shook her head. "No, why?"

Callan told her about finding the storeroom door unlocked the night before. He didn't elaborate.

"Maybe one of our people was careless. I'll mention it in my next staff meeting."

Callan acknowledged that the announcement would help.

Mary detected his skepticism, however. "There's something more, isn't there?"

"Yes, but I don't know what to make of it." At that, Callan turned and walked briskly toward the storeroom.

Intrigued, Mary followed. By the time she'd caught up to him, he'd unlocked the door and was standing in the doorway, peering warily inside at the inventory of furnishings and documents.

"What is it?" she asked.

"Have you ever seen anyone other than our staff come in or out of here?"

"No, never."

"It would be easy to do, though, wouldn't it? I mean, all they'd have to do is watch closely, slither around the corner of the hall, down the hallway and ..." Callan interrupted himself to walk to the corner of the hall. Spotting an exit sign, he returned to Mary, who stood with a bewildered look on her face.

"... and down the stairwell," he finished.

"Oh, Cal, we'd have surely seen someone if they were going in and out of the storeroom on a regular basis."

"Not if they're good at what they're doing."

Mary stared into Callan's eyes as if to get a read on his thoughts. "Why would anyone do that? Why would they care?"

"That's what I want to find out. I was in here last night. I thought I heard a noise that led me down to this room. I didn't see anything."

Mary touched his arm. "Go on."

"Except that I *felt* someone was here, and now I'm sure of it. This room, for instance. Something is different about this room since last evening. Tell me, Mary. That door on the opposite side, do you know what's in it, and who has the key?"

"I'm afraid I don't, Cal. I can find out for you."

"Would you? I'd appreciate it."

"Sure," she said and started to return to her office. A few steps down the hall, she stopped abruptly and faced him. "So was it you or this *presence* responsible for the coffee pot accident in the break room?"

Callan had completely forgotten about the coffee pot incident. He neglected to clean or to alert housekeeping of the mess in the kitchenette caused by his carelessness the night before. He darted for the break room before Mary stopped him.

"Don't worry; it's been taken care of. I called housekeeping, and they took care of it right away. By the looks of the room, it must have been very unnerving here last night."

Callan gave her a smile to show that he appreciated her understanding. She nodded in return, turned, and marched quickly toward her office. He walked back to the storeroom doorway and carefully perused the room, studying the shelves, the cabinets, the door on the opposite side, and the window.

"Yes, the window," he muttered to himself and walked into the room. The metal-basket cart that he'd moved to access the door now sat below the window, yet he distinctly remembered moving the cart back to its original place before he'd left to call safety and security.

Callan walked back toward Mary's office and noticed Aysha's door still tightly closed. So she still wasn't in. He wondered what was wrong.

He entered Mary's office without knocking. She was on the phone, talking to someone for information about the ownership of keys and access to the storeroom. Callan tried to pick up what he could from the conversation but gave up when he saw her tape dispenser. He reached across her desk and pulled off two long pieces of transparent tape strips. Mary lifted her head to give him a quizzical look.

He left quickly and entered the storeroom, heading straight to the doorway on the opposite side. Callan stooped in front of the door to be close to the floor. He attached one end of one of the pieces of tape to the door and the other end diagonally to the door frame, then he placed the remaining strip across the door and frame diagonally in the opposite direction. He stood and looked at his work. The transparent tape formed an 'x' that should be unnoticeable. Just to be safe, he scraped his thumbnail along the tapes' surfaces to ensure they blended invisibly into the door.

He rose again and walked toward the hallway, turning around to see if the tape would be conspicuous to anyone walking in from the hall. It wasn't. Though neither sophisticated nor reliable, the scheme should be enough to alert him when someone accessed the mysterious door.

Mary finished the last of her phone calls as Callan walked into her office.

"So who owns the door?" he asked.

"It seems this office space was occupied before my time."

"I didn't think there was a 'before your time.'"

"Smarty. You're almost correct. I've been with the company so long they think I knew the Wright Brothers. I don't remember much about this part of the building, though, before I was told to move into this office."

"So what did you find out?"

"Well, interestingly enough, operations has claims to the door in the storeroom."

"Not surprising. Somehow, all my misgivings about this company are focused on operations right now."

"Uninterestingly enough, however, is that the closet is charged to safety and security's cost center."

"Safety and security?"

She smiled as if Callan would be relieved.

"It's a closet?"

"That's what he called it."

"Who called it a closet?"

"Max Dennison. Max called it a closet."

Callan reflected thoughtfully. "Max. He's a good guy, isn't he?"

"I consider him to be, yes."

"Me, too."

"Well, that's something." Mary laughed. "Max will be happy to know he's on Callan Morrow's list of good guys. I suspect that it is a very short list. Max should consider it a huge honor."

Mary's phone rang, breaking the bright moment. She looked at the caller identification display and reached for the phone.

"Hey, does Max have a key so that we can get into the closet?" Callan asked, leaning over her desk.

Mary tried to shoo him away with her hand. The phone rang again. "I didn't ask. We'll have to talk about this later," she said. "I need to get this."

CHAPTER FOURTEEN

By the time Callan left Mary's office, Aysha had arrived. Her door was cracked open enough for him to know she was in, but closed enough for him to know she still wanted respect for her privacy. Callan hesitated in the hallway before poking his head through the crack.

Aysha was on the phone in animated conversation.

She handled Callan's interruption graciously, but her look of irritation was hard for her to disguise.

He gestured if she'd like some coffee.

She shook her head, then quickly changed her mind.

Callan wondered if that was to delay his coming back. *Cream? Sugar?* He asked with charades.

No, black, she lip-synced.

Callan smiled and left.

The break room was spotless with a shiny floor and no evidence of an accident with the coffee pot the night before. The face of the machine looked cleaner than it had been before the mishap, and a new carafe sat in place. The coffee was hot and smelled fresh.

He poured the coffee into cups, one black and one muddy brown, then returned to Aysha's office. He poked his head through the crack of the doorway. This time, she was off the phone. Her glum demeanor hadn't changed, but she'd glossed it over with a professional smile.

"There we go," he said, setting the Styrofoam cups gently on her desk top.

"This is a treat," she replied.

He took a sip, then asked, "Are you okay?"

"Yes, why shouldn't I be?"

"I don't know."

"Everything is fine."

"You seem preoccupied, different, this morning."

She took a deep breath, but offered nothing.

Callan looked at the phone.

"Just a call, if you must know," she said.

"I don't need to know."

"It was a personal call. I assumed we were allowed a couple of them during the day."

Callan took another sip of coffee.

"If it's about me being late."

"It's not."

"Then what's on your mind, Callan?"

"Coffee. Coffee is all. Caffeine to be exact."

"Coffee?"

"Yes. I like coffee. I thought you'd like a cup, too, before we continue our discussion about Cliff from your phone call last night."

"Oh, well, yes, thank you. I was running late this morning. I apologize about that. I barely had time to peek into the break room, let alone to grab a cup."

"Notice anything about the break room?"

"I did, as a matter of fact. Housekeeping did a nice job for once. I thought I'd stepped out of a tornado and into Oz."

"Why look?"

"What?"

"I asked why you looked into the break room."

"Why shouldn't I?"

"You don't drink coffee."

"What?"

"I've never seen you with a cup of coffee."

"Sure, you have."

"No, I don't think so."

"You just handed me a cup."

"That didn't mean you wanted it."

"Are you being serious? What difference does it make? What is this about anyway? This conversation isn't about coffee at all, is it? You can be upfront with me."

"If you're going to work for me, Aysha, you have to give me the benefit of the doubt, the same benefit you want me to give to you."

"And how do you figure that I don't?"

"You woke up this morning wishing you didn't have to come to work, didn't you?"

Aysha didn't respond.

"Last night was one of the first revelations in auditing that you'd made. You did well, and you did it right. You went about it the right way, but you woke up this morning wishing you hadn't made a breakthrough with Cliff Pierceman because now that you did, maybe you'll never be able to get out of this department and back to marketing where you really want to be."

"I don't believe this."

"Am I wrong?"

"You think you know everything. I'm not like that."

"Then what's the matter?"

"Nothing's the matter. I just told you that. I don't know why I'm here; that's my only problem. I don't know why management agreed to put me here. I think auditing was a move to push me out of the organization. I don't know why, Callan, because I don't know what I've done to deserve this transfer. I don't understand it."

"Well, if it makes any difference to you, I don't understand it, either."

"But you accept situations like this better than I do."

"Not necessarily."

"Well, you think you know me already. You think you know what makes me tick."

"No, all I know is that you're not happy with the transfer from marketing. I understand that, but that's all I know. Don't peg me as an old school fuddy-duddy from Indianoplace. I don't care about personal phone calls when you have time for them. I don't care about you coming in late. I know you work long hours and those incidentals don't bother me. All I know is that I have a job to do, and I need you to help me do it."

"Doesn't sound like it."

"You're not listening to me then."

"But the two of us are so different. We're so, so different, Cal."

"So?"

"So I just don't see how this can work. I mean, in marketing, we were all ... we were all—"

"The same."

"Yes!" she responded with relief. "The same. We had the same background. We were the same age. We thought alike. We had the same goals. We were a team. We were in sync."

"Doing the same thing, the same way with the same people day after day all the time. Sounds very unimaginative to me."

"But it worked."

"It can work here, too, Aysha, because differences balance people, and challenges strengthen the balance. My challenge to you isn't a sign that I don't want you, Aysha. It's a sign that I want you better. I want you to see the possibilities within yourself. Right now, I see you as someone who is young and daring and good at what she sets her mind to do, but only if she sets her mind to it and everyone is on board with her way of thinking. I know you want to have the world by the horns to show what you can do. We all do. It's frustrating to feel like you're losing control over your destiny, but if you *can* adjust and adapt to what has been thrust at you, in essence you really have controlled it. You've beaten it. You're even better than you would've been on your own."

"That doesn't make sense," she said, rubbing the tension from her temple.

"What doesn't make sense? That adversity can make you stronger?"

She looked at him critically.

"Adversity doesn't keep someone from doing what they want, Aysha. Adversity prepares them for doing what they want better."

Aysha blinked rapidly several times. Callan could see her grit her teeth—the way a man often does when he's consciously fighting back emotions so the world can't see what's inside.

"The lessons you learn in adversity are the lessons you'll remember as you go forward. It's what keeps you from making the same mistakes over and over so you can move forward."

"And how would someone like *you* know?"

The question took him by surprise. Her voice was accusatory and so low that Callan could hardly pick up on the words. He set his cup of coffee on her desk and took a deep breath. "Oh, wow. Wow, Aysha. I wasn't expecting that. That's a loaded question. Not sure where that came from or why, but let me answer you. First, I'm not about to tell you that I know where you've been or what you're going through. I have no idea what it's like to be black, to be a woman, or to live in a large city like Chicago all my life as you have. I see your image, but I don't know you. I want to, but I can't see your soul ... or your God ... or your gods. But I'm going to tell you something. You don't know me, either.

"You don't know me white. You don't know me male. You don't know where I've been or where I'm going. You don't know my soul or my God ... or my gods. All you see is my image and you judge me like I judge you. So you ask me how I know adversity and suffering. Why do you ask? Is it because I'm white? Is it because I'm male? Do you think everything has been given to me on a silver platter all of my life? Do you not think I face challenges? If so, that's rather shortsighted, isn't it? I may not have experienced challenge and adversity in the same way as you, but as a human being, I still know what it's like to scream at the top of my lungs in the darkness and to realize that no one—absolutely no one—hears me. Or, worse yet, they hear me, but no one cares. So when it comes to knowing adversity, I mean really *knowing* about life and challenge, there isn't anything more a person needs to know to show they're human than that."

Callan took another deep breath, this time to fight back wanting to say more.

Aysha took a deep breath, too.

104

"I don't know why, Aysha, but the two of us are here for a reason—perhaps to turn our relationship as bad as it is right now into something positive. I need someone like you. I need *you* because our relationship represents the very reason why I'm here. You have potential."

Aysha closed her eyes and sat in her chair quietly. When Callan finished talking, she waited a moment, as if struggling to speak and then said simply, "His name is Paeng."

The statement took Callan by surprise. "Pardon me?"

"I know you wonder who I talk to on the phone. You don't ask me, but I can tell you wonder, and you want to know. You have a right to know if you want that kind of working relationship with me. His name is Paeng. He's from the Philippines. His real name is Rafael. He's my boyfriend, my best friend right now. I call him Ralph."

"I see," Callan said softly. "All right, okay, great. Thanks for sharing. I'd like to meet him some time."

Aysha tried to smile, but not much of it bore through the apprehension on her face. "Sure." She thought for a moment, then said, "Well, that was him on the phone before you came in. We usually go to this place after work. It's called Centro Margarita. It's on Clark if you'd like to join us. We're heading there this evening."

Cal didn't hesitate. He accepted the offer.

"Right after work," she said. "Five thirty, six o'clock, whenever."

~

Callan arrived at Centro Margarita closer to six. He'd meant to arrive earlier, but the workpapers Aysha had developed related to Cliff Pierceman's unauthorized transaction deserved another review in case they missed something crucial to prove his innocence.

The cold air followed him into the restaurant—a small place filled with the strong aroma of salsa and oven-roasted tortilla chips. Young adults surrounded tables of tequila shots, lightening the atmosphere and making the place sound busier than it was.

Carlotta Mendoza appeared from behind a wall to greet him. She had a pleasant smile, large, innocent eyes, and beautiful jet-black hair that draped over her shoulders. She grabbed a menu from the hostess podium while he told her about the couple waiting for him.

She looked surprised.

"The woman's name is Aysha."

"I know who she is," she said, appearing distracted. "Follow me."

Carlotta's hair flowed behind her as she maneuvered around a table of three young women who laughed gregariously as if they were the only patrons in the restaurant. Aysha slid off her stool to meet Callan as they approached.

Carlotta set his menu on the table, gave a forced smile and left quickly.

"She really is a sweet girl," Aysha said, noticing Callan's reaction to the hostess' demeanor.

"She looked a little out of sorts with my arrival."

"I don't know why. Maybe she's adjusting to the place. She just arrived in Chicago from Costa Rica to be with her sister, Cecilia, who got her this job. Other than that, she's usually very friendly. She always has our table ready for us. I guess this is our spot—Ralph and me. We've been here so many times lately, she thinks of this table as ours. Pretty chilly out there, isn't it?"

"Yes, but the wind has died down. That helps. It's supposed to snow, they say."

"Oh, I hope so. I love the first snow."

Callan provided Cecilia Mendoza his margarita order.

"Ralph will be here shortly. He was detained at work," Aysha explained. "So... are you getting ready for Christmas? Are you going to Ken Holloway's big holiday party?"

"Are you?" he asked hopefully.

She laughed. "Oh, no; I'm not one of the executives. His party is usually just for management."

Callan squirmed and covered his face with the palm of his hands. "Oh, yeah, well, I got the invitation, but—"

"You're not going?"

"It's not exactly my thing. I'm not crazy about corporate party affairs. I'd rather not know what goes on with some executives after they've had too much to drink and let down their guard."

"Oh, I think that's the best part about parties," she laughed. "It's the most interesting. You can learn so much! You could use it to your advantage as an auditor."

"Yeah, that's true, but ..."

"Another but?"

"Yeah, well, Christmas is the farthest thing from my mind right now. I'm afraid a holiday party will just remind me what I've lost with my family. I'm trying to get into gear, but I'm going to have to find the spirit somewhere or it's going to be a Tiny Tim Christmas for everyone, I'm afraid."

"Work hasn't exactly helped with the holiday spirit, has it? I mean, you've been preoccupied with something, I can tell. It's the same busy, faraway look I see in Paeng sometimes when, oh, and speak of the devil."

Callan looked up to see a handsome young man wearing a black leather bomber jacket approach their table. He gave Aysha a small kiss on her cheek. She introduced him to Callan while moving her coat and purse to another stool so Paeng could have a seat.

"So you were talking about me?" the young man said, and ordered a margarita after Cecilia gave Callan his drink. "You want another one, baby?"

Aysha nodded. "Salt, please. More chips, too."

Cecilia smiled and was off.

"Yes, we were talking about you," Aysha teased. "I was talking about both of you. I hardly get to see either one of you sometimes. You both are impossible with your work schedules and oaths of secrecy about what you do."

"I think paranoia is setting in," Callan retorted teasingly.

"From what I heard at the office today, you above all people should know paranoia. What's this about noises in the dark, supernatural presences, broken coffee carafes, things moving about unexplainably in a storeroom, not to mention the taping of doors shut, workpapers amiss, and executives with advance knowledge of audit findings? Fact or paranoia, Mr. Morrow?"

"Sorry for my ignorance," Paeng interrupted, "but what the hell is going on in those offices of yours? Sounds like something more on the lines of what goes on in my offices at the FBI."

"No, I think your office would be considered dull and routine compared to what has been going on in ours lately."

Curiously, Callan asked, "So what exactly do you do, Paeng?"

Aysha's boyfriend explained his job as a linguist with the FBI. Callan saw many similarities between their careers, and they exchanged the fascination and frustration of an investigation.

Aysha listened intently. The exchange of conversation between her boss and her boyfriend illuminated the importance of the kind of thing she was assigned to do in auditing, and Callan hoped she was learning more of what forensic accounting was all about.

Suddenly, Aysha reached for her coat and draped it over her shoulders. "Oh, my gosh, I'm freezing. Why does it have to be so cold? Are you guys cold sitting here?"

"I can feel a draft." Callan noticed her shivering.

"We're next to the window," Paeng explained. "It's always going to be cold and drafty next to the window."

Aysha looked at the seals surrounding the plate glass window that covered the front of the restaurant. "Yes, I suppose you're right. Still, wouldn't it be nice if they put those wires in restaurant windows like they do in the back window of a car? Flip a switch and the wires make it warm for the customers!"

The men agreed. Callan stood and grabbed his coat. "And speaking of the cold, I'm afraid I'm going to have to leave, and get out into it. I've enjoyed myself, and it has been a real pleasure to meet you, Paeng. Aysha, thank you for the invitation and, most of all, thank you for our conversation this morning. It helped me understand things better." He glanced at Aysha as he slipped into his coat.

She smiled at him, but she didn't respond.

He didn't like the smile. It seemed more out of courtesy than genuineness. And he liked her lack of response even less.

Callan left enough cash on the table to cover the evening's expenses, then glanced again at her face. Even after their discussion earlier that morning when he'd explained her worth to him and the lighthearted conversation they'd had this evening, he still saw sadness in her eyes. He sensed she wouldn't be with him long. He hadn't convinced her of anything.

CHAPTER FIFTEEN

Callan dodged pelts of sleet as he walked away from the restaurant. He slowed to pull his cell phone from an inside coat pocket, wanting to give Larry a call, but pedestrians on the sidewalk made it difficult for him to concentrate. Finding shelter in an alcove away from the elements and people, Callan dialed his friend's familiar number.

Still no answer. He decided to try Argos'.

The westbound L out of downtown was slow going, and after arriving in Oak Park, falling snow sticking to the sidewalks tempered his hurried gait. It was a pretty walk, though. The darkness of evening and the twinkling of holiday lights against the snow crystals reminded him how beautiful Chicago was during the holidays. He wished Terese was with him to share it.

The piped sound of *White Christmas* accompanied him through the entrance of Argos' where a bartender and a waitress sat at a bar eating an appetizer and watching a local meteorologist stand in front of a large map of Chicagoland. The sound was low, but the caption on the screen explained the reason for the meteorologists' excited animation and alarm. The season's first winter storm was imminent with an expectation of six-to-seven inches of ice and snow.

The waitress saw Callan, then covered her mouth and waved her hand rapidly as if the appetizer had scalded her tongue. She nodded towards a table where Larry sat by himself. Larry acknowledged Callan's presence with indifference and continued to stare into his drink.

Callan noticed its bronze hue. "Looks like your glass has more Seven than Seven in it."

"It's still not strong enough. I think I was given a Shirley Temple."

"That's not what I meant."

"I know what you meant."

"How many Shirley Temples have you had?"

"Not enough."

The waitress approached and asked Callan if he wanted anything from the bar. He shook his head.

Larry mumbled under his breath, unable to articulate words. Periodic phrases about Cliff Pierceman sputtered from his mouth. He mentioned something about contracts briefly ... budgets ... maintenance ... then something poignant about Alan Cavanaugh.

"It was meant for me," he said in harsh words that Callan could finally understand.

"What was meant for you? What are you talking about?"

"Cliff, that's what. His firing was meant for me."

"Cavanaugh wasn't out to fire you."

"I didn't mean it like that. I meant Cliff was fired to keep me in my place, to keep my nose out of where it doesn't belong."

"Why would he do that? What the hell is going on?"

"I don't know. That's just it."

"Are you on a special project?"

He shook his head.

"What are you working on?"

"Something I started myself."

"Go on."

"The review of aircraft maintenance contracts, employment agreements, and vendor purchase orders."

"For what?"

"Inconsistencies and ghost contractors. Alan told me I didn't need to do that, said he'd have Mark Reasoner do it, but that's my job, not Mark's. When I told him that, he said he could make it so that it wasn't my job anymore."

"I see," Callan replied, watching the snow fall heavily against the restaurant's window panes.

"I can assure you that Cliff had nothing to do with any wrongdoing."

"Well, we're going to need that assurance."

"What do you mean?"

"Celia Hart requested proof of his wrongdoing. I had Aysha go to accounts payable to pull the documents in question. We found a requisition that Cliff signed."

"For what?"

"Consulting services."

Larry prompted his friend for more information.

"He paid some individual for consulting services."

"That's bullshit. Cliff has nothing to do with consultants."

"That's why Alan fired him."

"Who was the consultant?"

"I don't know. Aysha made a copy of the requisition and sent it to Celia before I had a chance to look at it."

"Was it Cliff's signature?"

"Aysha said it appeared to be."

"Not a forgery?"

"If it was, it was a good one."

Larry took a drink and slammed the bottom of the glass on the top of the counter. "Then it was a good one, Cal, because Cliff didn't sign it."

Callan sighed. "I don't know what to tell you. If the requisition is a forgery, then it would imply Cliff's termination was a smokescreen for something else. And there's one more thing. Tony seems to have some advanced knowledge of some other work we're doing. I hadn't discussed it with him, and I don't believe Aysha has mentioned it to anyone who would have told him about it, either."

Larry grinned. "Sounds like we've got a drone following us, doesn't it?"

"Don't laugh," Callan replied candidly. "You don't know how close to the truth that feels." He glanced at his watch and then assessed the mounting snow outside. "Hey, I'd better get going, but I want to make sure you're okay first."

Larry tipped his glass. "Feeling no pain, bro."

Cal waved to the waitress to calculate the check as he helped Larry off his stool.

After he paid the bill, the men stepped onto the front stoop of the restaurant and bundled their coats to keep the falling snow from finding its way under their collars. They walked to the street corner.

"Hey," Larry said as he kicked snow with the toe of his shoe, "I should probably tell you something."

"What's that?"

"I asked her to marry me last night. I asked Marlene."

"Wow, that's a surprise."

"Well, she's the best thing going on in my life right now. I didn't want her to slip away like everything else seems to be doing lately."

"That's great, Lare. Congratulations. I'm very happy for both of you. I really am. I'm just surprised."

"The two of us are going Christmas shopping Saturday if you'd like to come along. It would be good for you. You could be the only bachelor in Chicago ready for Christmas before Christmas Eve."

Callan grinned, but said he'd have to think about it. The thought of holiday shoppers on a weekend and of being a third wheel in Larry and Marlene's shopping excursion didn't thrill him. Having Christmas without Terese thrilled him even less.

"I'll let you know," he said.

The two shook hands.

Larry walked west, kicking up snow, bending down periodically to see how well the icy crystals packed in his bare hands.

Callan watched him maneuver down the street before making his own solitary journey to his apartment. He stomped the snow from the top of his shoes before entering the foyer of the Wingate-Powers Building. The door of Mrs. Powers' flat opened slowly, and Cal waved to the elderly landlady.

"Oh, it's you, Mr. Morrow," she said, dabbing at her hair.

"I'm sorry if I startled you. I had a late night."

"No apologies necessary, Mr. Morrow. You're okay?"

"Yes, I'm fine,"

She nodded. "I'm glad. Have a good evening." She hesitated before closing the door.

"Everything okay, Mrs. Powers?"

"What? Yes, well, no, not exactly, but nothing I should worry you about. Good night."

"You can tell me, Mrs. Powers. Is there something wrong?"

"I'm not sure."

She focused her apprehension on the front door.

"Please, Mrs. Powers, what is it?"

"Well, if you insist, Mr. Morrow. Earlier this evening when the snow started to fall, a gentleman called. At least, I thought he was calling, but he wouldn't tell me for whom. I didn't want to pry, Mr. Morrow. My business isn't to keep track of my tenants' gentleman friends, but it is to mind the safety of others, if you know what I mean. Not to pry, mind you, but, you know, for the safety of others."

"By all means; it's very kind of you."

"Yes, well, as I said, this gentleman appeared to be calling for a tenant, but he wouldn't say for whom. That nasty sleet and freezing rain was falling. Oh, I do hope you weren't caught in it, Mr. Morrow. I thought it odd because the streets were practically bare of pedestrian traffic as they have been for most of the evening."

Callan gave her a moment to continue, but the sight of the door interrupted her train of thought once again. Fear reflected from her eyes. He turned to look at the door, but saw nothing. "But you don't believe that was the case?" he asked.

"Oh, you're quite right. I don't believe he was here to call on anyone at all."

"What makes you say that?"

"I don't know. I honestly don't know, so I've been listening and watching very closely for him ever since."

"I think that's very prudent, Mrs. Powers, however, I can assure you that I just walked from Argos', and I saw no one the entire way. The walk was just as you described. Hardly a car passed me. Not a soul on the sidewalk. Whoever he was, I'm sure he's gone for the night."

Mrs. Powers tried to smile. "That is reassuring, Mr. Morrow. Thank you for the information. Good evening."

Callan waited until she closed and deadbolted her door before ascending the wooden steps to his second floor apartment. Mrs. Powers' description of an unknown man lurking outside the Wingate-Powers disturbed him a great deal given recent events, but with the weather as it was, there surely would be no additional cause for concern.

He removed his snow-drenched coat, using only the light from the street lamps through the windows as a guide, and spread it across his wing-back chair, the only chair he had.

The apartment was empty. More than just void of furniture and accessories, it was lifeless. He sighed. It wasn't the apartment that was lifeless. It was him, him without Terese.

The empty feeling inside grew stronger, and suddenly he could smell her perfume and feel her cool, smooth skin brush against his face and whisper how much she missed him. Nights like this made him miss her more. On cold and snowy nights like this, they turned on the gas logs in the fireplace and snuggled together under a soft, warm blanket. Nights like this, they shared their inner secrets and hopes for their boys as they sipped wine and listened to soft music. Nights like this, the love they made was the sweetest, most passionate moments of his life.

It was nights like this that he needed her. He also needed to take a deep breath, but he couldn't breathe. He needed air. Callan unhooked the window latch and opened the pane until the crisp air of the December night stilled his reflections.

The snow continued to fall, though the rate of snow had tapered. It was quiet, too. He looked at the apartment buildings and homes along Putnam Street. Most were decorated for the holidays with lights of red, white, and green on hooks along the tops of their porches. The branches of trees and shrubs that adorned the landscape also reflected a quiet, festive mood. The peacefulness of a Christmas snow never ceased to amaze him.

No cars passed along Putnam Street. How odd to have streets where no cars passed in a metropolitan city of eight million people. He was glad, though—grateful. The virgin snow remained intact—pure, white, and untouched—his own set of footprints the only disruption to the surface of the wintry covering.

Callan squinted at the prints he'd made leading to the Wingate-Powers below. He blinked his eyes to refocus and counted his steps, following the trail of footprints as far as he could see to the street corner.

He was wrong. His weren't the only footprints in the snow. Another set, fresher than his, followed his path to the door of the building, paused, and then returned the way they'd come.

CHAPTER SIXTEEN

"Mr. Perry in?" Callan asked as he stepped into Velma Hofmeyer's office.

The executive assistant sat at her computer terminal, typing. She pulled her reading glasses from the bridge of her nose and greeted Callan upon hearing his voice. "May I ask who's interested?" she teased.

"You wouldn't know him," he replied. "He hasn't been around to visit lately."

"The prodigal son returns without bearing gifts of Christmas, I see."

"No, I have no gift with me, but, oh, you're an unconditionally forgiving soul just the same."

"Often misconstrued and underestimated."

Callan grinned and nodded. His good sense of character agreed with her evaluation. Velma Hofmeyer was indeed often misconstrued and underestimated by many at GrandAire. It was why he spent so much time nurturing his relationship with her. Of all the people to ignore or to take advantage, she was not one of them. If he'd thought in advance, he would've brought her a gift for no other reason than to surprise her, being one who received so few gifts.

As it was, he gestured that he'd come empty-handed. "I am but a drummer boy, pa rum pum pum pum."

Velma Hofmeyer leaned back in her chair and allowed herself to have a good laugh. "You have a line for everything, don't you, Mr. Morrow? Is that what keeps you afloat?"

"It has served me well, Velma, I'll admit. Although somewhere along the way, I think I came up a line short." His thoughts turned to Terese.

The wide, jovial smile Velma had carried throughout their teasing turned into a sympathetic gesture of empathy.

"I'm sorry," Callan said. "You're probably not aware of the situation with my wife."

"I am. Mary DeFrantz and I are good friends. Our conversations about what you refer to as your 'situation' are completely harmless and are kept to ourselves with the strictest of confidence."

Callan believed her. Velma Hofmeyer and Mary DeFrantz were two of the most genuine people he knew at GrandAire.

"What may I do for you?" she inquired. "Oh, you asked about Mr. Perry. He's out of town, I'm afraid, on early holiday."

"Isn't there a Board of Directors' meeting scheduled soon?"

"Yes. He's planning to fly in from Palm Beach especially for the meeting. He'll fly back once the meeting is over."

"I see," Callan said under his breath. "I must admit I'm a bit bewildered."

"Excuse me?"

"So much is going on within the company. I find it odd that he's away."

"I'm sorry you came down from your office for nothing."

"Oh, I didn't come to see Mr. Perry. I have a meeting with Ken Holloway. I thought that if Mr. Perry was in the office today, I'd wish him a good holiday."

"I see," Velma said, her smile returning. "Will you be at Mr. Holloway's party tomorrow evening? I believe Mr. Perry is coming into town in advance of the Board meeting and will be at the gathering."

Callan barely allowed any enthusiasm to surface. The political awkwardness of corporate holiday parties with people who often made fools of themselves was not to his liking. He'd rather sit alone in his apartment staring blankly at his bare walls.

"By the way, Mr. Morrow," Velma inquired. "Were you able to meet with Ms. Chambers?"

"Meet? No. Was I supposed to?"

"She asked about you. She asked if I knew where you were. I said I was not privy to your calendar. I found it odd that she should ask me."

"She was fishing."

"Whatever for?"

Callan ignored her question. "Tell me something."

"If I can."

"Is there a history between the two of you by any chance?"

"Excuse me?"

"I'm sorry to ask this, Velma. It sounds impertinent, I know, but it really is important that I ask."

Velma straightened her posture and organized a few papers that had been scattered across the surface of her desk. She appeared perturbed by Callan's inquiry and seemed to consider a response then decide against it. She eventually handled the comment by saying, "Mr. Holloway's assistant is out of the office running an errand for the moment. I'm sure if you knock on his door you can go in."

Callan didn't press the issue and did just that. He left Velma to her typing and knocked solidly on Kenneth Holloway's door, then escorted himself into his large, elaborate office. Holloway leaned back in his leather chair as if talking to the ceiling, indulged in a conversation on the phone.

Kenneth gestured for Callan to sit. After looking at a plaque recognizing Kenneth's contributions to a committee of the American Bar Association, Callan walked to a burgundy chair in front of the lawyer's desk. He sank deeply into the leather cushion, allowing his back to be caressed by the curvature of the high-back chair.

"Yes, Mr. Dunham, I understand," Callan heard Holloway say. "Yes, sir, they *are* large contracts. Mr. Cavanaugh has his management team on top of them." Kenneth Holloway closed his eyes as Zane Dunham spoke. Weary frustration penetrated the tone of his response. "As a matter of fact, Mr. Dunham, Callan Morrow has just stepped into my office for a meeting on this very subject. I'll inform him of our conversation and get back to you on our action plan. Yes, sir. I understand. I'll be happy to get on that. Yes, sir, right away. Yes, sir. Good day, sir."

Kenneth placed the phone's receiver in its place and stared at it momentarily before turning to the auditor. "That was Dunham," he said as if Callan hadn't been paying attention. "He's concerned about recent large-dollar maintenance contracts executed by our operations team to support our line of aircraft. We've also entered into agreements to fund capital acquisitions that are a major part of our strategic plan in the New Year. He's concerned that our due diligence toward these arrangements has not been thoroughly communicated to the board and disclosed to our lending institutions."

"Is he right?"

"It's true that we haven't done a good job in communicating to the board the process of these acquisitions and maintenance contracts. The lack of communication has created distrust and uncertainty with some members of the board, so they now believe proper due diligence hasn't been performed."

"That's not good."

"Of course it's not good, but that's why he wants you involved."

"But I haven't been privy to these acquisitions or maintenance contracts to form an opinion."

"I thought Larry Southard would have kept you up to date."

"Larry understands confidentiality even with close friends."

"But you have a duty to be informed to do your job. We're in the process of buying some aircraft to expand our market and to increase flight schedules. This has created a need to review and modify current maintenance contracts with our third parties. While these contracts represent a large expenditure, they'll allow us to recognize a significant savings over previous contracts. Our third parties have been willing to work with us in achieving our marketing strategies and financial goals."

"So ... the problem?"

"I think Zane believes they are *too* willing to assist us."

"That's not good, either."

"Damn right."

"What do *you* think?"

The lawyer took a deep breath before saying, "Just because a company works with another company to help them meet operational goals doesn't mean there's impropriety. This is where Alan should've been more transparent. Our lack of communication has played a major role in the board's discontent."

"Where are we with this project?"

"We've been approved for funding; the acquisition contracts have been signed; the planes will be delivered, and the maintenance contracts are being reviewed and modified by Cavanaugh's management team as we speak. Maybe you could ensure that the controls and processes Burris has recommended to be implemented have been completed by his people."

"Burris has plans?" Callan asked, surprised. He could tell Kenneth Holloway didn't appreciate his sarcasm.

"He presented quite an extensive action plan to the executive council this morning," Kenneth replied, "including the establishment of a viable investment committee, the incorporation of additional segregation of duties within the treasury function, the provision for additional staff in finance and accounting, and improvements over the management expense reimbursement process."

Callan was speechless. Those were *Callan's* recommendations, not Tony Burris'. Burris must have obtained his recommendations and taken credit for doing so. Ken elaborated on what Tony had presented to the executive team. He recited findings and recommendations that Cal and Aysha had shared only with each other. But where did he get the information? Who leaked the information? More importantly, who'd been lurking around the audit offices after hours to gather this information?

"Callan?"

Callan looked up, realizing that he hadn't been paying attention. "I'm sorry. I was just thinking about Tony's recommendations."

"Alan Cavanaugh worked with Tony on them, apparently."

"Cavanaugh? What does he know about financial controls? That sounds rather odd, don't you think, Ken? I mean, where did he get his information to be able to work with Tony on this?" Callan stopped asking questions. It dawned on him that he'd answered his own questions about how the information was obtained. It also confirmed specifically who'd been lurking in his offices.

It also dawned on him who broke into his home and took the *Monon* folder.

CHAPTER SEVENTEEN

The atrium felt unusually chilly as Callan walked toward the elevators. He didn't get far before he heard a stern female voice calling his name above the echoing noise of other nearby employees. Callan turned and wondered how he'd missed the menacing march of the woman's shoes that dug into the floor's tile, clamoring loudly above all other sounds.

It was Carol Chambers. Crisp, meticulous and poised, she approached him quickly. "Good day, Callan," she said, more out of courtesy than sincerity.

Callan acknowledged her greeting.

"Didn't you get my message that I needed to talk to you?"

"Velma gave it to me just as I was going into a meeting with Ken."

"It's important."

"Shall we go to your office?"

"That's not necessary. In executive council, Tony Burris presented changes in the way expense reimbursements will be handled. Apparently, these improvements were based upon an audit you performed. I use the word improvements very loosely, I might add.

I'm not sure you fully understand the ramifications of what you're proposing."

Callan lifted a finger. "First of all, Carol, they weren't my proposals. I was asked by Tony to perform an audit, and I did so. The action plan he implemented was his proposal, not mine. I haven't even been given the opportunity to review what he proposed."

"Then that angers me even more," she replied with venomous inflections. "If you have findings, as you call them, and management has prepared an action plan, I believe you have an obligation as the organization's chief audit executive to determine the effectiveness of those action plans against the findings you discovered. Isn't that a part of your normal follow-up activity?" Before Callan could say anything, Chambers added, "If not, it should be."

"What did Tony recommend that you disagree with, Carol?"

"Do you think you can possibly change anything now?"

"I can give it a shot."

"Don't bother. You should've done it right the first time."

"Carol, if I'm going to be accused of developing inappropriate recommendations to the executive council, I at least have a right to know what the accusations are."

"Approval limits, for one," she retorted. "We had appropriate limits prior to Tony's recommendations. I don't see any reason to restrict them further. And is it necessary for all expense reimbursements by senior vice presidents to be approved by Mr. Perry? That is a complete waste of time by everyone involved."

"You don't believe that."

The whites of Chambers' eyes bulged. "I'm not in the habit of saying things I don't believe, Callan. That is one thing you better get straight."

"I'm sorry, but requiring appropriate approval limits is a basic control."

"So you think Hamilton Perry has the time to determine the validity of all our reimbursements and payable invoices? My point is, Callan, the additional restrictions proposed inhibit our ability to do what we need to do to get the job done. If you can't understand that, then I don't believe you truly understand the direction this organization is going."

"Or perhaps you don't understand the principle of fiscal responsibility. I'm sorry you're offended, Carol, but the work performed during the review was solid. I suggest you take your disagreement directly to Tony rather than stand here rallying your cause just because you didn't like the results of our findings."

"I'm rallying, as you put it, because your findings are flawed. The errors directly impact the way I'm able to do my job."

Callan gritted his teeth and stood defiantly. "Like I said, I stand behind Aysha's work."

"Oh, I'm sure you do," Chambers replied smugly as Callan turned toward the elevator.

She followed him as he pushed the elevator down button, hoping the elevator door would open quickly and whisk him away. "What do you mean by that?" he asked.

"I don't doubt for a minute that you stand behind her work."

"Your point?"

"Very simply. Does she stand behind *yours*?"

The comment caught him off guard.

"Ooh, you don't know what I'm talking about, do you?" she asked indignantly. "Well, I'd love to stand here and *rally* some more with you, but I've got a meeting to catch. Perhaps we'll both find out what I'm talking about soon enough."

Callan entered the elevator alone. He punched the button to his floor six times in rapid succession, but his impatience did little to speed the door's closing and the elevator's pace. Chambers' final statement haunted him.

Perhaps we'll both find out what I'm talking about soon enough.

What did that mean? And why?

The elevator opened, and he trotted toward Aysha's office. He could ask her what Chambers meant by the comment, but if Chambers was playing a mind game, questioning Aysha would be unfair. Aysha wasn't the problem.

Callan passed the storeroom and slowed to a halt. The thought of the tape at the bottom of the closet door entered his mind. He'd checked several times over the past few days, but the tape had always remained undisturbed. The lack of activity puzzled him. He unlocked the door to the storeroom, strode to the opposite side of the room, and, stooping down, he reached with his right hand toward the bottom of the door to feel the tape. This time, it was no longer intact against the surface of the frame. Someone had been in and out.

Callan tried the door, but couldn't open it.

"It's locked," a deep voice said from behind.

Callan turned abruptly.

Alan Cavanaugh loomed in the doorway of the storage room. "Why are you trying to get into there?"

"Is this yours?" Callan asked. "Do your people own this room?"

"It's not a room. It's just a closet, Morrow, barely big enough to hold my coat. Don't you have other things to do than to lurk about coat closets?"

"I was just looking for additional space to store audit workpapers. I need something that locked."

"Get a cabinet. You can place it over there in that vacant spot. Sounds simple enough to me."

Callan nodded, but he didn't believe the executive. He believed the door led to a space much bigger than a closet based upon eye-balling measurements of the storage room and adjacent offices.

Unless, of course, Alan Cavanaugh had a very large coat.

CHAPTER EIGHTEEN

"I thought you said you'd be right down," Candice scolded.

Terese finally came down from her room to the breakfast table of their downtown Chicago hotel. She agreed to come to Chicago with Ellen and Candice for a holiday shopping excursion, but wished she hadn't. She glanced at her watch to see how late she was running. *Oh, goodness! No wonder they're angry.*

"Where are we going first?" Ellen asked eagerly. "And what are you two wearing tonight?"

"I'm not going," Terese blurted as she searched her purse for a tissue.

Ellen slumped disappointedly in her seat.

"If you're talking about your son's holiday party tonight, I'm not going."

Candice winced. "I'm sorry, Ellen. I told Terese she didn't have to go if she didn't want to."

"All I want is for you to meet my son and his wife, Terese."

"I don't mind meeting them, but tonight isn't the right time or place. Do you think it is? Put yourself in my shoes. It's more than just meeting your son and his family, Ellen. I've separated from my husband, and I've refused to tell him I'm in town, yet he finds me at a corporate party where he now works. How uncomfortable is that for either one of us?"

"Another time, then."

"What do you mean, another time?"

"Another time. I'm not going to argue with you. I'm here to have a good time."

"Well, so am I."

"Then another time."

"You're making me out to be the grumpy Gus here," Terese said, looking into Ellen's defiant eyes. "I came to Chicago to have fun, too."

"Well, you're doing a very poor job of it."

Ellen slid out of the booth to go to the restroom.

"This isn't Ellen's fault, you know," Candice retorted angrily.

"Fault for what?"

"The crack in your porcelain life."

"I don't know what you're talking about."

"Contrary to what you think, this trip has nothing to do with you and Callan. It's about shopping and being together. It's about being with friends, and it's about having a good time. Tonight, it's about Ellen being with her family. It's not about you or Callan or how miserable you are."

"That's why I shouldn't be here, Candice. It's not fair for Ellen not to enjoy her family, and it's not fair for Callan to see me at the party even for Ellen's sake."

"But you're curious, aren't you?"

"Curious isn't the word. Of course I'm curious."

"And you care. Don't tell me you don't love him anymore."

"Of course I love him. I never said I didn't love Callan. I do. I never said that I don't care. What I'd like from him, though, is some semblance that he feels the same."

"But he does, Terese. That's what I don't get about you. Just because he has this passion to understand how his friend died, you get all bent out of shape."

"It isn't passion, Candice. It's an obsession. There's a difference between the two, and he has to make a choice whether he wants to follow his obsession or to do right by his family. He's obsessed with righting a wrong to his friend at the expense of doing what is right for his family."

"And what is that?"

"Providing us stability and security. Is it so wrong for me to want some security at this stage of my life?"

"Is that what you call *your* obsession?"

"Security isn't an obsession, Candice. You're talking nonsense."

"Am I? Your search for a porcelain-perfect life is an obsession, too, Terese. It affects your behavior and your family as much as Callan's quest affects you. Nothing is perfect in life. Nothing is sacred or secure. Don't you see that? It can all be taken away in a blink of an eye. For crying out loud, Terese, look at the world! There's hunger, poverty, deceit, discrimination, and dishonesty all around us, and you're content ignoring it for what you call security. Ignoring issues in life doesn't strengthen stability, Terese. It makes you vulnerable, and vulnerability, my friend, is the exact opposite of stability."

Terese sat cemented in place, considering her friend's statements.

Candice didn't let her think long. "I'd like to know something," she added. "Is Callan the only one who has a choice to make in your relationship?"

Terese stared, awestruck, at the exclusive homes in the north shore village of Kenilworth as Ellen drove her and Candice to her son's holiday party. Kenilworth, a planned city, meticulously planned and detailed, had homes with huge, exquisitely manicured yards, void of utility poles, set amidst an attractive landscape of seasonal adornments vibrant against the snow. Young and middle-aged couples in fashionable ski jackets walked their pets along the footpaths, talking casually as they passed.

Although a small community by Chicago standards, the eight hundred households maintained a staunch reputation as one of the wealthiest and most exclusive villages in the Midwest. The large, opulent houses impressed Terese, but oponents of the trend called these newly developed homes McMansions. The controversy divided the citizens of Kenilworth. Village political parties emerged based upon platforms of architectural design, historical preservation and zoning reform.

Kenneth and Lisa Holloway owned a McMansion.

Terese stared at the house as Ellen maneuvered her car to a halt and announced that they'd arrived.

"Wow," Candice said in a low whispery voice that expressed her awe. She looked at her outfit and attempted an excuse for staying in the car.

"Nonsense, Candice, you look fine," Ellen said. "Really, you do."

Terese opened her car door and scowled. "Stand by me all evening, Candice, and you're assured to look your best."

"Stop it, you two," Ellen scolded. "You have nothing to be ashamed of in my son's home. They're down-to-earth people from Indiana, for crying out loud."

Ellen was right. Terese and Candice were greeted warmly immediately upon entering the foyer, and Lisa Holloway remarked sincerely how festive they looked.

Terese marveled at the enormity of the entertainment room adorned with custom furniture and window treatments, textured walls and lush, sculptured carpet.

"Please come in and make yourself at home," Kenneth said, taking their coats. "Let's grab some drinks and find our way to the buffet, shall we? What can I get you to drink? I have a full bar. I'm getting Mother a Tom Collins. May I recommend a martini?"

"Yes, thank you, Ken," Terese replied. "Cosmopolitan, please."

Kenneth turned his attention to Candice, who requested a light beer.

"She'll have a Chardonnay," Terese interjected. "You like Chardonnay, don't you, dear?"

Candice relented graciously.

When Kenneth left to get their drinks, Terese turned to Candice and said, "You'll look better with a wine glass in your hand, trust me."

The introductions seemed endless and exhausting. The attention focused on Ellen. Terese felt grateful when Kenneth arrived with their drinks. The act of holding a drink and sipping in tasteful eloquence gave the appearance that she was enjoying hersself.

Terese took Kenneth's cue and searched for the buffet tables, one of garden vegetables, salads, Wisconsin cheeses, and a variety of patés and breads and the other

135

of hot entrees and side dishes. She walked casually toward the tables, hoping not to look too eager.

"Quite a spread," a male voice announced from behind her.

Terese turned. Her culinary trance had been broken by a tall man with scruffy, gray hair and an intimidating demeanor. She froze momentarily, recognizing him immediately. The voice belonged to the man she'd seen talking to Callan in the café at the safety board hearing, the same man that gave her chills when she thought of ever seeing him again. "Excuse me," she said coolly, skirting in front of him on her way to the next table.

The man ignored her, standing perfectly poised, appearing to enjoy her reaction.

She reached for a bacon-wrapped giblet and popped it into her mouth to determine if it tasted as good as it looked. It did. She decided she must like giblets after all, at least when marinated with a spicy teriyaki sauce. Then, as the livery flavor burst on top of her unsuspecting taste buds, she remembered why she didn't eat things wrapped in bacon at parties.

"Did I hear you're Callan Morrow's wife?"

Terese spun around.

The man spoke to her, but continued to stare at the buffet table as if he didn't really care who she was. "Or ex-wife or something?"

"Wife," Terese responded pleasantly.

"How interesting."

Terese ignored him.

"And awkward, too, I'm sure."

She paused briefly to consider the comment, then resumed her attention to the buffet's selections. "No, not

136

really. I'm enjoying myself very much. It's a very nice evening. Oh, you must try these wrapped giblets."

"I sound rude, don't I? I don't mean to come across so boorish, but I couldn't help but notice that I hadn't seen Callan this evening and yet ... here you are."

Terese transferred her plate into her left hand and extended her right arm to shake the man's hand. "I'm sorry. We haven't been introduced, and I'm afraid I don't know your name."

He smiled apologetically, but to Terese it appeared superficial. "Alan Cavanaugh, and you're Teresa?"

"Terese."

"Very nice. Is Callan here?"

"I came ahead separately with my friend Ellen Holloway."

Alan appeared impressed at the mention of Kenneth's mother. He turned away, giving his attention back to the buffet table. "It's so nice for Mrs. Holloway to bring you all the way from Indianapolis. Is this your first trip to Chicago?"

Terese faked a smile. "No, I've been granted a visa to your city before."

Alan laughed lightly and what appeared to be sincerely. "I'm sure Callan has mentioned my name several times. It's good to put a face to a name."

Terese lifted her free hand to touch the side of her face and pondered his statement carefully. "No, I'm sorry; he's mentioned several people that he's enjoyed working with at GrandAire, but not you."

Any resemblance of a smile—fake or otherwise—left Cavanaugh's face immediately. "I'd love to spend time to chat with you some more, but I must get back to the party. It was a pleasure to talk with you, Terese. I hope you enjoy the rest of the party, including this wonderful buffet. I presume this is what you Hoosiers refer to as 'good eats'?"

Terese didn't give him the honor of watching him walk away.

Candice walked up and stood beside her. "Who was that?"

"Nobody." She returned to the buffet table to put another cherry tomato on her plate. "Hey, try these bacon-wrapped things."

Candice curled her nose. "He thinks he's somebody. That's pretty obvious. So what do you make of these people?"

"I try not to think about it."

"I just can't see Callan fitting in with this crowd, can you? I wonder what attracted him to this."

"I think it's rather obvious."

"No, I'm serious."

"I am, too. I'm very serious. It's me."

"You?"

"The job's distraction was worth more than its attraction."

"I think you're over-exaggerating, Terese."

"Am I?"

"You usually do. I think Callan came to Chicago for a purpose—a specific purpose."

"And what's that?"

"I don't know, but I really thought he'd be here tonight. I thought he might patch things up with you a bit."

Terese avoided her comment and recommended Candice pick up a plate and fill it from the buffet.

"You ought to eat something before you take another drink," she warned. "You're starting to talk jibberish, and I've heard enough jibberish for one evening."

From behind, a soft but perky feminine voice interrupted Terese as she placed an appetizer in her mouth. Terese acknowledged the woman as she swallowed her food, excusing herself with hand gestures.

"Please eat," the young woman encouraged. "My boyfriend and I have been grazing all evening. The food is delicious, isn't it? My name's Aysha Marks. I understand you're Terese, Callan's wife. I work for your husband in the auditing department."

"Yes, Aysha, Callan has mentioned your name, and it's a delight to finally meet you. This is my friend from Indianapolis, Candice Reid."

"I haven't seen Cal. Is he here?' Aysha said. 'I told him that because I wasn't a part of management I wouldn't be coming to the party, but out of the blue I got this invitatation. I was quite surprised and was hoping I could talk with him. I really enjoy working with Cal."

"Really?"

"You don't believe me?" Aysha teased.

"No, no, I believe you." Terese laughed. "Callan loves his work, and I'm sure he's thrilled to share his experience with you."

"Yes, he's very passionate about what he does. I've had to learn to appreciate that about him first."

"Well put," Candice added, finishing her glass of wine. She looked at Aysha and said, "Appreciating passion is not one of Terese's strong points."

CHAPTER NINETEEN

Callan grabbed his coat and hastily put his right arm through its sleeve. Two hours ago, he'd sat in the comfort of his recliner to rest his eyes. He'd never meant to fall asleep. All he'd wanted was to relax enough to get him through the social excruciations of a corporate party he didn't want to attend.

Kenneth's mother, Ellen, was going to be at the party. That meant there was a good chance Terese would be there, too. It was an excellent opportunity for him to catch a few words with her on neutral ground to rekindle their relationship. Here he was, though, running late from his apartment—very late, disheveled, thoughtless—an impression he didn't want to give Terese.

A rush of bitter air met him at the bottom of the stairs near the entrance. He saw a woman coming in from the cold. If he hurried, he could reach the open door before it latched shut. He noted something recognizable about the large, old woman stepping into the entry, but he wasn't sure what. Layers of color-coordinated scarves, mittens, mufflers and a pullover hat shrouded her, and a large, dark coat over the ensemble ensured that she was bundled warmly. Something was vaguely familiar about her, but it wasn't Mrs. Powers; he was certain of that.

The woman looked up as they drew closer, and recognition dawned. "Callan? Good Heavens. Don't tell me you're going out on a night like this," Mrs. Argos scolded in a firm, but motherly, tone.

Callan stopped to greet her, letting the door shut behind her. "And I could say the same for you, young lady," he said with a grin.

"Me? Why, this is nothing for me. I'm just calling on an old friend. It has to be colder than this to keep me from seeing a friend who has a mystery I can assist in unraveling."

Callan didn't understand much of Mrs. Argos' last statement. He didn't have time for translation, but he also couldn't let the statement pass. "A mystery, Mrs. Argos? What friend do you have in the Wingate-Powers that carries such a burden? You weren't coming to see me, were you?"

She laughed, but didn't have time to answer before they heard Bernadette Powers' door opening. The portly landlady emerged from her dark apartment, holding a deck of cards. Her dark, wide-rimmed reading glasses slipped on her nose as she tried to peer over the lens. She wore a burgundy house dress with paisley prints and a sweater that, though appearing warm, was worn on the elbows. Her pink synthetic slippers made Callan look twice.

"What's going on out here?" she called.

"Never mind that. Let me in. It's cold out here," Mrs. Argos bellowed.

"You two know each other?" Callan asked.

The two women glanced casually in each other's direction. "I guess you could say that," Mrs. Argos chuckled. "Forty-six years of friendship."

So Wynetta Argos and Bernadette Powers were best friends. That surprised Callan.

Mrs. Argos couldn't contain herself any longer. She turned to Mrs. Powers and raised her left finger into the air to gain her attention. "I've seen your man," she cried. "Put on a pot of tea, my dear. I've much to tell you."

Callan smiled at the thought of the two of them, like *Arsenic and Old Lace,* nestling down on a cold winter's night to a conversation about how to snare old men into their lair. He turned quietly toward the door to leave.

"And you've seen him, too, Mr. Morrow," Mrs. Powers called out.

Callan stopped, intrigued. "Seen who?"

"Our man."

"What man?"

"You know the man, Callan. Remember the man I saw poking around the premises the night it snowed?"

He remembered. It was the man who left his footprints behind Callan's on the sidewalk along Putnam Street.

Mrs. Argos said, "I'd bet my bottom dollar he's the same man who's been in the restaurant."

"Which one?"

"The one who sits but a table or two away from you each time you're in the restaurant. Dark hair, mustached, odd sideburns, big frame, a little chunky. Don't you ever notice him, Mr. Morrow?"

Callan admitted that he did not.

"And, sometimes," she said, lowering her voice as if the man she was talking about could overhear, "I see him standing under the canopy in the alcove across the street. It's fairly dark usually, but I can see enough to know it is the same man."

"Why haven't you told me this before?"

"Because it didn't cause me any concern, not until Bernadette relayed her fears of the man prowling around in the snow the other night. Then I remembered this man, and I remembered that he seems very interested in what you and Mr. Southard have to talk about when you're in the restaurant. I often see you two having serious conversations."

"What do you think this means?" Mrs. Powers asked, genuinely concerned.

Callan shook his head. "I don't know." Thoughts swirled in his head, and fear trickled up his spine. Was it the man who'd broken into his house? Was it the same man as the one who'd entered his office after hours to take information from Aysha's workpapers? Was he the same man who'd left his footprints in the snow after he'd followed Callan home? Callan didn't know what to think. In fact, he didn't want to think. He had to get going. "Look, I'm running late, and I have a forty-five-minute drive ahead of me to Kenilworth."

"You're leaving?" Mrs. Powers asked with trepidation.

"We'll be fine," Mrs. Argos replied.

"Yes, you'll be fine. Nothing will happen tonight."

"How can you be so sure?"

"I can't," he confided, "but there's a holiday party going on right now, and I suspect that will take precedence even for our mystery man. You must do me a favor, however. You must keep the information about this man a secret. Can you do that? I don't know who he is or what he wants, but if he finds out you suspect him as a person of interest, it may put you both in harm's way."

"Do you really think that could be the case, Mr. Morrow?"

"Let's not take any chances, shall we?"

Mrs. Powers nodded and Wynetta Argos stood looking defiant against the unknown.

Callan bid the women goodbye and bolted for his car, thinking all the while of the man making footprints in the snow and lurking quietly in the shadows of a cold, dark alcove.

His chance to mend his relationship with his wife at Kenneth Holloway's party vanished by twenty minutes. He discovered that Terese had left the party with Ellen and Candice just before he'd arrived. Larry and Marlene tried to entertain him with small talk, but Callan wasn't interested in small talk. In fact, as he looked about the room at the guests, he decided there was very little that interested him at all. "I should go," he said.

"No, don't," Marlene implored. "Larry, get him a drink while I take Cal to the buffet. Far be it from me to believe a stiff drink is the answer to anything, but I think you deserve it right now."

Callan shook his head. He didn't want a drink if he was going to drive away soon.

"Then follow me. Something to eat will do you good."

"Did she ask about me?"

Marlene gave him a sorrowful look. "Cal, I didn't really get to talk—"

"Did she?"

"It wasn't so much about you. She talked about herself. She felt uncomfortable being here. She said it wasn't fair to you for her to be here. It was *your* corporate party, and she said it would be awkward for you."

"No, this is awkward, Marlene. Having my wife here without me, then leaving right before I arrive without her is what's awkward. I'm sure people have noticed."

"She said Mr. Cavanaugh did."

"Oh, good. That's just great."

"It's not her fault, Callan. Why couldn't you have gotten here earlier?"

Larry approached the couple and handed Callan a cocktail.

"I was detained. I was leaving the building when Mrs. Argos stopped by to see Mrs. Powers. Apparently, they've got it in their heads that there's a mysterious dark-haired man hiding in alcoves and listening in on our conversations at the restaurant."

"They're watching too many Vincent Price classics," Larry replied. "All mysterious men have dark hair and hide in alcoves in the old movies."

"I hear ya, but this time I believe there's something to their imagination. Have you noticed anybody—anybody at all—that looked suspicious to you when we've been there?"

"No, but I haven't been looking for someone."

"Exactly. I hate to admit it, but I haven't, either."

"Guys, let's not talk about it, okay?" Marlene asked. "Not here. Not tonight. You're starting to creep me out. How about we change the subject? Larry, get us something to munch on; do you mind?"

"Why am I always sent away when you want to change the subject?" he teased.

"Just go, please. Thank you. Then when Larry comes back, Cal, I suggest we find Aysha and her boyfriend and—"

"He's at the buffet."

"Pardon me?"

"He's at the buffet, and there's Aysha."

Callan pointed to a settee where Aysha sat next to another woman. "You get Paeng. I'll get Aysha." He took a few steps, then stopped abruptly in his tracks. Aysha was sitting with Carol Chambers, and their conversation wasn't a lighthearted one; it appeared serious—almost business-like.

Marlene approached Callan with Aysha's boyfriend by her side. "There," she said cheerfully. "Isn't this nice?"

Callan continued to stare at the two women talking intently on the settee. Nice wasn't the word that came to his mind.

CHAPTER TWENTY

Snow fell within the Mile Square of downtown Indianapolis on the afternoon of Christmas Eve, but only a couple of inches, and it soon started to melt. At thirty-eight degrees, hopes for a white Christmas in the Circle City grew dimmer by the hour. Even the remnants of snow earlier in the week were only a memory.

Fog shrouded Callan's walk south on Meridian Street from Monument Circle. He'd driven straight to the Circle from Chicago—a tense journey, fighting tiredness, visibility, and anxious travelers. The bustle of holiday shoppers had waned by the time he arrived downtown. That was just fine to him. He'd come to Indianapolis for only one reason: he wanted to spend time with his sons and see Terese.

While they had a nice Christmas Eve together as a family, it wasn't exactly what Callan had in mind. They had the Christmas ham and persimmon pudding, of course. There were presents and Callan's attempt at singing carols, but there was no reconciliation with Terese. That part of his expectation eluded him.

He tried another angle by inviting her to join him in his hometown of St. Joseph for the annual New Year's Dine

147

and Dance. She declined, though seemingly reluctantly. So he went alone with Larry and Marlene, hoping the revelry of music, noise makers, confetti, good food, and drinks would be enough to dissipate the sting of his disappointment.

Callan loved the Braun Haus where the party was being held. The Haus spent an enormous amount of time and energy sprucing the banquet hall for the occasion, and he enjoyed the aged building and fond memories tucked in every corner of its old-world architecture.

Larry broke Callan's trance by tapping his cup to show that it was empty. "Want anything from St. Louis?" he asked, referring to beer.

Callan shook his head and watched Larry waddle slowly to the bar. "Something's not right, Marlene."

"I know," she said from her seat next to Cal.

"What's going on?"

"His mom for one. She wasn't very coherent at Thanksgiving. Larry noticed it immediately. He wanted to enjoy his mom's home cooking again, but she couldn't put two and two together on the recipes. It was very apparent something wasn't right. She used baking soda instead of salt for the gravy, and it had a nasty taste.

"Then she made a pineapple honey glaze for it as if she was baking a ham. She bought a ham for dinner, but didn't bake it. She thought she did, though, and asked which one of us hid it. She was very upset that the postman didn't deliver the mail on Thanksgiving even though it was a holiday. We noticed, though, that there was no mail to be found anywhere in the house. We found out that she kept it hidden under a cement block off the back stoop so no one could steal her identity."

Callan shook his head and expressed how sorry he was for her and Larry.

"The most troublesome was Christmas Eve when we arrived from Chicago. We turned up the lane leading to her house. After we drove past the wood-lot clearing, Larry said, 'Is that Mama on the front porch?' I looked and couldn't believe my eyes. There she was, Cal, sitting in her front-porch rocker, rocking away like it was summertime. She had her coat on, thank goodness, but it was still cold, and Larry was extremely upset."

"I don't blame him. Is it Alzheimer's?"

Marlene shook her head to indicate that she didn't know. "Then, of course, there's Cliff Pierceman," she added, looking to see how close Larry was to returning to the table. "He's still very upset about Cliff. That has been the icing on the cake for him."

"Icing on what kind of cake?"

"Regret for dragging you into this mess at GrandAire."

Callan lifted his hand a little to let Marlene know that Larry was close. Larry approached slowly and set his Seven and Seven on the table, then clumsily sat across from his wife and friend.

"Things are looking up, Lare!" Callan said in a positive voice, more for himself than his friend.

Larry smirked. "Why? Has that mystery guy stopped following us? Is Cliff going to be back at work on Monday? What about that creepy stuff going on at night on your floor of the office building? Has all that been resolved?"

Callan didn't answer.

"Then it doesn't sound like it's looking up very much," Larry responded sarcastically, lifting his drink to toast.

Callan said he still didn't know the identity of the man following them, but Aysha's boyfriend, Paeng Ramirez, offered his services at the FBI. That's what he meant by 'looking up', he explained.

"Oh, yeah, well, there's nothing that screams the good life as when the FBI has to open a case to protect your ass. Maybe now you'll have more time to deal with your next problem."

"And what's that?"

"Finding out what's going on between Aysha and Carol Chambers."

"I don't know anything about that."

"You should. From what I saw at the party, Carol and Alan made it very obvious there was something seriously in the works. You saw it, too, and don't say you didn't."

"It was all for show, Larry. The conversation in front of the whole party wasn't for Aysha as much as it was for me."

"I'm not so sure about that." Larry moved closer, and his elbow slipped off the table, causing his hand to accidentally spill his drink.

"Larry!" Marlene scolded, reaching for stray napkins on the table to soak up the beverage from her lap. "Look what you're doing! Put the drink down. If you can't talk to us without getting sloshed, I'm leaving!" Larry pleaded for her not to go, but without saying a word, she rose from her seat and walked away.

"I better lay off the Shirley Temples," he joked with Callan.

"Yeah, I think you should. Set your drink aside, and tell me what's going on with you."

"Nothing's going on with me except having a good time."

"Is that what this is? Is this what you call a good time—pissing off your woman like that?"

Larry pushed the drink aside. "Hey! I gotta lot of shit going on, okay? And nobody's giving me a break about it, either."

"Larry, we're with you, man. We really are, but you have to lay off the booze if you're going to think straight. Don't call them Shirley Temples any more. Call them what they are. And call your job to task, too. Call it like it is."

Larry smirked at the mention of his job. "I'm going to beat them at their own game. I swear it, I'm almost there."

"What are you talking about?"

Larry slurred as he tried to explain. "I've been going through maintenance contracts, vendor service agreements, and purchase invoices against Cavanaugh's knowledge. I've been copying this documentation and sending them to a consultant who reviews the information and sends to me what he's found out."

"I'm not sure I like this idea, Larry. All this copying and mailing will eventually raise suspicion."

"I have that covered. I smuggle the documents out in my briefcase at night. The consultant only calls me at night when he needs to talk with me, but only if he needs to talk. We don't speak otherwise."

"I'd be careful just the same. Is this guy emailing you at your company address?"

"Not that dumb, bro. Give me credit."

"Is he emailing you at all?"

"No, I don't even want to take the chance of being hacked."

"So how's he getting the information back to you?"

Larry laughed.

"Don't tell me he snail mails it back," Callan guessed. "He's mailing information back to your home? Is that how he's doing it?"

151

"Best way, if you ask me."

"You're running a risk, Larry. How do you know someone isn't going through your mail box after the postman arrives? My mail is secure inside the Wingate-Powers Building, but you have a free-standing mail box."

"Got it covered."

Callan looked at him, unconvinced. "How's that?"

"He sends it to my mama."

"Your what?"

"It's okay! Who would think of my mother down here in St. Joseph? Besides, Mama's not doing so well."

"Marlene told me."

"This gets me down here more often to check up on her. It's perfect."

"I'm not sure it's perfect, exactly."

"Cal, the woman was sitting in a freaking rocking chair on her front porch in forty-degree weather, for crying out loud. She takes the mail from the mail box and hides it under a cement block outside the back door."

"But those documents could put her in greater danger than what her health will."

"The danger of the documents is overrated. It's okay, Cal. It's working out great. Trust me."

Callan stared at him.

"Trust me," he repeated.

"Who's your consultant?"

"Someone Alan would shit a brick over if he found out who it was."

"No," Cal said, reading the expression from Larry's face and realizing who the consultant was without Larry saying a word. "I mean it. No."

"Why not? Cliff is perfect, Cal. He's the only person that knows as much about the company as Alan does. He's been in the trenches. He knows what to look for."

"No. Don't you think they know Cliff's address? Mailing information to his address in Chicago will raise a red flag."

"Who said anything about using Cliff's address in Chicago?" Larry said with an arrogant tilt to his chin.

"Then where's it going?"

"Cliff and Liz moved to their place in Wisconsin. The company name we're using is officially located in Rhinelander as a bona fide LLC in the state of Wisconsin, recorded appropriately with the Secretary of State with his sister as President and CEO who doesn't know a damn thing about aeronautics, by the way, but doesn't care. She just wants to help out her little brother."

"I don't know about this, Lare. It sounds risky. There's got to be a better way."

"No, Cal, it's perfect, and we'll be sticking it back to the son of a bitch where it hurts the most—in Cavanaugh's wallet."

"His wallet? Wait. You didn't mention anything about his wallet. You're taking money in addition to confiscating documents?"

"Yeah, I'm sending invoices into the company for time billed as a consultant so that Cliff can bring some money into the house to support his family."

"No, Larry; that's not a good idea."

"Sure it is. We use consultants all the time at GrandAire. They'll never notice one more. Besides, I have the authority to hire whatever consultants I want or need."

"You don't get what I'm saying, buddy. You think you're sticking it back at Cavanaugh, but what you're really doing is stealing money from GrandAire, through a fraudulent company. Larry, you're not talking about a lemonade stand between an older sister and her little brother. You're talking about a scam—an embezzlement scam—a big, fat, fraudulent embezzlement scam."

"What else could I do? Cliff wants to do this. It's worth the risk to him. Besides, what's the worst that could happen—that they fire my ass for circumventing company consulting policies? As far as I'm concerned, that wouldn't be such a bad thing for me right now."

"No, Lare, it's not just getting fired. It could mean prison time for you and Cliff."

"That's if we're caught. I told you. Consultants are a dime a dozen at GrandAire."

"I don't like it."

"Then have another beer. That's how the idea came to me. I was having a Mythos at Argos', and *voila,* out popped this great idea. I suggest you catch up with me and get yourself another beer." Larry looked at the time on his watch. "Hey, I gotta go. It's half past eleven. I've got just thirty minutes to patch things up with Marlene. I can't afford to start the new year off on the wrong foot with her."

Callan waved him off and watched as Larry high-tailed it to the stage. Marlene stood near the band, holding a soft drink in her hand and talking to a woman Callan didn't know. As soon as Larry approached, the woman bid Marlene goodbye and left.

Callan watched Larry's dynamics to see how he could sway Marlene from walk-away angry to kissably loving in less than thirty minutes. Cal was never able to work

Terese like that. Terese wasn't prone to manipulation based upon sweet words.

He was like that, too, not being swayed easily by words. Not by Terese. Not by Cavanaugh, Burris or Holloway. Not now by Larry.

Marlene set her soft drink on a nearby table and put her arms around Larry's neck. He, in turn, wrapped his arms around her waist. They hugged and savored a long, premature New Year's kiss before moving toward the dance floor to dance to a romantic country love song.

Larry didn't need thirty minutes. Less than ten and all was well.

Callan shook his head. No, he wouldn't be taken in by Larry. He empathized with Cliff Pierceman, felt sorry for him, in fact. However, creating a fraudulent consulting company and submitting invoices so Cliff Pierceman could be paid to support his family was too serious to be taken in lightly by sweet words and empty promises of redemption.

CHAPTER TWENTY-ONE

The thought of Larry's bogus consulting company crawled under Callan's skin. He liked the idea that Larry was pulling contracts and maintenance agreements of vendors and manufacturers for Cliff to review in private. The information would be invaluable with the information Callan received in the mysterious folder by that Thompson man. He even liked the enthusiasm and dedication that Larry was putting toward the endeavor. Callan wasn't crazy, though, about Cliff sending his results and reviews back to Larry through Larry's elderly mother. That was a risk Callan believed Larry shouldn't be taking.

Also, he was all for taking contracts, copying documents, and sending them to Cliff, but charging GrandAire for the "work" and passing it off as a consulting fee so Cliff could support his family was fraud punishable by fines and prison terms. More specifically, it was theft through embezzlement. The legal implications of the invoices and getting paid for no real value to GrandAire would be hard to justify in court.

Callan sat in his office during the early morning hours on the first business day of the new year and tried to think how he could determine how deeply Larry and Cliff were charging GrandAire from a financial basis.

Aysha arrived late, but Callan didn't blame her. The thought of a new year at GrandAire made him think twice about coming back to work, too. He cornered her the first chance he could get. "Who helped you when you did the management expense work in accounts payable?" he asked her before she had a chance to take off her coat.

"Oh, um, Marcia. Marcia Downing. Nice lady. You'd like her."

"Good. Could you get me a list of all payments aggregating greater than $25,000 to any one company in the past six months?"

Silence. Callan asked her what was wrong.

"She's not going to like that," Aysha replied.

"I thought you said she was a nice lady."

"That's when I thought *you* were going to go see her."

Aysha relented and assured Callan she was on top of his request.

"Would you also mind having Tina pull an invoice file for a company called Northwoods Aeronautics Services Company? We've been doing business with them for about a month. I use the term 'doing business' loosely, though. I want to see their file."

"By *seeing* the file, Cal, does that mean you want me to hang onto the folder until you come down to look at it?"

"No, I'd like you to bring it to me."

"That's what I was afraid of. I'm telling you, Cal, Marcia isn't going to let any files out of her department, not after the allegations of false documents and signatures were made regarding Cliff's firing. She took all that very personally."

"Find a way," he said firmly. "I have to meet with Tony Burris now."

"So the answer is that you want me to steal her file folders?"

Callan exaggerated a gasp. "It's so harsh to hear you say it like that."

"Yeah, right. What next? After I steal her files, do you want me to write an audit report recommending that she get better control over lost files in her department?"

"That's an idea," he teased. "She'll be so mad about the report, she'll forget all about the files we took."

He reiterated his instructions to be sure she understood. One more thing came to mind. He wanted to know the name of the document required for a director or vice president to have a company approved as an authorized vendor within GrandAire. Aysha knew the answer and did her best to explain the form and the process.

"I'll need this vendor authorization form, as you call it, for Northwoods," he said. "Do you have access to the AP system?"

"You mean online real-time access?"

Cal said, "Yes," but she replied that Marcia Downing did not allow her such access.

"Signature controls over access to accounts payable are very poor, Cal," she explained. "That's why Marcia keeps close tabs on it. I've been working with IT to establish better controls, but it's a homegrown system. It's been customized so many times that IT can hardly figure it out any more."

"Get it."

"Get what?"

"Access!" he said. "I want to be able to monitor what's being requested from Northwoods to accounts payable for payment and compare it to what is actually being paid."

"Oh, Cal," Aysha pleaded. "Now you're asking for something I can't do. Getting access to the AP system will be next to impossible. IT has to get Marcia's approval before they'll grant any access to the system. Believe me, she keeps a tight diaper on that baby."

Cal laughed at the analogy. It was something he would've said given the chance. "Talk to IT and see what you can work out. Who do you normally talk to over there?"

"A guy by the name of Kenton Voss. Heard of him?"

"Actually, I have. Larry works with him when he needs some decision support. He'll be a good connection."

There was a moment of silence before Aysha asked if there was anything else he needed. She seemed relieved when he said, "No."

"May I ask what you're going to do with this information, Cal?"

"Would love to talk," he said sarcastically, "but Tony Burris is waiting."

"How about later at Centro Margarita?"

"Later?"

Aysha grinned. "Yeah, like I mean where we go for drinks. Centro Margarita."

"Oh, that, sure. Any particular reason?"

She hesitated. "No, not really. Just to talk. You know, just to talk."

Callan nodded. There was something in the tone of her voice he didn't like. His thoughts reverted back to the conversation he'd seen between her and Carol Chambers at Kenneth Holloway's holiday party. "Yeah, okay, I'll probably need a drink by the time this day is over anyway."

Soon after, Velma Hofmeyer escorted Callan into Tony Burris' office. She announced his entrance, retreated quietly, and closed the door.

Tony didn't look up. He continued to focus on paperwork. After studying a document closely, he lifted it up for Callan to see. "Ask Larry about this, will you?" He scribbled what appeared to be his signature across its face, and with a flick of his wrist, the paper floated across his desk toward Callan, falling short of his reach and landing facedown.

Callan leaned over the desk and picked up the document. The moment he turned over the paper, a sudden rush of blood from his face sank to his stomach. He felt lightheaded, almost nauseous.

In bold letters, the words *Northwoods Aeronautics Services Company* spanned the letterhead of what looked to be an invoice. At the bottom of the invoice, the amount of $2,550 was noted as being due, payable upon receipt, for consulting and and minor expenses.

Tony said, "Ask him what the hell they do for us."

Callan waited for further instruction to determine what the CFO knew of Northwoods Aeronautics. His fear was that senior management was already aware of the façade and had now called in the auditor to investigate.

"What I don't understand is why we're having all these consultants doing what I thought we hired vice presidents to do," Tony said. "We have management teams throughout the company hiring consultants to do their thinking for them. If these so-called executives are having a difficult time thinking for themselves, then maybe we need to find some people who can."

Callan agreed, but added, "What would you like me to do with this?"

Tony looked up as if his directions were clear. "I approved it already. Have Marcia Downing pay it as long as we're getting our money's worth."

"And if it's not legit?"

"Not legit? Why would it not be legit?"

"Oh, I'm sorry, sir, wrong choice of words. I meant if we're not getting our money's worth."

"If you believe the invoice is crap, I want to know about it."

"Yes, sir, I'll get on this right away. Is this what you needed to see me about?"

The CFO emerged from a trance as he read other papers on his desk. "What? Oh, hell, no. I just got sidetracked. You don't report to me anymore."

"Excuse me?" Callan wondered if he'd heard properly. He had.

Effective immediately, Callan now reported to Kenneth Holloway. Tony didn't have much more to add than that. He was direct and nonchalant about the change in organizational reporting and continued to work on his paper pile as he talked. "It was the board's request," he added.

"Protection of attorney client privilege," was all Tony said when Callan asked him the reason behind the board's decision. "To protect us from whatever comes out of your audit reports."

"But reporting structure won't protect GrandAire if a regulator subpoenas my audit records."

"You're preaching to the choir, Morrow. Like I said, it was the board's request. I think all they want is to have your audit work looked over by a lawyer in the event of legal problems down the road." Tony looked up as if he read Callan's mind. "Of which there are none right now. What's the matter? Are you not happy about this?"

"It doesn't matter if I'm happy or not," Callan responded honestly. "I wonder why the board believes attorney client privilege of my work is necessary."

Tony Burris didn't look up. He didn't answer the question.

Callan assumed there wasn't an answer.

CHAPTER TWENTY-TWO

Later that day, Callan returned to his office after getting a coffee. He logged in to his computer and noticed Aysha had confidentially emailed him the vendor report from accounts payable. He scanned it quickly. One company name caught his eye immediately—Northwoods Aeronautics Services Company.

Callan picked up the phone and dialed Larry's number. Larry answered the call on the first ring.

"I asked Marcia Downing to pull me a list of vendors," Callan said bluntly. "Your fake consulting firm hit the list as a big expense item."

"What do you mean, big?"

"I mean greater than what we pay to other consulting companies similar in scope as Northwoods."

"What does that mean in non-accounting terms?"

"Your company could pop up on a variance report for review or investigation by management."

"That's not good, is it?"

"Hell, no, it's not good. Larry, I'm so damn mad at you right now I could spit nails into a two by four. These amounts you're charging GrandAire are off the charts. You even charged them for incidental expenses."

"We had to buy paper and stuff."

"Oh, for Pete's sake."

"You know why we're doing this, Cal."

"Yes, I do, and I'm with you all the way, buddy, except for sending in bogus invoices. It's called fraud. It's called embezzlement. Do you realize that? Don't do this to me, man. Don't make me choose between you and doing what's right."

"What are you talking about? Are you going to turn us in?"

"No, of course not, but your scheme can get me into trouble, too. I'm certified as an auditor, a fraud examiner, and a systems' professional. I could lose my certifications and my livelihood if it was discovered that I knew about an embezzlement scheme within the company, but did nothing about it. That's not going to go very far with Terese if I not only lose my job, but I lose my credentials and the ability to get another job."

"It's not fraud, Cal, or embezzlement. I mean, not technically."

"You're banking on technicalities to keep you out of jail? How do you figure that?"

"We're just reclaiming what Cliff deserves."

"Okay, I understand, but I doubt that the authorities will care about your technicalities. Larry, you gotta promise me you're going to quit this shit. I'll tell you why it's so important that you do. I met with Burris this morning. He shoved a piece of paper under my face. It was an invoice from your company. I thought I was going to heave my breakfast on top of his desk."

"What did he say?"

"He wanted me to ask you if this consultant company was necessary or not. He wants to know what they do. I

164

said I'd have to find out and get back to him. The real problem is why he asked. He wants to know why management is using so many consultants to do their jobs."

"Or he may be asking because he already suspects we're a fraud," Larry added.

"It's a big problem, Larry."

"I know. I'm beginning to realize it."

"I don't think you are. You don't know what's going on within GrandAire that makes your charade so volatile. This is dangerous stuff. You didn't open up a junior achievement company, you know."

"How do we find out what he knows?"

"I don't know."

"Then what are you going to do with the invoice?"

"Send it through for payment."

"What? Why would you do that if it's on Tony's radar?"

"Because Tony left it up to me to decide the legitimacy of the invoice. If I don't send it in for payment, he'll know that I knew it was bogus."

"Oh, shit, this is becoming a mess."

"It's not becoming a mess, Lare, it *is* a mess. You need to stop it now."

"I better tell you that Cliff reviewed some contracts that Mark Reasoner worked up. He sent them off to me. I was going to pick them up this weekend."

"How often does he send information back to you?"

"Once a week, sometimes every other week. He has this fishing expedition job in Rhinelander. In the winter, they do ice fishing on the weekends. He stops by the post office on his way to work on Thursdays so that I can get it by Saturday."

Aysha popped her head through Callan's doorway, diverting his attention. He held the receiver away from his mouth so Larry couldn't hear. "Is it quality time already?" he asked her, looking at the clock and noting the time— five fifteen.

"Yes, I'm going to go now," she said. "Will I see you at Centro?"

Cal nodded and returned to the phone to close his conversation with Larry. "That was Aysha. She wants to talk about something, so I gotta go. If I have time, I'll see you later at Argos'."

"Okay. On top of everything, maybe we'll see our mystery guy there, too."

"Enough," Cal said, exasperated. "You could have talked all day and not said that."

CHAPTER TWENTY-THREE

Aysha entered Centro Margarita with apprehension. Carlotta Mendoza met her in the foyer with a broad smile. After grabbing a menu from the podium rack, Carlotta led Aysha to her normal table in the dining area.

"Just you?" Carlotta asked.

"Have you seen my boyfriend?"

"No, I'm sorry. I'll let him know you're here when he walks in." Carlotta strode to the table by the window where she always seated Aysha. "Can I have Cecilia order you a margarita while you wait?"

Aysha felt a cold draft from the window. "Carlotta, do you mind if we sit against an inside wall tonight?"

"Why?" she asked as if her evening routine had suddenly been disrupted.

"It's chilly here. The last time I sat here, it was very drafty and cold. How about over there? There's a table near that couple."

"It's reserved," Carlotta said instantly. "Would you like my sweater? I'll go get it."

Aysha thought Carlotta was kidding. "You're very sweet, Carlotta, but I could never fit into your sweater. It'd be easier to move."

"Around your shoulder would work."

"No, please, Carlotta. If that table doesn't work, anything will be fine."

"I must sit you here," she said abruptly. "How would your boyfriend find you? And Cecilia likes to take care of you. Those tables are not her tables. Her tables are by the window."

Hearing her name being used as she delivered drinks nearby, Cecilia walked toward them and put a comforting hand against her sister's back. "What's the matter? Is everything okay?"

Aysha explained to Cecilia and apologized if moving to another table meant she wouldn't be their server.

"We can do that," Cecilia responded, "and I can still be your waitress."

Cecilia took the menus Carlotta had laid on the table and moved them to a table near a staircase leading to the second-level private banquet rooms. Carlotta remained by the window with her arms folded across her waist, visibly shaken. After settling Aysha into her new table, Cecilia approached her sister.

"What is the matter with you?" she asked in Spanish. "You've been acting very strangely all evening."

"You don't understand, Cecilia. I have my way of doing things!" Carlotta bolted from her sister towards her post at the hostess station.

Callan appeared through the doorway to the dining room in search of Aysha and bumped into the teary-eyed waitress. Without missing a step, Carlotta continued on and ran into the women's restroom.

Aysha watched the scene unfold, embarrassed by her part in the scenario.

Callan walked to the table and stood by the chair Aysha had pulled out for him. "What's going on?" he asked.

"Oh, I created a scene, Callan."

"What happened?"

"It was rather odd," she said and then explained the story.

Callan laid his hand on top of hers where they rested on the table. "She's an odd person, Aysha. Don't give it a second thought. Usually things that happen like that have nothing to do with what you think. What happened doesn't sound like it was because of you."

Aysha sat back in her chair and shook her head. "I don't agree. Some things are exactly what they seem. I think you know it, too." She glanced at Callan's expression as she dunked a chip into the salsa and placed it in her mouth.

His eyes softened, and he pursed his lips as if he was about to hear something he didn't want to hear. "You're going back to marketing, aren't you?" he said first.

Aysha stopped chewing. "I didn't say that."

"But you're going back just the same, aren't you? You asked me to come here to tell me that you're going back to marketing with Carol Chambers."

Aysha stumbled for words. She looked about the table as if a satisfying response was written somewhere on one of the menus. "Oh, Cal," she finally said, "you understand what I'm going through. You have such passion and desire for your work. I do, too, but it's with marketing, not auditing. I find auditing interesting, but I'm not good at it. Not really, and Alan—"

"What about him?"

She took a deep breath. "He, uh, he made it compelling for me to go back to Carol."

169

"Of course he did. That's how he works. That's how he and Carol work. They both get what they want."

"Not Carol."

"Of course Carol. She and Alan are two peas in a pod. She's as bad as he is."

"No, you can't characterize her like that. She's a very powerful leader in the organization."

"That's not what I meant."

"I know what you meant. You meant she's selfish, self-centered, and controlling just like Alan Cavanaugh. I get it. She's a bit of all that. That's what makes her so good. She's a powerful leader, Callan, and just because she's powerful doesn't mean she should be considered selfish, self-centered, and controlling."

"Alan is."

"Well, that's Alan. I can't help what Alan is. Carol isn't. If you're saying you believe Carol is unethical and treats her employees the way Alan treats his employees, then you're wrong. You're very wrong, Callan. She isn't like that at all."

"Okay, whatever, I believe you."

"No, you don't. If you do, you don't believe me very much."

"Aysha, I have a general distrust of GrandAire executive management right now. Carol Chambers is a part of executive management. Maybe time will prove me wrong about her, I don't know at this point. We'll both have to wait and see."

Aysha reached for a chip to dip into the salsa. She didn't want the chip, but it kept her from arguing.

"The bottom line is, Aysha, no matter what we believe of Carol or Alan or any one of the members of management, you have to follow your passion. You need to do what your heart tells you, and if going back to marketing is your passion, you must follow it."

Aysha was suprised by what appeared to be a sudden change of heart.

"When do you start?"

"As soon as possible."

"You mean right away? Immediately?"

"Upon your approval."

"Any reason why I don't get the normal two- or three-weeks' notice?"

"Have you heard about Operation Spring Forward?"

Callan responded with a disgruntled expression. "No, I haven't heard about that one. Did the idea come from marketing?"

"Yes, but it's confidential—at least for the time being. I thought maybe Ken might've told you about it."

She explained that management was introducing a new service line related to executive travel to coincide with some large capital acquisitions of new aircrafts. Originally scheduled to debut in the spring, the promotion date was accelerated two months to be held on February 2 for unknown reasons, necessitating additional people in marketing who could organize and produce an extravaganza of entertainment and technical showmanship that would make investors and potential customers take notice.

Callan remembered back to his recent conversation with Kenneth Holloway about Zane Dunham's concern regarding due diligence. He wondered if Operation Spring Forward was the reason for the lack of transparency to the board due to its critical timing.

"February 2 doesn't give you much time, Aysha. Are they setting you up for failure?"

"Please, Cal, don't be negative."

"I'm being realistic."

"Okay, but don't. This is just a temporary assignment, I'm told. I'm hoping that if I do an exceptional job, there'll be a place for me permanently after it's over. Carol promised me she'd try her best to work it out."

"No doubt she will. As we discussed earlier, Carol seems to get what she wants."

Aysha shook her head. "Please, Cal, let's not go there again."

Suddenly, a commotion interrupted the conversation. A woman screamed from the direction of the kitchen.

"Did you hear that?" Aysha asked.

Sobbing followed the scream.

Callan turned his head toward the entrance and studied the patrons closest to the entry.

"I hope it's not about what happened with me," Aysha sighed.

"Surely not," he replied, keeping his attention on the entry.

Through the confusion, Aysha saw Paeng walking through the commotion to join them. She moved her chair to fit another one in between her and Callan.

Paeng approached their table, shaking the cold from his face, hesitant to remove his coat.

"What's going on in the entry? What's all the noise about?" Aysha asked.

"I don't know," he replied. "When I entered, the manager was shouting out orders to the staff, yelling that someone will have to take over at the front. That was about it."

"We thought we heard a woman scream."

"It was Cecilia. The manager said she was fired and told everyone to get back to work. Then Cecilia wailed and started crying."

"What? That doesn't make sense," Callan said.

Aysha shook her head in disbelief. It was such a simple request, the desire to change a seat in the restaurant. "Cecilia was fired? Oh, this is terrible. It's my fault." She placed her head into the palm of her hand and wondered if there was something she could do to rectify the situation.

Cecilia burst through the dining area and strode toward the trio.

Aysha stopped her as she passed their table. "Cecilia! Are you okay? What's happened?"

"I am sorry," Cecilia cried. "I am sorry you had to hear that. We will make it up to you."

"No, no, don't worry about that. We're just concerned. We heard you were fired. Tell us it's not true."

"*Que?* Me? No, not me, Aysha, not me. I am okay. It is my sister—my sister, Carlotta."

"Carlotta? Is it because I wanted to switch tables? But why? It was such a silly request!"

"No, not because of the tables," Cecilia explained. "It is because she is gone! Carlotta is missing!"

CHAPTER TWENTY-FOUR

"It was the damndest thing!" Callan said to Larry two evenings later while sitting at the bar of Argos'. "There's something very odd about Carlotta's disappearance."

The waitress took their order of two Mythoses.

"I wouldn't worry about it." Larry said. "She probably got fed up, and they fired her for leaving the job early."

"Or something frightened her."

Larry shook his head. "I don't see it."

"You weren't there."

"I've been to Centro Margarita before, Cal. There's nothing about that place that would suggest foul play. Solid owners. Honest, hard-working people. Professional clientele. I know who you're talking about. Carlotta's a cute little thing, but I have to tell you, I think she's a little off her rocker."

Callan conceded. "I've said that before, too, but Carlotta isn't the reason why I believe there was foul play. It's her sister, Cecilia. She specifically said that Carlotta was missing."

"Exact words?"

"Exact words. Now, it doesn't make sense to me that she'd say it like that if she didn't suspect it."

"Have you talked to the sister since?"

"Aysha has. She called Centro the next day and talked with Cecilia in person. Paeng helped them file a report with the police. Furthermore, Carlotta hasn't been home. You'd think that if she purposely walked off the job, she'd at least go home or call Cecilia."

"I see what you're saying."

Wynetta Argos passed by the men at the bar without saying hello.

Callan watched her pass. There was something different in her manner. The spirited, often uproarious Mrs. Argos was unusually subdued. Callan watched as she reached the corner of the bar where her son was standing. Before turning the corner to go into the kitchen, she put her right hand to the side of her head and rubbed her temple with the tips of her fingers.

"Are you listening to me?" Larry asked as Callan watched Mrs. Argos. "I asked how Terese was doing."

"Terese? She's fine. Really fine," he said, taking a large swallow of draft Mythos. "I talked to her last night, as a matter of fact. Gil's coming to Chicago soon. We're going to a Blackhawks game. I came across some pretty good tickets."

"How'd you manage that?"

"I went online and paid a pretty penny."

Larry shook his head. "Man, the company has tickets all over the place. You can get them through marketing. Aysha could get you some, if you'd just ask."

Callan didn't want anything from Carol Chambers' office.

"How's it been going without Aysha the past couple of days?"

Callan didn't know how to answer. In fact, he contemplated whether he should answer Larry's question at all. He hated to admit that the past two days were tougher than he'd thought they would be. He'd grown accustomed to having her in the department. Her willingness to delve into GrandAire's managerial and operational issues was valuable to him. He knew it took months, sometimes years, before young auditors with the proper aptitude became a viable member of an auditing department. Aysha was already making contributions and had been willing to do more. Marketing had offered her what she'd needed, though. From that standpoint, he didn't regret losing her, but losing to people like Carol Chambers and Alan Cavanaugh made the transition unbearable.

"Aysha's in the thick of this Groundhog Gala," Callan finally said. "She won't have time to miss me a bit."

Larry burst out laughing. "Carol would hit the roof if she heard you refer to her spring promotion as a Groundhog Gala."

"It is what it is. It's on Groundhog Day, for crying out loud. Spring is never six weeks away from Groundhog Day in Chicago. This promotion is supposed to be the grand opening of GrandAire's elite line of executive charters where we spring into a fresh new charter line for executives. It could be huge, yet Carol's tying it to an obscure holiday like Groundhog Day, and no one is going to tie Groundhog Day to an elite line of business charter flights, let alone to springtime. It's cold in Chicago on the second of February. I don't care what some furry rodent in Pennsylvania says."

"Or it could be the stroke of a genius. Let's face it, Cal. She's doing her job. She's marketing something exciting in a time of year that is less than exciting for Chicago in an industry that has become less than exciting. I hear the company's going all out for this thing. The atrium will be decked out like the Waldorf-Astoria. The focal point will be the large window that looks out toward the lake. We have flights synchronized from different cities served by the *Elite* line. They'll all converge over the lake and will fly in together so that invitees to the party can see the impressive aerial entourage."

"You're really caught up in this hoopla, aren't you?"

Larry shrugged his broad shoulders and smiled faintly. "Oh, I don't know, maybe a little. I mean, who wouldn't? It's the most exciting thing that's happened to this company since I arrived. I feel like a boy with a new set of toys with this new line of aircraft."

Callan rolled his eyes and belched loudly. "That's all I've got to say about that."

"It's what makes Carol so successful at what she does. She could put lipstick on a pig and people would kiss it."

"And don't forget that, either. I don't care how much lipstick she puts on this gala, in the end it's still a pig. Heck, she can put a tutu on the damn planes for all I care. It won't change my mind."

Callan downed the remainder of his liquid gold and called for another.

"I haven't forgotten," Larry said out of the blue.

Callan didn't catch the meaning. "Forgotten what?"

"Red, and I know you haven't, either."

Callan picked up his mug to see if enough brew remained at the bottom to be swallowed. He wanted a taste large enough to get the thought of Red out of his memory.

"And I haven't forgotten Cliff, either," Larry added. "They're both victims of corporate god-playing. They were victims before we even knew what was going on. I get caught up in this whole gala thing, Cal, but I haven't forgotten them."

Callan took a deep breath and tried to sit upright on the stool. He placed his hand on Larry's shoulder. "Then you also can't get caught up in the glitter of this promotional gala. It's a show. You got it? It's just a show. Besides, you're in your own game right now with this consulting company you're trying to pull off. If you let your guard down now, you're through. Both you and Cliff are through, and you'll be saying your wedding vows to Marlene through iron bars with Bubba as your maid of honor. I'm serious, Larry. Don't laugh at it. You don't want to be somebody's bunk muffin on your wedding night."

The bartender arrived with two frosty brews and set them in front of the men.

"Drink your beer," Larry commanded, taking his in his hand and following through with his own advice. "To be honest, Cal, I'm probably closer to being Bubba's roommate than you think. Marcia Downing stopped by to see me this afternoon. I know it wasn't good."

"What did she want?"

"All she said was that Alan wanted some supporting information on some invoices she paid, and somehow she didn't have it. She wondered if I knew anything about it so that she could get back to Alan with the answer."

"What supporting documentation was she missing?"

Larry hum-hawed before saying, "Something about Northwoods."

"Okay, so did you give it to her?"

"Give what to her? Hell, Cal, there was nothing to give. I didn't have it. I just prepared the invoice and sent it in. I didn't think about creating documentation to support the invoice."

"Oh, great, so now it looks like this invoice appeared out of thin air all by itself. Good work, Larry."

"So what do you think it means?"

"It doesn't matter what I think. It's what Marcia Downing thinks and what Alan thinks after she tells him. What did she say to you when you told her you had nothing to provide?"

"She just stood there in the doorway for a few seconds, looking at me with her beady little hawk eyes."

"And?"

"She said thank you and left."

Callan grabbed his beer mug by its handle. He tipped it just enough to look onto the thin layer of foam that floated on top before setting it back down hard, sloshing beer over the top of the glass.

"She's smarter than that, Larry. She processes thousands of invoices. Aysha told me that her policies and procedures are strict and solid to protect the company against unauthorized payments. If Cavanaugh was asking Downing about your company's invoice, and Downing was asking you, and you gave her nothing to substantiate the invoice, you can bet your bottom dollar that she went to Cavanaugh to tell him that to prevent her own ass from getting in trouble."

Larry squinted as if the whole situation was too complicated for him to understand completely.

Callan pointed his index finger at him. "There. Do you feel that stupid look on your face right now? I hope it's the same stupid look you gave Marcia Downing. That's exactly what she came to see, Larry. She came to see if you're scared, cocky, or just plain stupid, so I hope you gave her that look of confusion as if you couldn't imagine what happened to the supporting documentation."

"Look, Cal, it's almost over. I swear. This gig with Northwoods is almost over. I ran down to St. Joseph to get a package from Cliff. Not much was in it. There were some documents tied to transactions that he wanted more information on, but for the most part, it was all pretty much benign. So I told him this whole thing needed to end. It's over. I swear to you."

Callan listened and wondered what his own facial expression revealed about Larry's promise.

"We cool?" Larry asked.

Callan simply looked at him—no expression, no response.

Larry picked up his glass to consummate the treaty between them.

Callan lifted his mug reluctantly, *clinked* the two together, and took a hearty swig that was less refreshing than he'd hoped.

Mrs. Argos lumbered to the bar and stood before them. "He's not here," she whispered as she leaned as far across the counter as she could.

Callan realized she was referring to the restaurant's mystery man.

"He's not in the restaurant or in the alcove across the boulevard," she added. "I'm telling you I've seen him in the past. I'm not making it up, Mr. Morrow."

"I believe you. I never thought you made it up."

"But you haven't done anything about it."

"What am I to do? I don't have the time to stake out your restaurant, Mrs. Argos. I'm up to my neck in my own work and problems. So far, he hasn't acted up or been aggressive. The police aren't going to give a shit until he does, so what am I to do?"

She closed her eyes, then opened them slowly, reflecting anxiety and sorrow.

"What is it?" Callan asked.

"Bernadette. That man has her worried sick. She's ill in bed."

"In bed?"

"Ever since she heard that poor Mexican girl went missing, she's been sick with worry. She knows you were all involved."

"Carlotta Mendoza is from Costa Rica, not Mexico, and we were not involved, as you put it. We were merely at Centro Margarita at the time of the incident."

"Missing nonetheless, Mr. Morrow."

"Gone, just gone," he said, trying to tone down the woman's anxiety.

She ignored him. "I told Bernadette, as distressing as it is for all of us, that it should not cause her to be bedridden. I got her up this morning and gave her breakfast. This afternoon, however, I found her back under the covers, wailing in misery."

"It's unnecessary for her to be carrying on like that."

"Bedridden nonetheless, Mr. Morrow."

"I'll check up on her when I return to my apartment."

Larry climbed off his stool. "You check on Mrs. Powers, Cal. I'll settle our bill with George."

Mrs. Argos looked intently at Callan when Larry left. "I don't approve of these cards she uses, Mr. Morrow."

Callan sensed the concern and seriousness of her voice, but told her he didn't know to what cards she referred.

"Those Tarot cards. She had them here the other day after that Mexican girl went missing. Miss Marks stopped by to see if you were here and told us about her."

"This is the first I've heard that Aysha was here."

"She wanted to see you. She thought you'd be here. She talked to us briefly. I told her I hadn't seen you. Bernadette took her cards from her purse and flipped three of them over one by one. Each time she flipped a card she placed her hand over her heart and wailed dramatically. It was embarrassing. I'm sure it startled Miss Marks. I finally said to her, I said, 'Bernadette, you must go home if you insist on wailing in front of our customers.' That's what I said to her. She became distraught with me that I would talk to her in such a manner, but I had no choice, Mr. Morrow." Mrs. Argos lowered her voice.

Callan leaned closer to listen.

"Bernadette left shortly after Miss Marks. They both went out the door and walked to the street corner. Bernadette crossed the street toward the Wingate-Powers, but Miss Marks went down the side of the building along Lake Boulevard toward the library."

"Okay," Callan said, "but of what significance is this?"

"Significance? Don't you see? The man! That man with the black hair and mustache and cap on top of his head followed her! When they left, he passed the front door and turned down the street behind Miss Marks. 'My God!' I said to myself. I quickly summoned my son, Georgie, from behind the bar. He went out and yelled for the man to stop. Georgie says the man ran across the street into Scoville Park. As far as I know, Mr. Morrow, Miss Marks was able to get into her car and drive away none the wiser."

"Did George follow him very far? Did he see where he ran to?"

"No, he has responsibilities here. He came back to the restaurant."

"You ready?" Larry asked, approaching them quickly from the register. "Let's go."

The two men walked out of the restaurant and into the brisk mid-January air. Callan looked up and down the dark street, surveying every shadow being cast by the streetlights.

Larry flipped the collar of his coat around his neck to block the blowing wind. "Hey, George was telling me about that guy."

"I know," Callan interrupted, not wanting to hear the story again. "Let's just go."

CHAPTER TWENTY-FIVE

Callan walked to the Wingate-Powers in the stillness of the cold evening. Once inside the building, he stomped his feet to break away bits of frozen ice that had accumulated on the soles of his shoes. He tapped on the door to the apartment that belonged to Mrs. Powers and pondered whether or not to knock again when she didn't answer. The apartment inside seemed to be very still, but she had to be in.

He turned to go, then stopped, hearing what he thought were sounds of life from within the flat. He waited and soon sensed her presence on the opposite side of the door. "Mrs. Powers?" he called.

"Yes, who is it?"

"Callan Morrow."

She opened the door slowly, cracked enough to stretch the brass security chain across the opening. "I'm not feeling well, Mr. Morrow. Perhaps some other time."

Callan pressed his hand against the door to prevent her from shutting it on him. "May I come in anyway, Mrs. Powers?"

She closed the door, unhooked the chain, and opened it freely to reveal her frail frame. She wore bedclothes, and the room was dark except for a dull, eerie stream of light coming from a Tiffany reproduction lamp in front of a window.

Mrs. Powers hobbled to the rocker that sat next to a Ragtime-period end table. She stretched her arm to turn on another reproduction lamp, releasing a small groan as she did so. This lamp provided more light, but it was still not enough to lighten the dismal mood within the room. It was enough, however, to see.

"I'm very sorry for the state of my wardrobe this evening. I retired early. I'm feeling under the weather, you see." Mrs. Powers said.

Callan smiled politely as he removed his coat and took a seat in a chair with an embroidered cushion of needlework. He wasn't sure how to explain the reason for his visit. "Mrs. Powers, we're all going to be okay," he said reasuringly. "A gentleman by the name of Rafael Ramirez works for the FBI and is well aware of our situation. He monitors it daily."

Mrs. Powers stared blankly in front of her, rocking gently as the floorboards creaked underneath. "That poor girl," she muttered under her breath. "So young. She must have been scared. It isn't good, you know. I'm scared for her."

"No, I don't know, Mrs. Powers. No one knows. No one knows what has happened yet. There's still much hope that she's only gone for a little while, angry for being fired or for believing that her sister betrayed her."

Mrs. Powers shivered as the rocker creaked in rhythm with the floorboards. "I beg to differ," she said. "She's dead."

"We don't know that."

"I do."

Bernadette Powers' declaration silenced him.

Callan used the silence and the soft, dull light from the lamp to scan the room that made up the living portion of her apartment. Mrs. Powers barely had a place to move or to set something upon. What level surfaces she had were consumed by loosely strewn magazines and plastic WalMart sacks containing their original purchases. Knick knacks of porcelain figurines chipped from years of neglect that had been handed down over the years from friends and family adorned the end tables. He browzed the covers of several magazines that lay on top of the stacks—*Midwestern Living, Cooking Lightly, Ladies Home Journal.* They appeared untouched. The clutter seemed so pointless and sad to him.

"Did Wynetta Argos send you?" she asked out of the stillness.

"No," he responded honestly. "I came on my own. All she said was that you were not feeling well, that you were distraught over the recent events."

She appeared satisfied and began to rock peacefully. "How is your wife?"

Callan didn't feel like getting into a conversation about his relationship with his wife. "She was fine the last time we talked," he said uncommittally. "I don't know when I'll see her next. My youngest is coming up to Chicago next week for a hockey game. They have some sort of winter conference for the teachers in Indiana, and he'll be off for a long weekend."

Mrs. Powers nodded. "And your oldest?"

"Brandon? Oh, who ever knows about Brandon? I suppose only Brandon knows. He seems happy. After all, he's young, self-assured, confident, and immortal."

Mrs. Powers didn't laugh, but managed a smile. "He'll be fine," she answered as if she already knew he would.

Callan looked at his tired landlady and sat uncomfortably in the melancholy lull. After a few minutes of silent repose, Callan rose slowly and reached for his coat. "I should be going to let you rest. Thank you for letting me in. I wanted to make sure you were all right. You'll be okay?"

She nodded.

"You'll lock the door behind me?"

She nodded again.

As Callan turned to leave, he stopped and looked at the elderly woman who resumed rocking. The bronze light from the two lamps revealed strands of hair loosening from the once-tight grip of her bun wadded on top of her head. The lines on her face appeared more pronounced in the shadows. He wanted to touch her, to tell her that the unfolding events would not get better by glorifying them with fret and anxiety. He couldn't, though. He didn't know himself how the events would unfold. Instead, he referred to the use of the cards.

"Mrs. Powers, please be careful of ways you use to comfort yourself."

"Do you believe I'm being deceived by the cards, Mr. Morrow?"

"I have to be honest and say that I do, Mrs. Powers."

"Are you familiar with the writings of Francois de la Rochefoucauld?"

When he didn't answer, she recited through the dim, stale air, "'The surest way to be deceived is to think one's self more clever than others.'"

Callan frowned with indignance. "Am I to guess why you're telling me this?"

"Only that I'm conscious of my misgivings, Mr. Morrow. I would worry less if I believed you were equally aware of your apprehensions and didn't think yourself cleverer than that of which you do not know."

Callan turned to take his leave, deciding it was best to do so before he said something he'd regret later. He left quietly with his coat hooked on his finger and draped over his right shoulder. He moved slowly up the dozen steps to his apartment, coming away from the flat below with a different feeling about the old woman. Until tonight, he didn't have a sense that she was anything more than a busybody, justifying her prodding under the disguise of a landlady. Tonight, though, he realized he was wrong. Mrs. Powers was deeply rooted in her beliefs. She had her own sense of spirituality.

Callan placed the key in the lock to his apartment and turned the knob. The familiar air of his belongings welcomed him in. He walked into the kitchen and pulled out a cold bottle of water from the refrigerator. Its icy freshness cooled the back of his throat, and the sensation of it lined the walls of his stomach, absorbing into his system instantaneously. He didn't realize he was so thirsty.

He couldn't help but think of Mrs. Powers again. She surprised him. What bothered him most was how she'd been taken in so easily by what Callan considered foolish play. Suddenly, though, he was struck by self-awareness, a revelation of arrogance and unawareness of his own doing that sickened him.

You judge Mrs. Powers by her beliefs. Tell me, what are yours? What do you believe, Callan?

He picked up the water bottle and took a sip to cleanse his guilt. How often had he turned to his God, a God he professed to be his source of power and strength? In the recent months of turmoil, he confessed that he hadn't turned to his own beliefs to help him with his relationship with Terese, to comfort Gil's anguish over their separation, to ask for protection and safety for Carlotta Mendoza, and, most of all, to help him unwind the mess he was in at GrandAire. Yet it was easy to judge Mrs. Powers.

Callan closed his eyes. For the first time in a very long time, he dropped to his knees and prayed for forgiveness. After doing so, he crawled onto the couch and slept soundly with a peace he hadn't known in months.

~

At the moment sleep arrived for Callan, Mrs. Powers awoke from her rocker with a start. She heard her name being called from near the chair that Callan had occupied—a deep, masculine, genuine voice—real and familiar. She looked slowly around the room illuminated only by low-wattage bulbs in her reproduction lamps. She saw nothing tangible to explain the voice, so she listened intently to determine if anyone could be lurking outside her window. No one was there, yet she was sure she'd heard a voice.

She must have been dreaming, she decided—an ominous response to the unanswered questions plaguing her subconscious.

Fully awake now, she looked at the small table beside her. The joints from her fingers produced a dull arthritic pain as she extended them to reach for the tiny knob on the end-table's drawer. The drawer complained at being opened. Wood scraped across wood in its tight compartment. From where she sat, she couldn't see the drawer's contents, but she knew by faith they were there.

Her cards.

She tightened her fragile fingers around the deck and pulled the cards from their wooden crypt, using her other hand to make she didn't drop any cards. "Is there cause to feel as I do?" she asked the cards, looking for guidance, believing an answer would follow.

She turned over a card, revealing the Seven of Cups, seven gold, hour-glass-shaped cups that signified choices. *Of course,* she said to herself. There'd been a number of situations recently where choices had to be made. The card comforted her, helped her realize that any reasonable person would feel restless and uncertain by the recent events.

She flipped her second card. The Five of Cups with its ominous black figure appeared. Sadly, Mrs. Powers agreed with the card of regret. There'd been opportunities missed that would've prevented or minimized some of the unfortunate events that had happened if only someone had been more aware.

Don't let it get you down, Bernadette. Her feelings were natural. The card said so.

The third card, however, caused a chill down Mrs. Powers' spine: the Moon. She feared the Moon the most. It lay squarely on her lap, representing the unexpected, a broad array of dangers still ahead. Despite Callan Morrow and Wynetta Argos' opinion to the contrary, Bernadette Powers did have reason to doubt and to be anxious.

The unexpected was going to happen again.

CHAPTER TWENTY-SIX

"Want some more coffee before you head upstairs?" Liz Pierceman asked her husband.

Cliff tipped his cup her way to show he was one step ahead of her. Steam rolled over his fingers.

"Looks nice out there," she said, peering through the frosty panes of the kitchen window.

"I don't think it's supposed to be for long."

"Really? That's too bad. I was hoping to run some errands today after school."

"Be careful," he warned.

She rose onto the tips of her toes, wrapped her arms securely around his neck, and gave him a kiss. When she released her grip, he stood back and thanked her for the impromptu display of affection.

"What did I do to deserve that?"

"You don't have to do anything," she said. "You're a good man, Cliff."

Every day, Liz Pierceman told her husband he was a good man. Each time she told him so, the look of shame and rejection seemed to lessen in his eyes. She reminded herself how engrained a man's career was to his self-worth, but she'd reached a point where she no longer knew what to do for him. Together, they decided their move to Oneida County, Wisconsin, to get away from it all was worth trying, but finding a job that paid commensurate with his qualifications was next to impossible. His Thursday through Sunday job at the sporting goods outlet in Rhinelander complemented her teaching salary, but it wasn't enough to fulfill the agonizing emptiness of a career lost through injustice.

What made the loss worse was the allegation that Cliff inappropriately paid an invoice to an unknown individual beyond his authorization. He screamed upon deaf ears that he did no such thing, that the signature on the document was a forgery, but Celia Hart and Callan Morrow could find no evidence to the contrary. His termination had been upheld through the corporate appeals process.

Liz grabbed Cliff by the arm just before he got out of reach to go upstairs. "Look at me," she said, taking his stubbled face into the palm of her hands. "What happened to you is no reflection of the man you are, how good you are, or what you mean to the kids and me. Do you hear me? Don't let Alan Cavanaugh define us, Cliff. Don't let him define you and hold you back from being who you really are."

He nodded. He knew it to be true intellectually, but his heart was having trouble understanding it emotionally.

"You're a good man, Cliff." And as if she knew the question before he asked it, she added, "Yes, I'm happy here. I'm really glad to be out of the city."

"Are you saying that because we have no other place to go?"

"No," she replied. "It was too much for us in Chicago. I worried about the kids getting caught up in what they had and how much they had of it. Don't you see? So what if we have to sacrifice to be up here? It's harder, but look at what we've gained. It's beautiful, Cliff, and we've got our lives back. That's okay for me. I want it to be okay for you, too."

This time he smiled. "It will be," he said. "I just need a little more time." Before turning toward the stairs, he looked at his wife leaning against the kitchen counter. He didn't know what to say. He didn't know how to thank a woman like Liz for her patience and understanding and her belief in him when everyone else had stopped believing, including himself.

Cliff held tightly to his coffee cup and climbed the flight of stairs to his office. He sat the cup next to the mouse pad and turned the computer on, typing in a password and a couple of commands before sitting back and admiring his comfortable domain—an office he'd constructed out of empty, nonfunctional attic space. However, it was also much more than that. Pictures of shiny new aircraft soaring proudly through the skies contrasted sharply against grisly crash scenes of fallen fuselages, smoldering in the aftermath of horrific mistakes, bad weather, or poor maintenance. It wasn't a shrine to honor aircraft and human life as much as it was a memorial against corporate indifference and the lack of accountability.

He looked at each picture with special deliberation. He knew the details of every accident: the crash out of Raleigh/Durham International near Morrisville, North Carolina; the downing of a cargo flight during take-off from Miami International; two fatal crashes caused by a defective and malfunctioning rudder at both Colorado Springs and Pittsburgh, and, of course, the fatal emergency landing of a passenger plane in Sioux City, Iowa.

In a corner to his lower right was a picture of a nondescript crater in the middle of a flat soybean field. Sunlight reflected off tiny specks of color from flags identifying human remains. Authorities had combed the site for clues to the crash's origin. Nothing about the picture bore any indications of its identity, but Cliff knew the site by heart—Midland Airlines' Flight 3182, Monon, Indiana.

He rubbed the bridge of his nose with his left thumb and wiped what sleep remained in his eyes before placing his focus on his computer monitor. He had a lot he wanted to review today. New information from Larry needed to be verified, and companies from his review of GrandAire contracts needed to be researched.

Before starting, however, Cliff had three rituals he performed every morning. One was to check the weather for the day. Another was to check online sports scores from the night before. The last was to peruse the news and events in Chicago—just to keep in touch.

The weather forecast hadn't changed. A winter-storm warning had been issued for Southern Manitoba, Northern Minnesota, Northern Wisconsin, Ontario, and the Upper Peninsula of Michigan. Projections predicted the warning would extend as the system moved progressively southeast into the other Great Lakes states.

Rather than be dismayed, Cliff reveled at the forecast and the chance to use the plow he'd installed to the front of his red and white Ford Bronco. Snows such as these were playtime for guys like Cliff and a chance to earn some extra money.

As much as Chicago seemed to be worlds away from him now, he switched to online news events of the Windy City. Idle curiosity drew him to articles he found interesting based upon key words and phrases he entered through the search engine. Today would be uneventful, he believed. It was too cold for people to make news.

Just as he decided to click his focus to sports, the words "private airplane" caught his attention. He read the news release intently.

Thompson was a trial and appellate research consultant at Kirklin, Bender & Associates in Austin, Texas, specializing in the handling of airline, military, and private airline crashes. In addition, he became well known for product liability cases and litigation arising out of industrial accidents and injuries. His death ...

Cliff stopped reading. *His death?* Thompson? Could it be the same Thompson? He scrolled back to the beginning of the article to read its headline:

Former Chicago Airline Executive Murdered While Jogging in Austin, Texas

"Dear God," he whispered under his breath.

The stark realization that his former boss was now dead struck Cliff hard. He sat back in his chair to think. Beads of sweat formed around his hairline. He wiped his forehead, then opened a desk drawer beside him and fumbled through its contents to search for a business card. He'd always meant to call Murray Thompson, but never did. Cliff pulled items out of the drawer in search of the card he wanted.

He slammed the drawer shut in frustration and reached for the phone, spilling his coffee in the process. With his mind spinning in confusion and fear, he reached for anything he could find to stop the murky deluge, but the coffee quickly spread across the desk and dropped freely off the edge. Cliff took the t-shirt from his back and used it to soak up the coffee. It had permeated everything in its path, including his old pair of jeans.

With the spill under control, Cliff reached for the phone again. A weary Larry Southard answered in a voice noticeably groggy from the morning commute. Larry barely got his routine phone greeting completed before Cliff interrupted him.

"Murray Thompson is dead."

"Who?"

"Murdered."

"What are you talking about?"

"I read it online. Listen to this. It says he was shot along a neighborhood street while jogging. Robbery may be suspected, but he still had some small cash in the pockets of his sweatpants. No suspects, no motive. Nothing."

Larry said nothing, silenced by the news.

"Murray had your job, Larry. You filled his position."

"But I don't know what that has to do with me or my job."

"He knew something we don't. I don't know what we're missing yet, but we have to go to the authorities with the information we have."

"We don't have anything substantive, Cliff."

"What do you think I've been working on up here? I've been busting my ass reviewing contracts and looking into aviation reports."

"That proves nothing so far, nothing that would link anything to Thompson."

"How can you be so sure of that?"

"We shouldn't be having this conversation, Cliff," Larry replied sternly. "Listen to me. Don't call me here. Not here. Someone could be listening. We'll have to talk later."

"No, you listen to me. Do you understand what has just happened? Murray Thompson was murdered in cold blood on a city street. This is critical, Larry."

"I'm hanging up, Cliff. Don't call me here."

"Larry, listen to me! We have to go to Austin now to find out what he knew!"

Suddenly, the line went dead.

CHAPTER TWENTY-SEVEN

Frustration welled inside Cliff's chest. He hit the top of his desk with a quick blow of his fist. Despite Larry's reaction, Cliff knew what he had to do. He'd research Murray Thompson's past on the web and send whatever information he uncovered to Larry's mother's home in southern Indiana. That should provide Larry with the information he needed to assess the urgency of the situation.

Flakes of snow outside the attic window fell upon a carpeted ground of white velvety crystals. The once sunny, blue skies of the early morning turned gray with the advancing winter storm, a storm still hours away from full force. Perhaps if he hurried, he could drive into Minocqua and mail his package this afternoon rather than take the chance that he might not have time to do so the next morning on his way to work.

Forgotting he'd spilled it carelessly across the top of his desk, he reached for his coffee, the impetus he needed to keep going, and stared into the empty cup. Unless he wanted to suck the caffeine out of his stained shirt, he'd have to make a fresh pot downstairs, but he had little time for that. He wanted to reach the post office before it closed. More importantly, he wanted to reach the post office before the storm gathered its full force over Lake Superior.

Cliff typed the name *Murray Thompson* into the webbrowser's search line and added the words *Austin TX*. A number of sites appeared outlining his former boss' accomplishments over the years, including one that contained a listing of important litigation and consultative cases in which he'd been involved. Cliff clicked on the site and reviewed each case individually, taking notes as he read and printing pages as fast as he could. Common themes and trends related to manufacturers and individuals involved in FAA safety inspections came up in his research.

Cliff studied his pages of notes. One name consistently stood out among the rest, a regulator with the FAA. He picked up his pen and circled the name of Michael Benning each time it appeared. In the end, ten of the twelve cases he reviewed with a Thompson connection included Benning's name. Cliff continued to search, printing pages of pertinent information, one after another. He did the same with manufacturers and other agents that appeared frequently on his list.

How much easier it would be to forward the articles to Larry's email address, but as Larry cautioned earlier, the chance that his email accounts were being hacked was as much a possibility as their phones being tapped.

After working through mid-afternoon, Cliff finished in time to drive to the post office in Minocqua.

~

It wasn't the alarm, but the howling of the wind and the ping of ice pellets against the window panes that woke Cliff Pierceman from a deep sleep the next morning. He opened his eyes and looked over his pillow to where his wife of eleven years usually cuddled close to him for warmth on snowy and icy mornings such as these.

Her side of the bed was empty, however, but he could hear the FM radio in the kitchen, listing in monotonic tones the names of school districts that closed class for the day. Sure his wife was listening, he reached toward the end table and turned off the alarm.

The rhythmical announcement of school districts soon stopped. Liz returned to the bedroom and sank deeply into the serenity and security of quilted coverlets and down pillows. Cliff reached out to draw her near. Taking his cue, she rested her head upon his chest, draped her arm across his belly, and pulled him close.

"I take it this means you and the kids don't have school today."

"Yes, and I think you should call it a snow day as well. They say there's at least ten to twelve inches out there, and it's blowing and drifting. The road to Rhinelander can't be good. No one's going to be ice fishing this weekend, Cliff."

Cliff laughed and started to climb out of bed before his wife playfully pulled him back.

"Kind of hard for a guy like me with a plow attached to the front of his Bronco to call in a snow day and get away with it. You don't know these guys, babe. Hell, these shacks on the ice are in better shape than some of their own homes. Besides, by Saturday this little powder duster will be history long forgotten."

"Don't you want to stay in bed with me?"

"Always," he replied, kissing the top of her head.

Eventually, Cliff managed to slide out of bed and assess the snow accumulation from their bedroom window. He determined that he'd seen worse storms in his life, so he got dressed and braved the elements.

Normally, Cliff took back roads on his way to Highway 47 toward Rhinelander, but he wasn't sure how the Oneida County roads fared. He didn't want to take chances even with a five-foot plow attached to the front of his truck, so he drove the extra four miles north to Woodruff before hitting 47 south-east on a twenty-five-mile scenic drive through the Northern Highlands State Forest.

The pre-dawn sky hadn't lightened much as he drove toward Lake Tomahawk, but there was enough for Cliff to see how the snow had attached itself onto everything exposed to the elements. His headlights glistened off snowflakes hitting his windshield. The curves were treacherous even with the 4x4 Bronco and the weight of the plow. The Oneida County DOT had plowed the highway well, but a thin layer of ice on top of the snow made the curves in the road a test of a driver's expertise.

He thought about his and Larry's consulting company. The idea to organize the Northwoods Aeronautics Services Company was foolish, but Cliff didn't regret doing it. In fact, he enjoyed every bit of its mission and the work he performed on its behalf. Dropping off the package yesterday at the post office to Larry's mother's house gave him much pleasure. It was worth the risk to him. Besides, he and Liz needed the money even if it was illegal.

He tossed around the idea to confess to Liz what he and Larry were doing. She wouldn't take the news well. He knew his wife. It would be best to tell her later after they'd quit. He would then concentrate on his job in

Rhinelander, as meager as it was, until he found something better, something he was qualified to do.

Gradually, Cliff could see the eastern horizon getting lighter. The snow continued to fall gently on the heavy blanket already covering the landscape. He passed the Lake Tomahawk area without incident. Very few cars passed his way, which was why the blue SUV with Illinois license plates caught his attention off to the side of the road. Cliff slowed down and looked to see if the driver was in distress.

There was no driver. He or she must have found a ride into town.

Cliff accelerated slightly, comfortable with his speed. No need to go any faster or slower at this point. He turned on the radio for some news and weather information to bide the time. While flipping the channels, keeping his eye on the road, Cliff saw the silhouette of a tall, stocky figure ahead. He squinted. The figure was silver gray, almost blending into the snow.

As he approached, he noticed it was a man with something in his hand. Cliff slowed even more, straining to see. Something was peculiar about the outdoorsman. His stature wasn't that of one with car trouble, hoping for a ride into town. Instead, Cliff realized very quickly that the man was waiting, in a cradle carry position. Cliff slowed, but before he could sort out the situation, everything changed.

The figure picked up a long 22-gauge shotgun hidden well alongside his stocky build and pointed it at the Bronco.

"Oh, shit!" Cliff yelled, accelerating to pass the man.

The first sound he heard was a loud *bing* into the front-right fender of the truck. The second was more powerful, a blast to the right-front tire just as he swerved and accelerated, causing the vehicle to careen violently. Without warning, the solidly built Ford began to fishtail on the ice as the weight of the plow pulled the momentum of the back of the truck to the front. The vehicle spun around to the opposite side of the road. The wheel rim sliced through the snow like a scalpel, hitting the pavement and causing the 4x4 to slide onto the shoulder and down an embankment that plunged deeply into the base of pine trees that lined the road. Cliff braced for impact as the truck flipped side over side. It ended up wedged upright between two pines.

Barely conscious, Cliff fought to stay awake. The spinning in his head made him nauseous and dazed. Blood trickled from his forehead above his left eye. Confused, he grasped for the door handle and felt his hand touch jagged pieces of glass where the driver side window used to be. Cliff fought to catch his breath as the frigid Wisconsin air whisked through the car.

Barely able to see through his own blood and the dizziness of his wounds, he managed to unlock his seat belt and find the door handle. It did him little good as the mangled frame sealed the door tightly shut. He would have to find a way to crawl through the window's opening.

The pure stillness and eerie silence outside the wreckage gave way to the sound of ice crunching methodically under the boots of the approaching figure in gray. Cliff reached underneath the seat for the .38 caliber handgun he kept on the floorboard.

He felt nothing, could find nothing. The Colt had dislodged from its place under the seat by the rolling momentum of the vehicle. The crunching noise stopped.

Cliff looked up in time to recognize the man through the blurriness before everything went dark.

CHAPTER TWENTY-EIGHT

Marlene sat in the passenger seat of Larry's Chevrolet Tahoe and stared out of the window onto the frozen landscape. Her sullen expression and the plump purple-like circles around her eyes revealed her troubled spirit. When asked if anything was wrong, Larry received a silent gesture indicating that she wasn't ready to talk. An hour away from St. Joseph, though, she couldn't contain herself any longer.

"I'm very troubled about this venture with Cliff," she said. "I don't like these jaunts to your mother's, and I'm worried about her. You've placed her in a dangerous situation by having her accept these packages on the weekends. She's not well enough to take care of her daily living routine, let alone anything that would come out of this business of yours."

"Aunt Rosie is doing just fine watching Mama, Marlene. I trust her."

"Oh, please, Larry. Rose is only four years younger than your mother. It has nothing to do with trust."

Larry drove and kept his mouth shut.

"Why haven't you stopped this charade? Callan told you to stop."

"Callan doesn't tell me what to do, okay?"

"Not even on the heels of this Mendoza girl's disappearance?"

"My business with Cliff has nothing to do with Carlotta."

"You can't be so certain."

"There isn't any evidence that her disappearance is anything but one sister being mad at another sister and leaving town."

"You don't believe that."

"I absolutely do believe it. Think about it, Marlene. What common denominator could someone like Carlotta Mendoza have with GrandAire Airlines that would put her in such danger?"

"Perhaps the same common denominator that killed that guy in Austin."

"Murray Thompson? Hon, he was shot along a city street near a park at night. It was a robbery gone bad by a couple of thugs."

"But, Larry, you can't help but think otherwise."

"Think what?" Larry asked, now angry. "The timing between the Mendoza situation and the Thompson shooting is pure coincidence. The two incidents couldn't be any more different. One is about a young Latino girl running away from home in Chicago, and the other is about a middle-aged white professional robbed while jogging in Austin. What common denominator are you talking about?"

Marlene was unconvinced. "All I want from you is an acknowledgement that you understand the danger of what's happening whether the events are connected or not."

"Do you think I'm so naïve and insensitive that I—"

"No, Larry."

"—don't have a sense of right or wrong, danger or safety, good or bad?"

"I didn't say that."

"Then what?" he yelled. "I get the same bullshit from Callan over and over. You two must think I'm some sort of stupid twelve-year-old playing Superman. That's not me at all, Marlene!" He sent her a piercing glance before focusing back onto the concrete highway. On the horizon, he saw stubbles of unplowed corn stalks and bean shoots rising from the dormant ground. After three hours in the car, the formations were now nothing more than a monotonous rerun, like the day after day stubbles of what had become of his life.

He took hold of the wheel with his left hand and reached out to her with his right, rubbing gently the top of her leg. When she turned to see his eyes pleading for a second chance, he tried to muster a smile to reassure her. It didn't work. A half-hearted attempt at making a joke to levity the moment didn't work, either.

The two didn't speak until Larry's late-model Tahoe pulled into the ice-covered lane leading to his mother's house. As he slid into the drive, he noticed that the mail box nailed to the side of an old, weathered post was wide open, revealing nothing inside. There were footprints, but they didn't appear to be those of his mother—larger, more like those of a man.

The white clapboard house where Larry was raised sat high on a small knoll at the end of a double-tracked lane with just enough gravel for a sport utility vehicle like Larry's to gain traction. It sat peacefully away from the old country road that county officials often overlooked. A small woodlot edged the right side of the lane for forty yards before diminishing to a thin line of oak and sycamore trees that divided the property between Larry's mother and her long-time neighbors, Ray and Harriet Lichtle.

The beauty of the snow didn't escape Larry—or Marlene, either, for that matter. They remembered snow like this as kids—fresh, clean, white—and they remembered the smell of cold. There was something special about the smell of virgin snow in the country. The snowfalls in Chicago were pretty, but only for a day or so. Here, in the serenity and obscurity of a place where no one came or went, the beauty remained postcard perfect for days.

Mrs. Southard peered through the front window as they came up the drive. Larry stopped the truck far from the house, not sure how deep the wind had whipped the drifts into place. The old woman opened the door, and a brown, wired-haired Airedale escaped and rampaged through the drifts, tongue flapping off one side between lips that appeared to be smiling to the familiar weekend visitor.

"At least your mom's not sitting on the porch," Marlene said.

Larry grinned as the tired, old mutt reached the side of the truck. Larry emerged from the cab's warmth, bent down, and returned the dog's loyalty with hearty pats to the side of his thick, scraggly coat. "Hey, Mr. Bee! How are you, boy? You treatin' Mama good? Huh? You keepin' 'er warm and comfy?"

Mr. Bee, his official name being Mr. Bolger, jumped as high as he could without falling on his worn back legs. He then made sure he greeted Marlene, who carefully trod around the front of the truck, arms folded across the opening of her coat for warmth.

"Okay, okay, Mr. Bee," Marlene called as the old dog bumped up against her legs and fell at her feet so she could scratch and pat his belly. "Oh, Mr. Bee, honey, it's too cold out here to bend down and give you any lovin' right now." Besides, she could smell the acrid odor of whatever he'd rolled in recently and didn't want to return home with her wool gloves smelling the same.

As they do when not given proper attention, the pet rolled around her feet until Marlene finally bent down and patted his ivory stomach. Satisfied, Mr. Bee got up slowly, scattering snow onto Marlene's pant legs and rushing toward Larry, who'd already started the slow trek toward the house to greet his mother.

"Heel! Heel!" Mrs. Southard commanded the Airedale from the porch. "Heel now, Mr. Bee. Heel!"

"Aw, Mama, that dog ain't gonna heel. He ain't heeled in years." Larry laughed.

"Heel!" she cried again.

"Mama, don't yell. What do you think you're going to get out of him?"

"Don't know, but he minds better'n you. Come on in now. Hi do, Marlene. Mr. Bee, leave them two alone and let 'em git warmed up once. You'ns come in now 'n git warm. Marlene, I made them sugar cookies you like so well, and, Larry, I made a fresh butterscotch pie. It's in the kitchen in the bread box."

"You mean the ice box, Mama?" he asked teasingly, inhaling the stale miasma of the old farmhouse as he entered the front door. He unbuttoned his coat immediately, perspiring from a thermostat set far above a reasonable setting.

209

She paused. "Yes. What did I say?"

"Nothing, Mama. Hope its better than that turkey you made last Thanksgiving."

"What was wrong with that turkey?" she asked indignantly. Then, as soon as the words left her mouth, she laughed and continued on her way. "Oh, *that* turkey. Yes, well, there were j'st too many cooks in the kitchen that day, that's what happened with that turkey."

"Yeah, Mama, I 'spect that's what it was." He turned to Marlene and winked. "Hey, Mama, you still keeping the mail under the cement block by the back porch? Shall I go get it?"

Mrs. Southard was too busy watching Mr. Bolger contorting to bite a flea off his back to hear her son. The old woman bellowed out a hearty laugh at her pet's antics. She sat upright on the edge of her chair, her hands folded securely in her lap. "Why, that dog's going to need a chiropractor before he gets to that itch, I'm tellin' ya."

Larry didn't wait for his mother to answer about the mail. He motioned to Marlene that he was going to the back door off the kitchen.

His mother laughed one more time at her pet before noticing that her son was no longer in the room. She looked at Marlene. "Did he ask me if I kept the mail under a cement block?"

Marlene nodded politely with a tinge of embarrassment.

"What an odd thing to ask," his mother said. "Why in the world would I keep my mail under a cement block?"

Marlene shrugged and looked anxiously through the doorway to the kitchen. She heard the metal screen door slam shut and soon felt cold air usher Larry into the room. Mr. Bolger's tail wagged excitedly as Larry walked through the doorway. Larry entered empty-handed, indicating to Marlene that there was nothing under the block this time.

"Eleanor, would you mind if I took a look at some of your bills to see what I can help you pay this weekend?" Marlene asked.

Mrs. Southard, who was normally eager for the assistance, eyed her skeptically. "I put them away," she said.

"Yes, I know. Where did you put them?"

"Certainly not under a cement block in the back yard." The old woman turned abruptly in her seat to face her son. "Phil Newton stopped by this morning to see you."

Marlene looked at her fiancé as he began to move cautiously toward his mother at the mention of the visitor's name.

Mrs. Southard continued. "He said you had something for him, and I asked, 'Who are you? You look familiar.' He said he was your friend. I asked him, 'From where?' He said from here in town. I said to him, 'You ain't Bimbo Newton, are you?' Remember how much trouble you had growing up with Bimbo Newton? Lord, he was a handful. I said I doubt that you had anything for him but words. He said he wasn't Bimbo, so I said he must be his older brother, Phil. I was right. He was."

Larry took a deep breath and went to his mother's side. "Mama—"

"You remember Phil, Larry. He was the nice one, always respectful and polite. Used to help me, he did, out back when the muskmelons were ready for pickin'."

"Mama," Larry interrupted sternly. "Phil Newton drowned thirty years ago in the Patoka. That man wasn't Phil, Mama."

211

Fear entered Marlene's eyes, but Eleanor Southard was not convinced. "He said he was," she insisted.

"But he couldn't have been, Mom. Listen to me. It's important that you think. Try to tell me what he looked like. What did he want? What did he say?"

It was evident as soon as Larry's mother started babbling that she didn't remember what the man looked like. She used so many conflicting adjectives of his physical appearance in her description that the man sounded more like an ogre living under a bridge down the road.

"Mama, did you give him anything?"

"Larry, we have to get her out of here," Marlene said, looking at the door. "Where does she keep your Aunt Rose's phone number?"

Calmly, Larry faked a smile for his mother to hide his panic. He told Marlene a phone book could be found in the top left drawer of the kitchen counter. "Her last name is Dillon."

Mrs. Southard's attention again focused on Mr. Bolger as the old pup stretched out on a braided floor rug in the middle of the front room. As she bent forward to pet the dog's wiry coat, Larry stopped her and pulled her back.

"Mama, I need to find your mail. Do you understand?"

"Yes, dear," she said politely as if she couldn't fathom why she wouldn't.

"Did you give the man who called himself Phil any letters or envelopes when he visited today?"

"No. Why would I give him my mail? Phil Newton has no business taking any of my mail."

"Good, Mama, now what did you do with today's mail?"

She laughed. "Why, Larry, I didn't do anything with it."

"But there was no mail in the mailbox down by the road."

"I know. That's because there weren't none. Mr. Lichtle next door told me so."

Larry took in an involuntary breath of air—a sign of relief—or so he hoped. He knelt in front of her so he could see directly into her face. "Mr. Lichtle?"

Mrs. Southard took her soft hands and caressed her son's face. "Yes, Larry. Mr. Lichtle keeps an eye on me, sweetheart. With all this ice and snow, Mr. Lichtle says I have no business going down to the road to get my mail. He says I might fall and break my hip or something, and with the bitter cold I might just lie out there for hours and die. So he gets the mail for me when the weather ain't so good."

"That's wonderful, Mama. Mr. Lichtle's a good man. He said there was no mail today?"

Mrs. Southard smiled.

"No big brown envelope?"

She shook her head.

"Think, Mama. Are you sure?"

"Yes, Larry!" she scoffed. "Goodness! Yes, I'm sure! There was no mail today, no big brown envelope, no bills, no letters, nothing."

"But that doesn't make sense."

"Well, it certainly does."

"How, Mama? I don't understand."

"Because they all came yesterday, dear. The big, brown envelope came yesterday. It usually comes on Saturdays, and I place it over there on the end table for you, but this time it came yesterday. Friday. It's still over at Mr. Lichtle's house."

Just then, Marlene came through the doorway from the kitchen. Larry looked up to hear what she had to say. "Your Aunt Rose is coming right away to take your mother to her house for the night. I'll get a few things packed."

Larry explained to Marlene the whereabouts of the mail and Cliff's package. He hurried out the door to the frantic sound of his mother, calling out his name.

Ray Lichtle answered the persistent pounding of Larry's fist upon the door of his small country cottage nestled next door on the knoll. The elderly tobacco grower with his slight frame, weathered face and witty, observant eyes took his time unlatching the lock to the metal storm door. The musty smell of memories greeted Larry once the latch broke free.

"Lord, have mercy," Ray Lichtle said, practically skipping in place at the sight of the grown neighbor. "Who do we have here? Come in, come in a spell, you young rascal. Why, Miss Harriet and I were j'st talkin' about you."

"I hope it was all good, Mr. Lichtle."

"Oh, it was, it was. Not very flattering, though. Shoot, how many times did I have to rescue you from that ol' rooster we had out in the back lot because you thought you could outsmart him? Lord, no smarter than a chicken you were when you were a little squirt, and yet here you are—a dad-burn pilot, no doubt. Come in, come in! Git out o' the cold. I'm j'st teasing you about that rooster, y'know. You were smarter than a mad chicken, boy, you know that. I was j'st teasing you."

Larry mustered a good laugh. "I can't stay long, Mr. Lichtle. Listen, could you tell me something?"

"Harriet!" the farmer yelled, then turned to Larry and grinned. "I have to yell. She can't hear too good. She ain't gettin' any younger, y'see."

"I understand, Mr. Lichtle. I came to get Mama's mail."

"Your mother's mail, y'say?" Ray Lichtle looked around the living room of the modest house and scanned the surfaces of the forty-year-old furnishings as if he was trying to decide what he did with the letters and envelopes. Larry wasn't sure if the old man couldn't remember where he put the mail or if he was holding it hostage to prolong his visit. He suspected the latter. "Now where in the confound tarnation did we put that pack of letters? Oh, and one big envelope, too. I remember you had an envelope. Harriet! You coming?"

A frail voice from a back room called out in response.

Larry interjected, "That envelope you mentioned, Mr. Lichtle, did it have a return address from Wisconsin?"

"Wisconsin, son? Well, I don't know anything about that, but it's the one that usually comes on Saturday mornings to your mother's, it does. Y'see, I pick up the mail for your mother. She has no business runnin' down to the mail box. Harriet! Bring the stack of mail next to my desk papers when you come out! She'll be out directly, Larry. Here, have a seat and tell me all about them big birds you fly."

"Yes, sir. Let me ask something first, however. Did the envelope come today?"

"Today? No, it came yesterday."

"Yesterday? Are you sure, Mr. Lichtle?"

"About as sure as the dadburn crick in my left knee."

"Did you happen to look out your window this morning and see someone come around to visit my mother?"

The old man's eyes lit up. "Yes, that was mighty peculiar to say the least."

Before he could say what was on his mind, Harriet Lichtle emerged from the small hallway, holding a few letters and a large brown envelope as she tried to balance herself with a wooden cane. Greetings from the old woman were short and quick. Larry couldn't help but take time to kiss the side of the face of the woman who used to wipe away tears because of skinned knees, bee stings, and deserved whuppings.

"Is this what you want, Larry?" she asked, lifting the documents as far up as she could without feeling the sharp stab of arthritis lodged in her shoulder.

"It is, Miss Harriet. Thank you. Now, if I promise to return very soon, may I come back to visit you later? I need to go and take care of Mama."

"Don't you want to hear about that man in that big, fancy blue tank that drove up your mama's drive?"

Larry had almost forgotten about his mother's visitor. He faced his neighbor and prompted him to tell him what he knew. Although Mr. Lichtle's memory of the man and his vehicle was more descriptive than his mother's, it revealed little more to help Larry sort out the identity of the man.

After saying his farewells, Larry ran from the farmhouse, package in hand. He stopped between the properties, unsealed the envelope, yanked a few pages from its opening, and scanned them quickly. It appeared on first glance that Cliff had taken the time to organize and highlight the specific facts he wanted Larry to see. Larry withdrew more papers from the envelope.

"Oh, God." Plumes of warm air puffed from his mouth and dissipated into the frosty countryside. For a moment, Larry stood in the snow, frozen with uncertainty about what he should do next.

The excuses and rationale he'd given to Marlene about Northwoods Aeronautics when they were in the car were now unfounded. Cliff's information changed everything. Larry stuffed the documents back into the envelope. Now he wished he hadn't cut Cliff off when he'd called. Larry was convinced. Cliff's firing, Murray Thompson's death, and Carlotta Mendoza's disappearance were now connected. He was certain of it. He ran into his mother's home and began grabbing what he could carry in his arms.

"What are you doing?" Marlene asked as if he were half crazy.

"We gotta go, baby. Now."

"But Rose will be here any minute. If we go now, we'll miss her."

"I said *now*!" he yelled, pulling his cell phone from his pocket. "We can't wait for Rose."

Marlene respected Larry's urgency and hurried into his mother's bedroom to finish packing. She scooped some toiletries into a bag and found the woman's coat in a side closet. She yanked it from its hanger and the hanger clanked to the floor.

Eleanor Southard looked nervously in the direction of the noise. "I'm not going!" she yelled amid the chaos.

"It will be okay, Eleanor," Marlene said as she walked into the living room.

"Where am I going, Marlene? Where are you sending me? I'm not going to The Manor."

"Rose will be here shortly to take you to her house for a nice visit. You're going with Rose."

Larry shut the cover to his phone and went quickly to his mother. "Mama, we're not going to the old folks' home," he said, placing both of his hands gently on her

217

shoulders. "We are going to Aunt Rosie's house, really, we are. I'd never send you to the county farm. We have to go to Aunt Rosie's, and we have to go now, and you can't argue with us."

The expression in his mother'd eyes turned from anger to bewilderment. She didn't say anything, just stood obediently, and listened intently as Marlene rummaged through her drawers and bedroom closet for appropriate clothing.

"If you have to go to the bathroom, Mama, go now. I'm going to give Callan Morrow a call. You know Cal, Mama. I want him to know what we're doing."

Whether Mrs. Southard had to go to the bathroom or not was irrelevant. She followed her son's orders and turned to go. At that, Larry grabbed his phone and punched in his friend's phone number. "Damn!" he exclaimed under his breath when he placed the call. He wanted Callan to answer, but it went immediately to voice mail.

"You 'bout ready?" he called to Marlene excitedly. "Mama? Got your coat handy?"

"It's not that cold out there," she replied stubbornly, folding her arms in defiance.

Larry took four steps in his mother's direction. "Yes, it is," he said. "I want your coat on."

"Larry, be patient," Marlene chided, toting an overnight bag and a small suitcase from the bedroom. "I'm sure Rose is on her way."

"I'll get the car warmed up," he said, wrapping his unbuttoned coat around him.

"You'll need gloves," his mother warned.

"I'm fine, Mama," he responded curtly as his mother balked at his hypocrisy.

The snow crunched beneath his feet as he stepped off the front porch and across the yard. The stillness of the snowy landscape was a sharp contrast to the confusion and urgency inside the house. When his phone rang from his coat pocket, he anticipated it to be Callan, returning his call. He withdrew the phone and noticed Cliff's number on the caller identification display.

"Hey, Cliff," Larry said. "Glad you called. Listen, this shit you sent me is crazy. We gotta talk as soon as I get my mother to a safe place."

The caller didn't respond.

"You there?" he asked.

A voice, different from his friend's, answered Larry weakly. "This isn't," the caller started to say, his voice faltering. "I'm using Cliff's phone, but this isn't Cliff. I'm his brother, Rob. Rob Pierceman."

Larry stopped to listen.

From the front window of the house, Marlene looked out to see Aunt Rose's large, burgundy sedan burrowing through the snow toward the house. She was relieved to see that Aunt Rose had arrived before Larry could load the car and they'd left the property. Otherwise, they'd have been sure to miss his aunt in passing.

Eleanor Southard came alongside Marlene to look out the window with her. Snow began to fall gently outside. Rose took her time getting out of the car, age and cold temperatures contributing to her lethargic actions. Larry continued to stand still in his tracks, his back squarely to the women looking out of the window.

"What's he doing?" Mrs. Southard asked.

"Shhh," Marlene said. She noticed Larry's posture change. Something was wrong. The solid, towering man she knew was diminishing, sinking into the snow as if he

219

were being swallowed by a drift. Her stomach began to churn and her heart nearly squeezed the breath out of her chest. Marlene lunged for the door.

"What's going on?" Mrs. Southard cried. "What's happening to him?"

Rose reached Larry first, unable to comprehend the agony within his sobbing, corpse-like body that had crumpled like a child into the whiteness. By the time Marlene wrapped her arms across his back, his grief—the kind born from an awareness of regret and guilt that could never be forgiven—had fully consumed him.

Marlene let him lie, resting her head on his coat between the blades of his shoulders as she held him. She began to cry, too, covered in snow and surrounded by sorrow, not because she knew why, but because she knew him.

CHAPTER TWENTY-NINE

On Monday morning, Aysha Marks rose early and rushed to her GrandAire office in the pouring rain, feeling exhausted from another long evening the night before. The news of Cliff Pierceman's death had alarmed her to the point that sleep was next to impossible on top of her professional worries.

She struggled to concentrate. Temporary workers hired specifically for the gala waited patiently for assignments. She was slow to delegate.

Aysha wiped her head and rubbed her temples as she moved quickly toward her cubicle. Thirteen-hour days, seven days a week since she transferred to marketing were starting to take their toll. She was up for the job, she knew she was, but she was unable to deal with the constant needs of her people, who sapped her energy and ability to concentrate.

Before reaching her cube, Aysha saw Carol Chambers walking in her direction, talking intently to a peer and gesturing at a document. The last person she wanted to see this morning was Carol. She didn't have time for her whirlwind orders and chaotic manner. She ducked into a side cubicle, burying her face into a stack of stray papers as if she was busy studying their content.

"These must be signed by tomorrow," Carol argued as the two stopped short of the opening to the cubicle where Aysha was hiding. "It's becoming increasingly difficult to get approvals from Hamilton with his schedule taking him out of the city. At first, it was convenient having him out of the way. Lately, though, it's been making my job impossible. These have to be signed by tomorrow."

"What about Velma Hofmeyer?" the other woman asked.

"What about her?"

"Isn't there some way she can contact him to send the documents out for his signature?"

"I'm not going to hold my breath for Velma Hofmeyer. She's been part of the problem to begin with. She scrutinizes every document that comes across his desk to sign. She filters what she thinks he needs to see. Her controlling maneuverings increase the complexity of things."

The two moved on, and Aysha exited the cubicle, nearly bumping into a young woman standing in the opening.

"I'm sorry, Aysha," the woman, her assistant, said. "Your boyfriend, Rafael, is on your line. Do you want to talk to him?"

"Oh, Debbie, I'm stretched right now. Ask him if I can call him back."

"It sounds important," she said.

Aysha didn't know how to answer. She didn't think she could handle more bad news. Not today. Not even from Paeng.

"I have him on hold," Debbie added.

Aysha relented and moved quickly to her cubicle. Picking up the phone, she greeted her boyfriend without her usual lighthearted spirit.

"Are you okay?" he asked immediately. "You don't sound okay."

Holding her hair back with one hand and talking closely into the receiver, Aysha looked to see if anyone was in the near vicinity. "Ralph, I'm scared. This thing about Cliff is getting to me."

"I know, baby. It'll be okay, though. We've got a couple of guys here working on it right now. The reason I called is that a woman telephoned before I left the house. She was asking for you. She said her name was Ellen Holloway. Is she that lawyer's mom? Anyway, she received her invitation in the mail to the Gala and just now realized that it included two inaugural VIP flight tickets from Indianapolis to Chicago and back. Were two tickets intended for her?"

"Yes! Ken wants his mother to be there when we unveil the promotion. He felt she would be more likely to come if she brought a friend."

"Any restrictions on the person she brings?"

"No, whoever she wants."

"That's what I was afraid of."

"What do you mean? What's wrong?"

"Nothing's wrong, but the guest she wants to bring may cause a stir."

"Who's she inviting?"

Paeng told her.

Aysha's eyes bulged. She wondered how she was going to keep the information a secret from Callan.

CHAPTER THIRTY

The Protestant church in the Milwaukee suburb of Brookfield was small, but easily held the gathering of friends and family who came to pay final respects to a man who'd loved airplanes, fishing, and the solitude of the North. As much as Cliff Pierceman also loved the snow, Liz hoped it wouldn't snow on this particular morning. Her wish was granted, although disappointingly so. A rare late-January warm front replaced the snow storm. The rain began to fall around eight o'clock in the morning.

At the advice of the pastor on behalf of Cliff's aging parents, Liz opted to have the graveside service near the front entrance inside the church. Both Callan and Larry sat silently near the front row behind Liz. They sat as they did during the drive to Milwaukee shrouded in a daze of disbelief and impending horror. The service presented little solace. Even though the pastor knew Cliff well as a boy and had much to say, Callan felt the service was uninspiring.

Perhaps the preacher was as shocked and dismayed as everyone else.

Liz chose a passage from *Hebrews* to consummate Cliff's memory. "Faith is being sure of what we hope for and certain of what we do not see." It professed faith as an act of believing when, in all practical purposes, there appeared to be nothing to believe.

"I don't care what Alan Cavanaugh thinks," Liz said to Callan with tears in her eyes. "God knows Cliff was an innocent man."

Larry and Callan assisted four other men to lift the casket containing their friend's body and carry it from the steps of the altar to a wheeled cart in the Narthex.

The procession wasn't a long one, but the walk made in rhythm to the pattering rain on the roof of the church felt as though it were. The casket was heavy. Callan didn't remember caskets weighing on his arm as heavily as Cliff's did, and he found he needed all the power he had to lead the way behind the pastor.

Then, as Callan was about to face forward before entering the Narthex, he saw a man wrapped in a heavy overcoat, sitting in the back of the church.

Larry saw him, too.

The man was Mark Reasoner, Larry's counterpart at GrandAire, and Alan Cavanaugh's right-hand man. Mark caught the two men's puzzling stares and offered no apologies by his expression for his presence.

"Surprised to see him?" Callan asked Larry after the service as they cowered under umbrellas, walking from the front steps of the church. They could see Mark walking swiftly ahead of them, away from the church, unprotected from the elements except for the overcoat.

Larry didn't respond.

"I don't care for him," Callan offered. "He's too quiet."

"You don't like 'em windy, either."

"I don't like extremes. I don't like Alan because he's a hot-air balloon, and I don't like Reasoner because he slinks in and out of places and doesn't say a word. He's Alan's puppet."

"Why are you all of a sudden interested in Mark Reasoner?" Larry asked. "You've never been interested before. In fact, you've never had any meaningful interactions with him at GrandAire."

"I know, but remember the first time you told me about your job at GrandAire? I said something bothered me about the company. I couldn't put my finger on it, Larry, but something did bother me. I remember now. It had to do with inspection procedures and problems with testing by third-party companies. Even Cliff referenced it in his last documentation to you. It's one reason why I don't trust Reasoner. He's responsible for plane inspections."

"Guilt by association?"

"Maybe, but it makes sense. What do you know about him?"

Larry shrugged off the question.

"He's gotta be one of Alan's cronies. Do you think he came to the funeral to see the result of his work?" Callan asked.

"You think Reasoner is the killer?"

"That's what I'm asking. I wonder if he's here on Alan's behalf like a pyromaniac watches his fire."

Larry didn't say anything until they were well on the road south of Milwaukee. "Drop me off at O'Hare once we get to Chicago," he said as they crossed into Illinois.

"What for?"

"I'm going to Austin."

Callan shook his head vehemently. "I know why you want to go, but it's too dangerous. Not a good idea."

"It is if you keep your mouth shut and don't tell anyone. No one knows I'm going, Cal. I haven't bought my ticket yet so there's no record of me leaving. No hotel reservations have been made in Austin. I purposely didn't tell Marlene. Come to think of it, you didn't know until just now. So who would know of my plan?"

Callan bit his lower lip and clutched the steering wheel with a white-knuckled grip as he deliberated the proposal. Larry could be right. No phone calls, no tickets, no reservations, no documentation, no paper trail of any kind. No one would suspect where he was, and he would be back in town by tomorrow evening with no one the wiser. He glanced into his rear-view mirror and got a good look at the cars behind them.

"Being followed?" Larry asked.

"No, of course not."

"You're making sure, though, aren't you?"

"Yes, I think it would be a good idea," he said, accelerating the gas pedal, "especially if I'm taking you straight to the airport."

Larry leaned his head on the head rest and closed his eyes. "Thanks, buddy."

CHAPTER THIRTY-ONE

"Mr. Bender and Ms. Wyatt will be with you shortly, sir," said the receptionist who sat beneath large bronze letters spelling the words *Kirklin Bender.* She motioned for Larry to have a seat. "Care for some coffee?"

"No, thank you."

It was early the next morning. On a routine day, Larry would have sucked down enough cups to jolt a generator into action, but today he refused. A meeting with the associates of Kirklin, Bender was enough of a rush.

When Larry had arrived in Austin, Amelia Wyatt was eager to forward Larry's phone call to the firm's partner, Randall Bender. Bender accepted it immediately and rearranged his calendar to meet him with the hopes of exchanging information.

Larry sat nervously in the posh but desolate room of pecan-paneled walls and bronze fixtures. The plush décor of the lobby stood in stark contrast to his office at GrandAire.

The receptionist politely ushered him into a small, rectangular conference room near the lobby, and he accepted a subsequent offer of some bottled water. Randall Bender greeted him first. Amelia Wyatt and another middle-aged gentleman named David Lampton rose from the table to introduce themselves and shake his hand. Exchanges of information about their backgrounds illustrated their extensive knowledge base and experience.

"It's necessary for us to hire individuals from multi-disciplinary fields for our pre-trial consulting role related to litigation matters," Mr. Bender explained. "Many of our cases involve complex legal and scientific issues, so we have to be well versed in all aspects of these cases to develop factual defenses for our clients that judges and juries can identify."

"And prosecutors, too," Ms. Wyatt added.

Bender turned to the woman and nodded. "Prosecutors, too."

"Amelia worked with Mr. Thompson on a variety of cases related to aviation."

"Murray had a juris doctorate from Illinois, an engineering degree from Purdue, and vast practical, hands-on experience within the field," Amelia said. "His most recent experience was that of Vice President of Operations at GrandAire."

"A position you currently hold, if we understand correctly," Mr. Lampton added.

Larry concurred.

"Did you know him in that role, Mr. Southard?"

"No, I replaced him when he left. I have a commercial pilot's background, but very little operational experience before taking the position. However, Thompson left behind some excellent people under my employment who have supported me in my management role."

"We understand completely," Bender said. "That's how Mr. Thompson happened to join our firm. Where we don't have the experience and hands-on knowledge related to the cases we serve, we find it. In Mr. Thompson's case, he found us. We also contract with individuals who are leading experts in various disciplines. We must have viable, knowledgeable people in areas such as toxicology, psychiatry, chemistry, and geology."

"Metallurgy, too," Lampton interrupted.

"And risk management," Amelia Wyatt added. "Not only are people and relationships important to us, but our technology must be superior to stay on top of cutting-edge development. We have excellent documentation support, and we find software and analytical tools to assist us."

"I want to stress one other thing," Lampton said. "We aren't just attorneys. We're also advocates."

"What does that mean?" Larry asked.

"We're proactive as well as reactive," Ms. Wyatt explained. "Murray Thompson was passionate about his work at Kirklin Bender. With that passion was a strong desire to prevent corporate disasters before they happened. That meant monitoring corporate activities by staying abreast of their research and development. It meant monitoring their ethical policies and the regulations they lobbied for or against on a state and federal level. It also meant determining how they used their dollars to protect and maintain the welfare of the consumers they served. To do that, Murray established a network of individuals in the private and public arenas who worked undercover, if you will, to provide us information on those activities."

"Moles? You used moles?" Larry asked.

Amelia looked at Randall Bender for his guidance on the proper response.

"We have informants throughout many industries, yes," he said. "We don't refer to them as moles."

"Is that why you were eager to see me? Do you need me as an informant?"

The three looked at each other again before responding.

"Not at this time," Bender replied. "Don't get us wrong. We are interested in what you have to say, and based upon our telephone conversation to establish this meeting, we are also willing to provide you with information in return. This meeting, however, isn't contingent on a condition that information must be provided to us on an ongoing basis about what's happening within GrandAire Airlines."

"Why not?" he asked bluntly.

When they didn't answer, Larry nodded. "Okay, I see," he said. "I think I understand. You already have an informant within GrandAire, don't you?"

"We hope you understand that to divulge the identity of the individual would be counter-productive. It's evident that we share the same objectives. We are both advocates. For years, Kirklin Bender has been interested in uncovering bribes and kickbacks within the airline manufacturing industry and the Federal government. We're probably more interested in the government's relationships with manufacturers and maintenance contractors."

"We lost a dear advocate when Murray was shot," Ms. Wyatt said sincerely, "and we suspect and will prove that he died at the hands of corporate professionals because of his work and knowledge of the issues."

She looked at Larry sympathetically.

"But then, so did your colleague," she added.

Larry sucked in a deep breath of stale air and exhaled slowly. "How did you know about Cliff Pierceman?" Larry looked into their icy, professional stares. After releasing the question, he realized that answering would reveal the informant, something they wouldn't do.

"So," Randall Bender said, opening the thick, brown folder of documents that had been lying on the table throughout their conversation. "Are we ready to begin exchanging information to get to the bottom of their deaths to prevent future tragedies?"

Larry nodded.

"Confidentially, of course?" Bender added.

Larry put his hand on top of the folder of documents David Lampton slid across the table to him. Opening the folder and exchanging information would change everything. It wasn't a simple game of revenge anymore. It wasn't internal auditing as Callan knew it, either. Opening the folder meant that Larry and those around the table were personally responsible for the lives of thousands of future airline passengers and individuals who upheld ethical behavior within their companies. Opening the folder meant he couldn't return to Chicago the same man as he left. He, his responsibilities at GrandAire, his responsibilities to those who worked for him—even his relationships with Marlene and Callan—would all change. They would *have* to change.

Larry looked into the eyes of Randall Bender and met his challenge. "Of course," he said and opened his folder.

CHAPTER THIRTY-TWO

Callan stood patiently at O'Hare International in anticipation of spending time with his son, Gil, at the Blackhawks hockey game that evening. He felt the vibrations of his cell phone in his pocket, but he had Gil in sight; his son walked swiftly down the corridor toward him. Whoever was trying to call him could wait until Callan greeted his youngest to Chicago.

His phone rang again as they drove in the vicinity of the United Center. "I better get this one, son," Callan said as he reached inside his pocket,

"Cal? This is Paeng," said the voice at the other end. "Can you meet me now at Centro Margarita? It's important." Paeng explained that he'd received a call from Larry about the conclusions Larry had derived from his visit to Austin.

Callan hung up and took a deep breath. He looked toward Gil, who was busy watching traffic and taking in the sights around the airport. He wasn't sure how he'd accept a sudden change in plans. "Say, Gil," Cal murmured reluctantly. "How would you like to eat at this Mexican place I like to go to?"

"Cool."

"Yeah, and how would you like to help me, uh, investigate something while we're there?"

"Really?" he asked excitedly. "Even cooler!"

Callan sighed in relief.

Thirty minutes later, they met Paeng inside Centro Margarita's entrance near the hostess podium. Cecilia came from the kitchen as Callan introduced Paeng to Gil.

"I'll be with you guys in a moment," she said, smiling and waving to the trio as she passed.

"That's a good sign," Callan said as he watched her movements. "She looks like she's doing well. Good news about her sister?"

Paeng shook his head. "*Nada.*"

Odd, Callan thought. He wondered what was behind Cecilia's new, uplifted spirit. "Maybe she's heard from her," he suggested.

"From Carlotta? No, I don't think so," Paeng replied. "From what we've been able to piece together, it doesn't look like she disappeared on her own."

"What do you have?"

"Nothing, really."

"Then how do you know? Look at Cecilia. She's waving and smiling. She's either won the lottery or found out that her sister is alive. What else is there?"

"Let's get a table, and I'll show you."

"So good to see you both again," Cecilia greeted as she approached. "Aw, *es su muchacho, Senor* Morrow?"

"Yes, his name is Gil."

"Welcome, *Senor* Gil," Cecilia said politely, pulling back her hair to reveal a beautiful smile radiating from her golden skin. "Care for your same table by the window, gentlemen?"

"Yes, please," Paeng replied energetically before Callan could intervene.

Cecilia escorted the three and wished them all a good dinner with thoughts of happier times ahead.

"Oh, yes, I see what you mean," Callan said sarcastically to Paeng when Cecilia slipped away. "She sure is downtrodden."

Paeng ignored him.

"Any reason why we're sitting at this particular table this evening?" Callan asked. "The last time Aysha was here quite a ruckus occurred."

"Stick your head under the table."

Gil was the first to do so while his father looked on.

"It's sticky," the boy said.

"Food? Gum?"

Gil said no and sat back to an upright position on his stool.

"Residue," Paeng replied. "We believe a surveillance recorder was installed to monitor conversations we had when we sat at this very table. We believe Carlotta Mendoza had a part in ensuring that we sat here each time we came in."

"Thus your reason for believing Carlotta didn't just disappear."

"Exactly. I think she's dead."

Gil sat silently, taking it all in with wide eyes.

"Did Larry learn some good information in Austin?"

"Yes, he did, but I haven't had an opportunity to talk to him completely. I've only had short phone calls here and there. When his plane lands tonight, I want to sit down with him and discuss his findings in greater detail. An agent at the FBI has been assigned to the case because of the Mendoza disappearance and the death of Cliff Pierceman."

"What have you got so far?"

"If you remember, Cliff was killed on a Thursday, the day he normally drove into Rhinelander to mail his research package before going to work. Whoever it was heard about Cliff's timeline when all of us were here at Centro Margarita. Aysha remembers discussing it here, but in the week Cliff was killed, he mailed the package on Wednesday instead of Thursday because of the snow storm. No one knew of the change in routine, especially not the killer. The killer, though, must have realized something was wrong after he killed Cliff because the package wasn't in Cliff's possession. It had already been mailed. The killer put two and two together and then made a quick visit to Larry's mother's house before Larry and Marlene got there on Saturday. It was fortunate that the old man next door to Larry's mother picked up her mail and kept it at his home that day. We're not sure, but we believe this explains the events. What we are sure about, though, is that Centro Margarita was the source of the killer's information."

Callan's mind went into a flurry of thoughts. "What else does Larry know?" he asked.

"What I've been able to gather is that there were certain names Kirklin Bender relayed that he says you've already researched."

Callan shook his head. "I haven't done any research. I've purposely not done any research."

"Yes, you did."

"You mean the audits Aysha and I performed?"

"No, the stuff you did before you came to Chicago."

"Oh, no, that research was done a long time ago. I'm sure it's not relevant anymore, and if it is relevant, I don't remember any of the details. I've not done any recent stuff. That's been Larry and Cliff's baby."

"But that's what we need—your old stuff."

Callan looked at his son. He was interested in hearing more, but apprehensive about delving into a past that had caused him and his family so much personal heartache.

"Prior to the Monon crash," Paeng explained, "Midland Airlines bought planes from the French company Lignes Aérienne de National. As a result of the crash, National went out of business when it was determined that improper testing of the aircraft in certain weather conditions was performed."

"You mean like the weather around Lake Michigan that brought down the Midlands flight?"

"Exactly. The aircraft shouldn't have been authorized or certified to fly in conditions more severe than those it'd been tested to perform. The manufacturer didn't test properly even though they knew there were problems."

"Problems with what?"

"Their de-icing mechanism."

"Are you saying they knew this before the Monon crash happened?"

"Yes, from a situation that happened in Wisconsin. An investigation was conducted following that incident, recommending that they modify the plane's structure, improve the de-icing capabilities, and provide pilots with updated training on how to handle icing problems."

"Wait a minute. Wasn't there any follow-up to make sure the manufacturer made the corrective actions based upon the investigation?"

"Apparently not by either the French Dictorate General or the U.S. government."

"If they had, the Monon crash could have been prevented."

"That's right."

"I don't get it. I don't understand why they wouldn't follow-up. We're talking about people's lives."

"That's where the allegations of bribes and payoffs to certain government personnel brought the company to its knees and destroyed the industry's trust in the planes the company built."

"So what happened to the planes?"

"What do marketing experts do when products fail or don't sell?"

Callan rolled his eyes. "Don't tell me they changed the name of the product, called it new and improved, slapped a brighter picture on the box, and put it back on the shelf."

"That's exactly what they did. They did it with the LAN-27 model aircraft. Lignes Aerienne de National didn't do it, but the company that bought them did. That company had trouble selling the plane. They changed their name, changed the craft slightly to accommodate executive flying needs, repainted the planes, and sold the crafts to the same market that bought the originals. The buyers trusted these crafts to be the future for executive charters."

"Are you trying to tell me that GrandAire was the buyer of these *new* planes?"

"That I am."

"So that's when GrandAire was born."

"And none the wiser," Paeng said, "until guys like Murray Thompson and Cliff Pierceman started asking questions and digging around."

"How much of this does Aysha know as she prepares for the Gala?"

"The situation is too volatile for me to divulge that information to Aysha right now. The less she knows, the safer she'll be. We need to act quickly, though. I'm hoping that some of the names involved in these transactions are the same names you determined were involved in your original research related to the Monon crash."

"Are we sure that one or more executives within GrandAire knew of this scam before purchasing the planes?"

"We need more evidence," Paeng said frankly.

"Okay," Callan agreed. "Write down the names of your suspects, and I'll see what I can find."

Callan took a deep breath and turned to his son. He promised him a long weekend—just the two of them—to visit sights and have some fun in the Windy City. He looked at the young man who'd been sitting patiently on his stool, sipping his soft drink.

"I've got this stuff in a storage area, Son."

"I'll help you, Dad."

Callan didn't know how to respond.

"Honest, Dad. We could go down there and pull your stuff. I could help you look through it. Honest."

"Sure you don't mind?"

The young man nodded eagerly.

"Okay," Callan said. "We'll go to the game tonight and head for Indiana early in the morning."

"Cool!"

CHAPTER THIRTY-THREE

Terese stood in the kitchen, dipping a spoon into a cup of non-fat vanilla yogurt as she hugged the phone to her ear. It'd been more than a week since she'd talked to Ellen Holloway. The sound of her voice was good to hear. She was also working a crossword puzzle, though, and found herself continually asking Ellen to repeat what she'd just said as she did two things at once. She finally set her pencil on top of the book and pushed it off to the side.

"No, you're not bothering me," Terese stated. "I'm just standing here, trying to curb my appetite with some yogurt. What I really want are those potato chips in the cupboard, but I'm being willfully strong. If I can lose a size and get rid of those flappers under my arms, I'll feel better about being seen at this party."

Ellen had been pleased that Terese had accepted her invitation to GrandAire's Gala and be on the inaugural flight from Indianapolis. Nine other flights would simultaneously converge over Lake Michigan to make a spectacular entrance into Chicago by flying over the GrandAire headquarters building on their way to Chicago Midway, she'd explained. A cocktail reception prior to each flight was being organized for each location in addition to the main affair.

Terese dipped her spoon one last time into the yogurt cup. Licking the back of the utensil, she listened to a description of the gown Ellen was planning to wear. Suddenly, she heard the outside screen door bang as if someone was trying unsuccessfully to gain entrance. Terese turned toward the sound. She heard voices, too.

Her heart started to pound. It couldn't be Brandon, she thought. Brandon and three other buddies had gone skiing in Michigan. It wasn't Gil. He was in Chicago with his father. She told Ellen she would call her back.

Suddenly, the door flung open, and a familiar voice called out, "Hey, Mom! We're back! Dad's here!"

Terese leaned against a kitchen counter and smirked as Callan bashfully poked his head into view.

"Dad bought you flowers!" Gil yelled as a dozen red roses appeared from around the corner.

"What's this for? Why are you guys back? You didn't come back to see me, did you?"

"No!" Gil laughed as he looked at his father.

"Okay, then, what did you do that requires flowers?"

"Nothing," Callan reassured her.

Gil couldn't contain himself. "We're investigating!"

"What?"

"No, we're not," Callan said. "It's nothing, really."

"We've got boxes and boxes out in the living room."

"Two boxes," Callan interjected.

"There's a couple more still in the car. Want me to go get them, Dad?"

Callan shook his head and tried to diminish his son's enthusiasm.

The look on Terese's face didn't match her son's excitement. "What sort of investigating?" she asked skeptically.

Callan started to answer, but didn't get the words out in time.

Instead, Gil did the talking. "There've been murders and girls disappearing and this guy, I mean, this bad guy has been following Dad places."

"Gil!" Callan said to get his son's attention.

Terese gestured for Callan to let the boy continue.

"... and they've been bugged at this Mexican place ..."

"Bugged?"

"Yeah, like in wire tap, Mom. You know."

"In Mexico?"

"No!" Callan blurted before the conversation got out of hand.

Gil laughed. "No, just this Mexican place, but the FBI knows about it so don't worry about that. It's cool, Mom. I met this guy from the FBI."

"Callan, what in the world is he talking about? The FBI? Murder? Missing persons? Stalking? Spying? You've left out gambling, drugs, and prostitution, for crying out loud! And Gil has met the FBI? Don't tell me you've introduced our son to this!"

"Calm down, Terese. The FBI is Aysha's boyfriend."

"And he's been trying to find out stuff about bribes to the government and something about contracts," Gil said.

"Government bribes?"

"Gil, let me handle this," his father said. "You've said enough."

"But *you* haven't, Callan," Terese retorted. She placed her hand to the side of her head in disbelief. "And put those damn roses down! I'm not looking at those things while you try to sweet talk your way out of this calamity!"

Callan immediately set the flowers on the counter.

"But, Mom!" Gil pleaded, suddenly realizing what was happening.

"This is bad, Callan," she said. "This is really bad. Do you realize that? Do you know why?" Terese pointed to their son. "How could you put our son in danger by getting him involved? Do you not remember, oh, my God, do you not remember that night when they broke into our home?" She became frightened and reached for the nearest chair at the kitchen table to sit down.

Callan started to walk toward her.

"Don't. Just stay where you are. Please, Cal, I don't know what to think anymore. We had our house ransacked and you moved immediately to Chicago to put us into more danger. What am I supposed to do now?"

Gil stepped back, inching his way toward the doorway. After a few steps, he bolted for his room.

Seconds passed before the next words were spoken. Terese sucked in air and started to cry. "Well," she said through cracks in her voice, "I guess I can eat that bag of potato chips after all. I have no reason to slip into any fancy gown or to impress any snooty-assed women in your company."

"What are you talking about? Why would you ever want to do that?"

"Because I was going to surprise you," she said. "Ellen invited me up to Chicago for that big party GrandAire is having. We were even taking that flight."

"What flight?"

"That flight!" she repeated defiantly. "That, uh, inaugural thing or whatever they're calling it. It's that flight with all those other flights."

"No," he said.

Terese stared at her husband. The tears stopped.

"What did you say?"

"I said, no, you're not, Terese."

"No, I'm not what, Callan?"

Callan searched for words to describe the disgust and disdain he had for GrandAire Airlines. He was angered that his wife was part of a potentially dangerous promotion that the company was planning. He couldn't express in words how he was feeling. Instead, he announced with authority that she was not going on any flight, getting on any airplane, or flying anywhere on anything associated with GrandAire Airlines—ever.

"How dare you," she said sternly. "What makes you think you can keep me from doing anything I want to do?"

"Terese."

"No, I'm not listening to you. That's what you do. You audit and you investigate and you tell people what they're doing right and what they're doing wrong. You tell them what they can do and what they can't do. Well, you can't do that with me, Callan. It's not going to work. Not any more."

"Terese, the flights occurring on inaugural night with GrandAire are in serious jeopardy. That's what Gil and I are trying to prove. We're uncovering evidence of improperly tested airplanes in inclement weather conditions—the exact kind of weather conditions this inaugural flight could experience. We're finding a lack of adequate maintenance and inspections. There's corruption and collusion involved with this gala. I know you're upset, but you can't get on that plane. I'm pleading with you."

"I'm pleading, too, Callan. I've been pleading for months. All I want is a normal, secure family home that's safe to be in where we don't have to fear who we are and who hates us for what we know. I'm sick of it. I was sick of Monon, and now I'm sick of GrandAire. Don't you get that? I've had it. I'm through with it, Callan, and I'm through talking about it."

Callan stood silently in the middle of the room.

"I'd like you to leave," she said.

Callan looked at her unbelievingly.

"Yes, I mean it. I'm through."

When she saw he wasn't moving toward the door, she calmly and deliberately presented an ultimatum. "I said I want you to leave. I mean it. I've had it with this hell you've put us through, and I want no more part of it. That means I'm through with you, too, so take everything when you leave, Callan, because this time, you're not coming back."

CHAPTER THIRTY-FOUR

Mary DeFrantz was crunching month-end closing numbers at her desk when Callan's call interrupted her concentration.

"I need to talk to Aysha, but I can't get hold of her," he blurted.

"I doubt that you will, Cal. She's busy, and it's late. She's in frantic mode right now with the celebration. Is there something you need?"

"Yes. Aysha did a management expense audit. Her workpapers are in my office. I need her to look up something."

"I can do that for you. You gave me one of your office keys awhile back. Does it still work?"

"Yes. Would you see if certain names appear on management expense reports for entertainment or other expenses?"

Mary jotted down the names, then walked across the hall, let herself into Callan's office, and quietly closed the door. It locked automatically. She found the workpaper file in two boxes on the floor. She couldn't imagine any of the executives being so careless as to include real names on their expense reports if the names were tied to illegal activity, but as Mary perused Carol Chambers' expenses, several names did appear for entertainment, meals, lodging, and other incidentals.

The name Michael Benning appeared frequently and the initials *T.W.*, presumably Ted Warmke, appeared twice on the sheets of Alan Cavanaugh. She studied the workpapers further, checking and double-checking her work to ensure the information Callan requested was correct.

She started to put some of the files back in their original place when she heard unfamiliar footsteps outside the office door. Whoever was standing in the hall had a key—or was using a mechanism that could be used as a key. The lock unlatched, and the door opened slowly.

Mary grabbed Callan's black stapler from his desk and held it tightly in her hand. When the door opened enough to see the intruder, Mary sighed with relief and dropped the stapler.

Max Dennison stood poised as if to challenge an intruder inside the office. "Ms. DeFrantz?" he asked, surprised by his find.

"Oh, God, Max, I'm glad it's you."

"I thought I heard some noise in here, and then I noticed the light under the door. Mr. Morrow told me he was taking a couple of days off to be with his kid, so I thought it was odd to hear noises and see lights in his office."

"Yes, but I'm glad you did. Sorry, Max. Cal called and asked me to check his workpapers for something."

"He's supposed to be taking time off. I told him he needed to get away from this place. Why isn't he with his boy?"

"He is, I think."

"Then what's he doing thinking about work?"

"My point exactly."

"You don't mind if I verify your story with him, do you? I hate to do that, Mary, but his work is very confidential, and I don't believe I'd be doing my job if I didn't."

"Absolutely, Max, I understand."

"Otherwise, is everything okay with you before I finish my rounds and the next shift begins?"

Mary assured him that all was well and that he could go.

He tipped his cap and began to close the door.

"Max!" she called just before he closed it completely. He reopened the door, and Mary responded with a simple and sincere, "Thank you."

He closed the door again, leaving Mary with boxes of workpapers that made her nervous just knowing they were there. She organized her work and left the office, carrying two folders from the box of management expenses.

Max was nowhere in sight in the hallway. He'd obviously finished his rounds on the floor and left to go home.

She found Aysha in the atrium, helping workers set the stage and decorate the room, answering questions posed by the electricians, and ensuring promotional signage was properly situated.

Aysha saw Mary and greeted her with a hug.

"Things must be going well," Mary said. "This is the first smile I've seen out of you in a very long time."

"Yes, it is." Aysha giggled. "Things *are* going well, actually. It's finally coming together. I think it'll be the event of the year in this city. It's just how Carol wanted it.

Follow me." Aysha took Mary by the hand and led her to the atrium window that looked out toward the lake. "Sometimes, at the end of the day when everyone has left, I look at this great room and I marvel over the opportunity I've been given to put on such a show for our city. But it's not just the room that inspires me, Mary. It's this window and Lake Michigan as the stage!"

She stared with wonder over the darkening eastern horizon of Lake Michigan as the lights of the city twinkled in the view's foreground. "I stand here, and I imagine each of the ten planes converging over the lake one by one— dots of lights coming together—to fly in single file over the building to the airport. I hear the music strike; I see the balloons and confetti released, and I see myself reaching for a celebratory glass of champagne faster than anyone can say, 'I wonder what she has up the other sleeve'."

The two laughed and settled into their normal conversational tone. Soon, Aysha looked at Mary in more business-like fashion and said, "I bet my repertoire wasn't what you came to hear, was it?"

"No, but it's better than what I came to talk about. Cal called and asked me to look over your management expense audit workpapers. Is there someplace we can go to talk privately? It'll only take a moment."

Aysha eyed the room quickly to make sure everyone had enough to do while she was gone. "Let's go to marketing," she said. "I have to run back to the office for something anyway. Besides, no one is there."

"Carol?"

"She left. She said she had a dinner engagement related to the gala. I told her to go. I'd rather she not meddle at this late stage. It's easier for me that way."

249

The women returned to marketing where Aysha picked up a can of diet cola that was sitting on her desk. She took a sip and smiled. "What've we got?"

Mary spread Aysha's original worksheets on a nearby table, including three of the expense reports. "What do you make of these?"

"Cal had me pull and review these reports shortly after I transitioned into auditing. Quite frankly, Mary, I didn't know what I was looking at or what I was looking for at the time. I glossed over everything. They didn't mean anything to me."

"Would you mind taking a second look now that you have a different perspective?"

Aysha took the workpapers and closely studied each page. She shook her head often and then gasped suddenly.

"What is it?" Mary asked.

Aysha wouldn't say. "Come in here; I need to show you."

Mary gathered up the spreadsheets and followed. "Where are we going?"

Aysha led her to Chambers' office. She walked to a burgundy hardback book sitting at eye level on a built-in bookshelf, pulled it out and opened it. Inside the front cover was a master key held in place by a small envelope glued to the backing. She lifted the key for Mary to see. "This opens all the cabinets in the file room we just passed."

"How did you know it was there?"

"I did learn a thing or two from Cal when I was in auditing. He taught me to be aware of my surroundings and trust my instincts about anything that seemed odd, out of sequence, or outside of a person's normal routine or character."

"And the key was odd? I don't understand."

"Not the key, the person that held the key."

"You mean Carol?"

"Yeah, sometimes when I walked into this office to ask Carol a question, she'd have this book in her hand. That wasn't odd by itself, but when I walked in, she'd close the book and hold it tightly, like she was preventing something from falling out. One day I got close enough to the book to read its title. I asked myself if Carol was the type of person who'd be inclined to refer to a book on business law. So one evening after she left for the day, I let myself into her office and took a look."

"But how did you know they fit the file cabinets?"

"I didn't. I had to wait, and watch, and put two and two together. I watched her come out of her office and go into the file room, come out and go back into her office. The only items with locks in the file room that contain anything of any value are the file cabinets. So I took a hunch and was right."

"What's in the cabinets?"

"I'll show you," Aysha answered, leading the way.

"Are you sure this is a good idea?"

"Do you want to find the answers to Cal's questions?"

"Yeah, sure, but are you sure none of your staff will come back?"

"They may, but they're not going to be interested in the file room. They're too busy elsewhere. Trust me. They won't think anything of it. I'll just say this is Mary from accounting. They know of you. You always ask stuff from us whether we have time for you or not. It'll be natural."

Mary frowned. "Am I really that big of a pain?"

"Oh, Mary, I didn't mean it that way, but sometimes, yes, you are."

The lighthearted levity did little to calm Mary. She couldn't put her finger on it, but as she stood in Carol's office, she had a hunch that something wasn't right.

"Come here!" Aysha called, entering the file room. "In these cabinets," she explained, "are contracts of vendors and agencies we use all the time. There's nothing sexy about them, but you're free to look. I don't know what's in the cabinets over here. I haven't looked in them before."

She walked to the latter cabinets and used the key. The locks opened easily. She pulled open the drawer of one cabinet, revealing brown folders of regulatory documents and federal contracts.

"Shouldn't these be stored in our legal department?" Mary asked.

"One would think so, unless our legal department didn't draw them up. Oh, my goodness, Mary, look! This one says *FAA,* and this one is of ... oh, I can't make it out very well, can you?"

Mary strained her eyes. "No, I can't tell. It looks like information of aircraft manufacturers and maintenance contractors. Why wouldn't they be with Alan Cavanaugh?"

"Let's pull them." Aysha began to yank them out of the cabinet.

"What are you doing?" Mary exclaimed. "We can't take these."

Aysha opened one of the folders out of curiosity. "Yes, we can," she said confidently. "I want Cal and Ralph to look at these documents and tell us what they mean. Mary, this is a serious situation here. People are getting killed. I want them to see these files tonight. After they look them over, I'll return them tomorrow morning. Look at this. Isn't this one of the names you were asking me about?"

Mary eyed the document closely. The name *Michael Benning* appeared as payee on a copy of a GrandAire check.

"And look, here's more copies of checks and wire transfers," Aysha said. "We've got to pull these and take them with us."

Mary hesitated, then relented. "Okay, but if we're going to take those, we might as well pull this other file."

Aysha turned her attention to the file Mary pulled from the drawer. The words *Security/Surveillance* appeared on the outside. They found another folder with the same title hiding behind the first one.

"Good Heavens!" Mary said. "These are documents related to the construction of a surveillance outfit, including equipment and monitors. There's even the design of a room somewhere in this building. I didn't know Max had such a room."

"I've seen it before," Aysha replied. "It's on the main level out by the docks. There's nothing secret about it."

Both women reviewed the plans.

"This isn't the room out by the docks, though. These plans are of another room. Look, Aysha." Mary pointed to the top of the blueprints. In bold letters, the words *Fifth Floor GrandAire* were clearly visible. "Oh, God," Mary said. "That's in the storage area down the hall from Cal and me. It's the room Cal has been watching and asking about for the past two months."

Aysha's expression hardened. "I'm calling Ralph."

Mary shivered. "We shouldn't have looked into these files, Aysha. We shouldn't have pried this far. We've gone too far; you know that, don't you?"

Aysha swung around and gave Mary an angry, determined look. "This is no time to melt down. I mean it.

We're damn lucky we found these documents. They're going to get us one step closer to what's happening around here. It may even save our lives."

Mary didn't refute Aysha's claim, but she didn't affirm it, either. Whether Aysha was right or not, she didn't care. Mary still wished she and Aysha hadn't discovered the secret surveillance room plans.

Aysha closed the drawers, locked the cabinets, and looked around the file room before exiting, checking to make sure the room looked exactly as it had when they'd entered. "You stay here," Aysha commanded. "I'm going to return the key to the book. Let me know if the front door opens."

"Hurry," Mary said, "because the next time that door opens, I want it to be my ass getting the hell out of here."

~

Aysha did as Mary asked. She hurried into Chambers' office, pulled the *Introduction to Business Law* book from the shelf and replaced the key in the tiny envelope glued to the front cover. As she closed the book, her hand rubbed across the top of the pages. The pages felt uneven as if there was a small bump in the middle of them. She hadn't noticed the bump before. She closed the book anyway and replaced it on the shelf. She, too, wanted to leave and get back to the atrium as if nothing had happened or had been found.

She turned to scurry out of Chambers' office, but stopped. *Follow your hunch,* she said to herself. Something wasn't right about the book. She returned to the shelf, pulled the textbook, and felt the bump again. There was definitely something in between the pages. Carefully,

254

Aysha flipped the pages until she reached another small envelope half way through the book. It bore the inscription *5th Floor* in pencil in Carol's handwriting.

Aysha opened the envelope and removed another key. *Fifth Floor*, she thought and remembered the blueprints. It must be the key to the storage room closet.

Mary burst through the office doorway. "What's taking you so long? Let's go!"

"Mary, look. It's the storage room closet key. I'm sure of it."

"Put it back!"

"But, Mary."

"Put it back! I'm scared half to death, Aysha. I want out of here. Just put it back where you found it and let's go!"

"No," Aysha said defiantly, closing the book and putting in on the shelf. "This key is a clue, and I'm taking it. We're calling Ralph." She flipped off the light to Chambers' office and exited.

~

Mary panicked. She was so scared she could smell the staleness of her breath. Something still wasn't right. She could sense it. It wasn't right.

The room was wrong.

Mary turned slowly in the darkness and stared into the corner of the office where Chambers' hall tree stood containing a couple of sweaters, an umbrella, and a winter coat. Why? She asked herself, if Chambers had gone out for dinner as Aysha said, why didn't she take her coat? There was no place to eat within the GrandAire Building at this time of evening.

The coat hanging on the tree had only one explanation. Chambers hadn't gone out to eat after all. She was still in the building.

Aysha reached for the nearest phone and punched in Paeng's cell phone number. He answered immediately. "Baby, I don't have time to talk," she said, "but you have to come to the GrandAire Building right away. Mary DeFrantz and I will be in the lobby waiting for you. Do you hear me? Can you come? Can you come right away? ... Great. See you soon." Aysha hung up.

"We gotta go now, Aysha!" Mary insisted, prodding Aysha toward the door. In her haste, she almost dropped the folders she had in her arms.

"Why? What's the matter?"

Mary didn't answer, acutely aware that Carol Chambers could return to the office at any moment. She heard voices outside the entrance to the marketing suite.

Aysha's eyes widened; she'd heard them, too.

A key entered the lock, and the door to the office suite began to open.

"In here!" Aysha whispered. "In the storage room!"

Mary obeyed, following Aysha, being careful not to close the door completely so the sound of the latch wouldn't alarm whoever was coming in. She recognized the voices.

"It's quiet in here," Cavanaugh said. "The party's tomorrow night. Where is everybody?"

"They better be in the atrium," Chambers replied curtly. "There was still a lot of work to do as of this afternoon."

"You mean it's not done? We're counting on this event, Carol."

"I didn't say it's not done, and I'm fully aware of what this event means. Do you take me for an idiot? I haven't risked my life and career these past few months to do a half-assed gala, Alan."

"If I need to be the one to direct how this gets done, I'll do it."

"No, I need you to stay the hell away. I've seen your handiwork at finishing things, and I'm pissed."

There was silence as the two walked past the file room to Chambers' office. Aysha and Mary could hear Chambers taking her coat off the hall tree as she and Cavanaugh started talking again.

"Aysha makes a better event planner than she does an auditor," he said.

Chambers sighed. "Yeah, she was disappointing in that role, wasn't she?"

"Disappointing? No, she was a failure."

"Okay, I didn't count on her being as loyal to Callan as she was."

"I took your word that putting her in auditing would provide us with the information we needed. I don't know who screwed up more, you for suggesting that she transfer to auditing or me for listening to you."

The two left Chambers' office and stood outside the file room door. Mary held her breath as she saw Aysha lean closer to the door to listen.

"I'm not going to worry about that now," Chambers responded. "We've got more important things than Aysha Marks, thanks to you."

"And what the hell does that mean?"

"It means Cliff Pierceman wasn't part of the plan, Alan. Let's face it. Your man screwed up, and we've got authorities in Wisconsin and agents in Chicago asking questions."

"Shut up, and make sure you keep your mouth shut. You don't understand. Our problems aren't going to go away unless those causing our problems go away. You hear me? Pierceman was causing problems, just like Morrow and Marks are causing problems now. You can stand there and gripe about what happened or you can do something to help. I suggest you do something to help."

"Like what?"

"Like take care of Aysha Marks and do it quick. We haven't much time."

"I'm going home," she said. "I'm going to rest tonight so I can get through this party. I'm not doing a damn thing until the gala is over, and I suggest you don't, either. You've screwed up enough already. We wait until Monday."

"We don't have until Monday."

"I said Monday. On Monday you can deal with Morrow as you wish, but not before."

"And Marks?"

Chambers paused before saying with conviction, "I'll deal with Aysha. Let's get one thing straight," she added. "You're the one who screwed things up in the first place."

Suddenly, the storage room door slammed shut in front of the two women, causing them both to jump and expect the worst. The last they heard before Chambers and Cavanaugh left the office suite was Chambers' voice complaining that she has to tell her staff constantly to keep the storage room door closed, but they never comply.

When it felt safe, Aysha and Mary emerged from the room and stared at each other in disbelief and disgust.

"I'm so sorry, Aysha," Mary said.

The light reflecting off Aysha's face revealed an expression of doubt, surprise, and dread. She quivered and seemed to be trying to catch her breath, then she exhaled and rage replaced the previous expression of dread. She spouted an expletive that made Mary blush. "Let's meet Ralph," she said confidently.

"But what about what we just heard?"

"Carol can't do a damn thing to us, not if we get to her first. I want Ralph."

On the lookout for both Cavanaugh and Chambers, the two made it to the lobby and waited anxiously. The lobby was cold and drafty, and the women, covered in a thin layer of sweat from their ordeal, responded by shivering.

"If that room on the fifth floor is really a security room," Mary whispered, "then I don't understand why Max Dennison doesn't know about it, or why he didn't tell us. Cal and I have asked about that room on a number of occasions."

"I don't know. I thought about that myself, but I bet senior management has purposely kept it a secret from him. You know Max. He's a nice guy and does what he's told. He's not going to rock the boat against senior management if he doesn't have to."

Mary agreed and watched as Paeng came through the revolving doors of the GrandAire entrance.

Aysha met him at the Security Information Counter and signed him in as a visitor on the entry log. "This is my boyfriend," Aysha explained to the woman sitting behind the counter. "I need extra help in the atrium. I'm drafting the poor guy."

The woman laughed and wished him good luck.

Aysha pushed the elevator button. Once safely inside the car, she punched the fifth-floor button. Aysha showed him the key she'd found in Carol's book and pointed to the folders Mary held. "We're going into a room we suspect could be the answer to a lot of your questions. I think this key will open the door to a closet in a storage area that we suspect holds some kind of surveillance equipment. I also need you and Cal to look at these folders tonight so I can bring them back tomorrow morning. Think you can do that?"

"What are they?" he asked as Mary handed them to him, then he quickly perused the documents to answer his own question. "Yes, we'll want to see these." He closed the folders as the elevator doors opened.

The three walked to the storage room and scanned the hall. It was late and dark. No one was on the floor working or cleaning. Mary used her key to enter the storage room, calmed by Paeng's presence, but still unnerved at what they'd find.

"That's the door," Mary said, pointing to the opposite end of the room. She took the lead and moved the metal cart that blocked its entrance.

Aysha handed her the key.

Mary hesitated slightly as she placed the key in the lock and turned the door knob. "Bingo!" she whispered and opened the door slowly. She prompted Paeng to enter first.

He uttered an expletive in awe of what was before him.

The "closet" wasn't a closet at all but a small room, eight by eight in diameter, complete with an integrated security management system. The system provided local and remote access to live and recorded video and audio settings from multiple locations, utilizing a standard internet browser to provide an interface to three personal computers installed around the room.

"This is incredible!" Paeng exclaimed.

Mary was speechless.

Aysha just stared. "Do you think we were being watched?" she asked her boyfriend. "We were, weren't we? Everywhere we went, whatever we said. Do you think my office was bugged? Our phone calls?"

"I don't know yet," he replied. "The important thing is that you two found this room. Now we've got to do something about it."

"Like what? You're not planning to do something now, are you?"

"Baby, this is too important to delay."

"Ralph, no. Please! This celebration has to go on first. Probing into this room may open a whole new can of worms that we're not prepared to deal with. There's no telling what they'd do to us if this gala doesn't go on as planned." Aysha took a deep breath and added, "We overheard them this evening, Ralph. We heard Carol and Alan. I'm convinced they'd kill us without missing a heartbeat if they believed we interfered with this promotion tomorrow night. Promise me you won't do anything until after the gala. Once the planes land at Midway, you can do whatever you need to do. But for now, promise me you'll keep the knowledge of this room in strict confidence."

CHAPTER THIRTY-FIVE

Callan and Paeng spent the evening at a small-business-services outlet in Lincoln Park that stayed open to accommodate their request to copy documents. Paeng offered to reward them well. The men reviewed the information and then turned them over to agents in Paeng's office who had an active interest and open file on the case.

Aysha was too busy putting final touches on the gala event to assist, but called periodically to see how they were coming along.

Callan crashed that night on Paeng's couch, a lumpy futon-like piece of furniture that Callan vowed he would never own.

Aysha came through the room the next morning clad in an oversized t-shirt and baggy pajama bottoms that belonged to her boyfriend. She yawned and rubbed her fingers vigorously through her hair to awaken the pores on her scalp.

"Today's the day," Callan remarked, pulling back a cover that had partially covered his face, leaving his denim-clad legs exposed as they dangled uncomfortably off the couch.

Aysha spun toward the voice. "Oh! It's you. I forgot you were here. Hope I didn't wake you last night when I came in."

"No, I was out. Paeng and I were up until two."

"Point taken. Whatever the time, it was definitely on the morning side of the clock, but the atrium is all done, all decorated. There are just a few little touches this afternoon. Coffee?"

Callan indicated that there was a half pot of cold black goo from the night before if that was good enough to get the blood flowing.

She heated two cups in the microwave and started a fresh pot of good stuff for later.

"So you do drink the stuff, don't you?" Callan asked, remembering an earlier conversation when he'd accused her of not being a coffee drinker.

"Yes, especially with this big to-do going on. I don't know where you got the idea that I didn't drink coffee. I guess it was the point you were trying to make that was important and not the fact that your supporting evidence was flawed."

"Oh, I bet you enjoyed every minute of my flawed evidence."

Aysha took the cups out of the microwave and walked into the living room. "A little, but let me ask you something," she said, handing Callan his cup. "What if this whole thing is not what it seems?"

"What do you mean?"

"I mean, what if *our* evidence is flawed?"

Callan took a sip and shook his head as he considered her questions thoughtfully. In his professional opinion, their evidence wasn't flawed. Instead, it was probably just the tip of the iceberg.

"I'm scared, Cal," she replied candidly.

Callan didn't know how to alleviate her fears. He was scared, too. Paeng told him about her and Mary overhearing Chambers' implication of Cavanaugh in Pierceman's murder. Paeng also told him about the possibility of impending harm to both Aysha and Callan.

"Do you want to know what's funny?" she asked.

"I can't imagine. I'm finding very little that's funny with this whole thing."

"I know, but through it all, I still believe in our mission at GrandAire and what we're trying to accomplish in spite of people like Carol and Alan. You know?"

"No, I don't know, but I think Larry feels the same way. I don't know how you two can say that. I'm totally disillusioned with people like Carol and Alan and their deceit. I'm disillusioned with people like Tony Burris who are so busy that they simply rubber stamp papers without knowing the consequences. I'm disillusioned by people like Hamilton Perry who lead by absentia, and I'm fed up with people like Ken Holloway who are so stuck on themselves and the prestige of being who they are, what they've done, and where they live that they're complacent about the suffering that made them rich."

"There are people like that in every organization, Cal."

"But their rubber-stamping, absent, complacent style of leadership isn't killing or kidnapping people who get in the way."

Aysha changed the subject. "Sorry you didn't spend the time with your son like you'd hoped. Have you talked to him?"

"Yeah. Gil's okay. He's a strong one. He's doing better than Terese and me."

Aysha stood and touched Callan's shoulder. "I better get ready to go. I've got a few more things to do to the guest tables in the atrium. After that, I'm coming back here to change for the event. Ralph promised to be there early to help me if I need something at the last minute. What are your plans today?"

Callan didn't answer.

Aysha set her cup down on a coffee table that had been pushed out of the way to give Callan room on the futon. "I shouldn't have asked."

He closed his eyes and rested his head on the back of the futon.

"Be careful," she said as she walked toward her bedroom. "I don't like that look in your eyes."

"My eyes are closed."

"I'm serious. Whatever it is you're planning, be careful."

CHAPTER THIRTY-SIX

Terese dedicated the entire morning and afternoon to preparing for the inaugural flight. Candice arrived around two o'clock to assist her and to take her to the airport.

"I know what you can do to help," Terese said. "You can help me with my hair. I don't like it."

Candice looked at Terese's hair and then at her evening gown. The gown was too elegant and sleek to be out-staged by hair that was doing its own thing. Rather than attending to the hair, though, Candice picked up an old photograth of Terese and Callan that sat on top of the vanity.

"Which necklace should I wear?" Terese asked, giving Candice a choice between a diamond pendant and a sapphire. When Candice didn't answer, Terese looked at her through the mirror. "You might as well tell me."

"Oh, I'm sorry. The, uh, the sapphire."

"I'm not talking about the necklace now. I'm talking about what's on your mind."

"Do you keep this photo here for a reason?"

"It's where it's always been. I just haven't moved it."

"But you look at it, don't you?"

"Every day, Candice. What difference does it make? Look, I've asked you to do something with my hair. I don't have much time."

"I wish you wouldn't go."

"Somehow that isn't what I thought you'd say. It's not like I'm moving away. All I'm doing is going to a party."

"And you're flying with an airline that has a short, questionable history."

"That's Callan talking, not you, and you didn't hear this from a photograph. You've been talking to him. When was that?"

"I know it's over between the two of you, Terese. This isn't about getting you two back together. It's about what he had to say. It makes sense to me. From my account, he's never been wrong about things like this. I think you wallow in your self-pity so much that you can't see the fact that Callan knows what he's talking about, and this time, he's doing it for *you*."

Terese smacked the hair brush against her opposite palm. "For me? Candice, you may think of him trying to forbid me to go on this flight as his way of saving my life, but I remember a night when an intruder entered our home because of him that almost cost me mine. I don't know what to believe, but I can tell you one thing; I'm going to this party in Chicago, and I plan to be wined and dined and pampered to my heart's content because, by damn, I'm alive right now despite Callan Morrow, and I'm going to live, and I'm going to live well."

Candice sat on the edge of the bed. She didn't seem to have the energy to argue any more, and she certainly didn't have the right.

She drove Terese to the airport and watched her take a satchel of essentials from the back seat of her car without saying a word.

"Terese!" Ellen shrilled as she met her on entering the reception of the terminal annex building. "I'm so excited the evening's finally here! Aren't you?"

Terese smiled and tried to present an air of dignity.

Ellen handed her some champagne. "Let me introduce you to the others who will be on the flight with us. They're great fun and good people."

"Who is this, Ellen?" asked a stately gentleman in a shawl-collared tuxedo with a woman, supposedly his wife, close beside him. He extended his right hand.

"Terese, this is Tom and June Elliott," Ellen said. "They're our designated hosts for the evening. Tom is an exclusive client of GrandAire and, as his name suggests, is partner of the law firm Burns & Elliott. And this way, dear, is Urban and Carolyn Snider and their two daughters, Amy and, oh, I'm sorry, sweetheart, I've forgotten your name."

"Chelsea," the younger daughter said.

"And last, but not least, this handsome young man is A.J. Risen. A.J., darling, come closer."

A.J. stepped timidly toward the group with his hands in his pockets and his face blushing at the knowledge that all eyes were upon him.

"A.J. is the son of Marty Risen, one of the supervisors in accounting at GrandAire. One of the Big Ten's best swimmers from Purdue, I might add. His parents are waiting for him at the GrandAire building when we make our grand entrance into the gala."

Terese pointed to a pilot, standing in another part of the room. "And is that our captain?"

"Yes," Ellen beamed. "Captain Aaron Lauder."

"It looks as if I'm in very good company this evening," Terese said, glad she'd decided to accept Ellen's invitation to the flight. She lifted her glass of champagne and toasted those around her. "To the evening—to a very fun evening!"

The Indianapolis delegation of the inaugural entourage relinguished their drinks in the termal annex, crossed the tarmac, and climbed the short flight of stairs to the passenger cabin of their invitation-only flight.

Ellen entered the luxury plane first and stood speechless in the doorway between the galley and the cabin. June Elliott followed and placed her hands on Ellen's shoulders.

"Tell me it's fabulous, Ellen," she prompted. "It's fabulous, isn't it?"

Ellen and June stood in the middle of the galley when Captain Lauder and flight attendant Laurie Banes greeted them. The galley, complete with a high-temperature oven, range, microwave, and refrigerator, enticed the women to want to see more. One by one the guests entered the cabin with nearly the same estatic reaction to their accommodations as Ellen and June had.

Captain Lauder was proud of the plane. The Lexcelle A-715 was touted by GrandAire as the ultimate luxury aircraft for discriminating business passengers. He was all too pleased to promote its branded reputation as each person entered.

The fortunate guests stood in awe of the lavish cabin interior, complete with a wet bar, a grouping of four club seats, two groupings of two club seats, and a four-place berthing divan. The entertainment center included aft and forward fifty-two-inch high-definition screens. For gatherings of a business nature, a conference area included a fax, copier, scanner, and three personal computers. To top it off, a twin-size bed with two lounging chairs for the ill or weary was sectioned off in the rear of the plane.

Laurie Banes took drink orders and personally welcomed each guest, then gave simple instructions on the location of exit doors and safety features, including flotation devices.

"I guess it's good to know in case we drop into the Wabash River," June replied. "Really, there's hardly a need for flotation devices between Indianapolis and Chicago, don't you think?"

Deanna McClintock looked at her and said, "Lake Michigan."

"I'm sorry?" June asked, not catching her comment.

"I said we'll be flying at some point over Lake Michigan."

June Elliott looked down at her seat and tried to gauge where the flotation device was located. "Oh, my goodness, you're right, dear. I completely forgot about Lake Michigan. Quite silly of me. Tom and I often vacation near Beverly Shores at the Indiana Dunes. How could I have forgotten?"

Deanna turned casually to her husband and said, "Perhaps you're drunk."

"Behave," her husband whispered teasingly as June Elliott described at length the vacation home she and Tom rented every other summer at Beverly Shores. No one paid attention. They were too busy admiring the luxury they'd experience during their short flight to Chicago.

The take-off went smoothly and according to plan— on time and without incident. The eleven guests munched on the remaining appetizers from the party and sipped drinks served by Laurie Banes. They all but missed the transition from land to air with the exception of a brief moment to cheer, toast, and talk about the excitement of their inaugural trip and the elaborate party ahead of them at GrandAire headquarters.

CHAPTER THIRTY-SEVEN

Callan entered the elevator off the lobby of the GrandAire building and pushed the fifth-floor button to his office. A gold balloon floated above his head. Revelers followed him into the elevator, laughing and teasing each other loudly. Callan closed his eyes to shut out the celebration. He looked at his watch and noticed the gala had just started, yet guests were already behaving like juveniles. When the door opened on the fifth floor, the balloon escaped through the opening with Callan. He let it float away as he walked to his office.

He sat behind his desk and opened a program on his computer. He also opened the accounts-payable application and pulled up a database of current vendors, then stared at the screen and contemplated what he could do.

With a few clicks of his mouse and the access discreetly provided to him, he was capable of modifying not only demographic information in those files but also of cancelling orders and stopping payment on any invoice to any vendor.

That's what he wanted to do. It's what he came to do. His heart wanted to sabotage the company's accounts-

272

payable system through his unauthorized access to stop the flow of money to those GrandAire paid off to circumvent inspection and maintenance controls. His brain reminded him that such deceit could backfire, escalating violence against him, his co-workers, and his family.

He placed pens and paper clips that were lying on the surface of his desk into his top desk drawer and slammed the drawer so fiercely that it rebounded back at him. Then, leaving his coat behind, Callan left the office and entered the elevator that took him to the atrium. He'd lost track of time. He told himself he had no interest in the gala, but he did want to see the decorated room, for Aysha—to say that he had.

People passed near him with cocktails and food, laughing and enjoying themselves amid big band sounds of music and revelry. In their jovial spirit, they didn't seem to notice him lurking conspicuously under the palms.

Callan moved to a spot where he could see the stage more clearly. He spotted Aysha looking up to the stage from below the platform ready to accept any order or request Carol Chambers darted her way. Chambers stood on stage and captured the party's energy with her million-dollar smile and celebratory spirit. Under his breath, Callan admonished the senior vice president for stealing the thunder that rightfully belonged to Aysha.

"Welcome, ladies and gentlemen; welcome!" announced Hamilton Perry. "Welcome to a night of history in the making, not only for GrandAire Airlines, but for the chartered airline industry and the city of Chicago. Never before has such a prolific and innovative service been offered to the American business community, and never before has such a new service been presented in the manner that you'll see tonight. Standing with me is Ms. Carol Chambers, Senior Vice President of Marketing and Public Relations, whose stunning ideas will dazzle you this evening. Will you please join me in giving Carol a round of applause?"

Chambers accepted the applause from the three hundred or more gathered guests.

"May I direct your attention to the window overlooking Chicago's lakeshore? In sixty to ninety minutes, an entourage of executive chartered aircraft from ten originating cities will converge in front of us over the lake. One by one the entourage will fly over our building in grand style, marking the beginning of GrandAire Airlines' newest service ... GrandAire *Elite!*"

At Perry's conclusion, the band broke into a hearty show tune and guests burst into a round of applause as streams of confetti were blown into the air. In addition, two units of balloons were released, the remaining to be released when the planes passed overhead.

Callan surveyed the span of the atrium as Perry talked. Tony Burris and his wife stood with Zane Dunham. Callan could tell that Tony had too much to drink already. Mr. Dunham, in his usual conservative stance, stood without beverage or food in hand.

Larry and Marlene strolled through the maze of party invitees. They meandered to a small circle of people that contained Celia Hart and Mark Reasoner engaged in a lighthearted conversation.

Mary DeFrantz stood with Velma Hofmeyer and looked about the atrium at the wide variety of guests. She spotted Callan near the palms. She patted Velma's arm, indicated that she would be right back, and walked towards him.

Callan saw her approach, but gave no outward sign that he cared.

"The invitation did say black tie optional," she said, "but I don't think Carol meant for it to be *this* optional."

"At least I showed up," he said, "which is more than I can say for a couple of executives."

"And to whom are you referring?"

"Where are Alan and Ken? I don't see them around."

"I heard they were sharing a private drink in Ken's office, but I wouldn't go in there if I were you. Run home and change, Callan. Come back to the gala. If you leave now, you can make it back in time for the grand entrance of the entourage."

"Why would I want to do that?" he asked. "If I want to see the show, I'll watch it from the edge of Navy Pier so I'll have plenty of room to walk away whenever I want."

Mary looked sadly at Callan. His attitude had turned from strong-willed and confident to hopeless and hateful.

"Tell me," Callan demanded. "Is she on the plane?

Mary responded with the same indignation she received. "I don't know. I heard that she might be, but I don't know for sure."

"Then I have nothing to lose by going into Ken's office and giving them a last rousing piece of my mind." Callan turned and walked down Mahogany Row toward the lawyer's office.

Mary followed and pleaded, "Cal, don't go in there."

~

Kenneth Holloway stood in front of his desk near his wife, Lisa, who sat in one of his high-back chairs in front of the windows. He'd just handed her a flute of exclusive Comtes de Champagne wine. As Kenneth lifted his glass, Lisa stood with Alan and Alan's wife, Julie, to join him.

"It's been rocky getting to this evening," he said, "and there were times we didn't believe we'd get here, but we did, and here's to all the hard work and the rewards to follow."

"Hear! Hear!" Alan cheered and he guzzled the wine as if it were a cold beer.

Kenneth frowned at the waste of such wine on Alan's palate, but three intense knocks on the door interrupted him and startled his guests.

"Who's that?" Alan asked indignantly.

Kenneth opened the door. The unshaven face of Callan Morrow, embroiled in anger, glared through the doorway. Kenneth placed his hand squarely on Callan's chest as Callan tried to enter the room. "What's this about, Callan?"

Callan caught Alan's wary eye and challenged the executive in a visual duel. "It's about him," he replied.

Kenneth stared in confusion.

"Get out of here, Morrow!" ordered a vehement Cavanaugh.

Kenneth glanced at the COO before facing Callan. "I don't know what you're talking about."

"I'm sure you don't, Ken."

Alan outstretched his arms to gather the spouses as they looked on, curious and bewildered. "Ladies, why don't you enjoy yourself in the atrium? Ken and I will be with you shortly after we take care of our employee's needs."

Lisa and Julie took his cue, setting their glasses down and leaving the office quietly.

Once the door was closed, Alan burst into flaming anger. "How dare you come into this office lashing allegations like a washed-up Hardy Boy?"

Callan turned his attention to Kenneth. "It's no Hardy Boy mystery, Ken. This is real. What's flying in the air as we speak is the product of payments to government authorities, the undercover reincarnation of faulty aircraft by a corrupt manufacturer, the falsification of aircraft maintenance records, and the murder of former GrandAire employees."

"Come now, Morrow!" Kenneth retaliated. "This is insane. Let's sit down and talk about this. Alan, sit down with us."

Alan didn't remove his glare from the auditor. He refused to sit, even though Kenneth moved three high-back chairs into a layout that facilitated a conversation.

"Alan, Callan, please. Let's sit and discuss this."

"There is nothing to discuss, Ken," Alan said. "I have no idea what Morrow is talking about, but I suggest he quit his little tirade before I call security or, better yet, the police."

"Oh, that would be the ultimate irony, wouldn't it, Alan? *You* calling the police?"

Kenneth paced in a half circle as he tried to develop a strategy to diffuse the tension. "Let's calm down, gentlemen. Let's enjoy ourselves at the celebration and address this on Monday. I'll make it a priority to review each one of the allegations in confidence."

"No. Monday will be too late," Callan said. "The planes from Des Moines and Cincinnati are in the air already. In a few minutes, the rest will be taking off with the blood of Murray Thompson, Cliff Pierceman, and Carlotta Mendoza as their fuel."

"That does it!" Cavanaugh yelled, heading for the door. "I'm not listening to any more of this."

"Alan, what is he talking about?" Kenneth asked.

"You're going to listen to him?"

"I didn't say that. I just want to know who these people are that Callan mentioned."

~

Alan exited the office without responding and walked two doors down the hall to his own office. He locked the door behind him. Guest chairs prevented a straight shot to the phone. He flipped one of the chairs on its side, making it an obstacle no longer, then reached for his phone and punched in a number. The man he wanted to talk to answered immediately.

"It's me," Cavanaugh said. "Callan Morrow is with Ken Holloway in Holloway's office. When Morrow leaves the building, I want him followed. I don't care when or how, I want you to send the son-of-a-bitch back to his maker. Do you hear?"

~

The man understood the order. He pulled out a .38 caliber Magnum and set it on top of his desk. In the drawer below, he started to pull out a dark wig and a fake mustache with matching sideburns, but slammed the drawer shut without them.

He had a hunch Callan would be none the wiser.

CHAPTER THIRTY-EIGHT

Kenneth Holloway wiped away the beads of nervous perspiration on his forehead. The man whose professional success was due to his quick thinking and proficient way with words didn't appear to know how to respond.

"Ken," Callan pleaded, "this whole gala event could backfire in management's face by the corruption in this company."

"I don't know what you're talking about, Callan."

"You're serious, aren't you? You really don't know what the hell is going on. The names of the people I mentioned mean nothing to you?"

"I'm not, well, I mean, Pierceman does, but I haven't been informed of the others."

"My God, you're as pathetic as they are."

"I don't know what you're accusing us of doing, Callan, but I can assure you that I've done nothing wrong!"

"Oh, I agree you've done nothing, but I don't agree that you've done nothing wrong. Doing nothing is very wrong." Callan pointed to the lawyer's certifications, awards, diplomas and memberships nailed proudly to the walls. "And this is wrong! Your education, your experience, your brilliant mind all used for what?"

"For the individuals and companies I've defended, that's what."

"What about justice? Where's the plaque on your wall for justice? What kept those airlines and manufacturers that you defended accountable for correcting their mistakes? Did they acknowledge that the lives lost meant something to those left behind? Did they not recognize that saving future lives should be their most noble mission of all? You don't know what's going on in this company, Ken, because you don't care to know."

Kenneth looked relieved when Callan walked to the door and placed his hand on the knob. "You won't be seeing me Monday morning for that little chat you recommended," Callan said. "I am not wasting my breath giving you information that'll be used to defend this company." Callan opened the door and, before exiting, added, "You better hope nothing goes wrong this evening with the flight from Indianapolis. You wouldn't want your mother and my wife's lives to be the wake-up call you need to correct your misguided professional motives."

Callan left Kenneth, found an empty box in storage, then made his way to his office. The room seemed more like a tomb. Nothing came alive for him as he sat at his desk. Nothing of importance seemed to matter anymore. His fiery resignation to Kenneth Holloway summarized his opinions thoroughly. Somehow, he'd always anticipated resigning his position at GrandAire to be much more fulfilling and gratifying than it actually was.

He finished packing his personal belongings and refused to take a final look around. It would be the proper and honorable thing for him to say goodbye to Aysha before he left. He pushed the elevator button to the top floor of the atrium.

The atmosphere and energy had intensified since he'd last stood among the palms. The number of guests had increased, electrifying the grandeur of the celebration as they swayed to nostalgic sounds, many by Chicago native Gene Krupa.

Kenneth and Alan mingled amongst the guests, appearing as if nothing had happened minutes before. Alan took a woman with whom his wife conversed and began to dance with her, laughing as he twirled the delighted woman to another gentleman so he could be with his own wife. Callan's visit to Holloway's office had done nothing to change the COO.

Mary hurried toward him just as he picked up his box of personal belongings to make his way toward the elevators. "Cal!" she called, bumping into two gentlemen who'd had enough martinis to dismiss her disturbance. "You're not going, are you? Please wait."

"Mary, it's no use."

She saw his box of belongings. "What's this? Are you quitting? You can't quit, Cal. We're too deep into this. You can't uncover this bedlam and then leave us to fend for ourselves!"

"I'll be around for a while before I head back to Indy, but I can't stay here. I burned whatever bridges I had back in Ken's office. I appreciate everything you've done, Mary. Thanks for everything. We'll keep in touch."

Aysha hurried up to where Callan and Mary stood by the elevators. "Cal, I'm glad we caught you," Aysha panted. "Do you know where Ralph is? He said he'd be here one or two hours ago, but I haven't seen any sign of him. I'm starting to get worried." Her gaze suddenly swept over Callan and his box of belongings. "What's going on here?"

Mary took her arm and explained.

Aysha's eyes widened and her mouth opened but then closed without saying anything. The three stood and looked at each other as the band changed tunes.

"Aysha! They need you up front!" someone called from the crowd. 'Executive management presentation."

Aysha didn't move. She continued to stare at Callan.

"Go," Callan urged. "Have a good time tonight. You deserve it. I'm going to watch the festivities from Navy Pier."

"Navy Pier? Are you crazy?"

"Aysha! Aysha! Front and center!" The woman who was yelling raced toward her, grabbed her arm, and escorted her to the stage. She glanced back once.

The audience burst into applause as Aysha crossed the stage to take her place in line next to Larry, who had joined a stage-frightened Mark Reasoner and the management team of Tony Burris, Alan Cavanaugh, and Carol Chambers. Hamilton Perry and Zane Dunham took the microphones and asked for the crowd's attention.

"I promise this won't take long," Dunham said as Hamilton Perry drew near. "I know we all want to get back to the celebration, but it would be a shame to go through the evening without introducing the management team that made this evening possible."

Callan stood in the back and decided to watch the introductions. He laughed at the sight of Larry and Mark, standing nervously on stage with their hands cupped in front of them like soccer boys anticipating a penalty kick.

~

"What's going on down there?" Larry whispered to Aysha. "What's Cal doing?"

282

"First, may I have a hearty round of applause for GrandAire's Chief Operating Officer, Alan Cavanaugh, and Chief Financial Officer, Tony Burris?"

The audience did just that as the two men walked to the front of the stage and waved.

"You have to talk with him, Larry," Aysha whispered back. "He's quit the company. He's on his way to the pier."

"And, of course, these men couldn't have done it without Alan's two reports, who have worked like a team from the get-go," Dunham announced.

"What happened?" Larry asked, forgetting he was being watched by three hundred boisterous and jubilant party-goers.

"Ladies and gentlemen, I now introduce to you Mr. Mark Reasoner, GrandAire's Vice President of Facilities and Mr. Lawrence Southard, GrandAire's Vice President of Operations!"

Mark took the cue and started toward the center of the stage. Realizing that Larry wasn't following, he turned and called out his name, waving him on. Some of the crowd laughed, believing Larry wasn't paying attention.

Hamilton Perry took the microphone from Zane Dunham and asked Carol Chambers to join him. An employee hopped onto the stage with two dozen yellow roses. After introductory words of praise, Perry announced, "And for putting this grand celebration together and making it the most glamorous and star-studded Groundhog Day the city of Chicago has ever seen, we present these roses to you, Carol, to signify a bright new beginning to one of the most exciting service lines to come from chartered aviation in recent history."

A fervent applause erupted from the crowd as Chambers emitted a sincere look of awe at the presentation. "May I say," she announced over the exuberant crowd. "Excuse me," she paused for the guests' attention. "May I, oh, my, it sounds like you're having a good time!"

The crowd erupted again.

"I'm so glad you're having a good time this evening. This is what this evening is all about," Chambers announced, radiating a presence of class and elegance. "I wish I could stand here in all good conscience and say that I am entirely responsible for the success of this evening, but I can't. In fact, this evening is the product of countless hours by dozens of fine GrandAire employees, most who work on my staff in marketing and public relations." Chambers indicated the roses. "They are beautiful," she said. "Aren't they beautiful, ladies and gentlemen? But the person who deserves our praise most of all is this woman to my right, standing modestly out of the spotlight."

Aysha's stomach suddenly became queasy. She'd worked and sacrificed for this moment. Now that it finally came, she felt as if she was going to throw up.

"Ladies and gentlemen, Ms. Aysha Marks!"

Aysha smiled and walked toward the microphone. She used the height of the stage to look to the back of the atrium to see if Callan was still watching. He was. He gave her two thumbs up and blew her a kiss as the band played an Earl Hines rendition of *Call Me Happy.* As Aysha stepped to the front, someone appeared with more roses, a dozen in each arm.

"I must say," Chambers announced. "May I have your attention? I must say that I couldn't have done this event without Aysha. She accepted a temporary assignment from the company toward the end of last year, but came back to marketing and public relations just in time to pull this entire extravaganza off without a hitch. Because of her efforts, this gala event is a success. And not only that." Chambers smiled broadly and drew Aysha closer to her. "Not only that but also, effective Monday morning, Aysha Marks will be promoted as my new director of marketing. So congratulations, Aysha! Not only is this evening all yours to celebrate, but Monday morning will be all yours as well, the beginning of a new era for GrandAire Airlines!"

Aysha was stunned. *Promotion? Director of Marketing? Monday?* The band continued and more balloons were released from the nets. Aysha tried to smile broadly, but she had every reason to be skeptical. She strained to look toward the back of the atrium to get a sense from Callan what he thought about the sudden turn of events.

He wasn't there.

Aysha surveyed the perimeter of the room as Chambers left her side to be assisted down the half-dozen steps from the stage to the atrium floor.

"Aysha!" a voice called, barely discernable over the revelry. "Aysha!"

She looked toward the sound, saw Paeng's familiar face, and hurried to the right-hand edge of the stage where he stood. She stooped to get as close as she could so she didn't have to yell. "Did you hear? Did you hear about Monday?"

"Yes!" he yelled above the noise. "Congratulations!"

Aysha rolled her eyes. "Why would she do that? I'm so frightened! What does this promotion mean?"

"I don't know," he said, shaking his head and looking skeptical, "but I need to find Callan. Have you seen Cal?"

"No! He was here a minute ago, but left!"

"I can't hear you!" Paeng yelled. "Did you say he left?"

"Let me come down off the stage and meet you, Ralph. Stay right there!" Aysha rose and walked toward the stairs. Mary stood there ready to assist her.

As Aysha walked up, Larry approached Paeng from behind and patted him on the back.

Paeng jerked at the unexpected touch.

"Whoa! Looks like you need a drink or something, buddy," Larry said. "A little jumpy there!"

Paeng turned, looking relieved. "Larry, I need to talk to Cal. Where is he?"

"He went to Navy Pier to watch the planes come in," Ayesha said.

"We have to find him. I know who our man is. I came across something and verified the information with our files at the FBI. I have good reason to believe I know the name of the man who killed your friend Cliff. I believe he's the same guy who killed Murray Thompson in Austin and who took care of the Mendoza girl. His real name is Ted Warmke, a hired killer from the East Coast. He's been a long-time associate of a guy named Michael Benning, who has been involved in government bribes and kickbacks associated with the airline business. We have to find Cal."

"I'm going to the pier now!" Larry screamed. "Aysha, tell Marlene I'll be back!"

"I'll go with you," Paeng said.

"No!" Aysha objected. "I need you here."

Larry nodded in agreement. "You stay here with Aysha and Marlene. I'll catch up with Cal and inform him. We'll meet later at your place." At that, Larry turned towards the elevators.

"Wait!" Paeng screamed above the noise. "Larry! I haven't told you who you're going to be looking for!"

Larry came back. "Yes, you did. Ted somebody, a Ted Warmke."

"No, Ted Warmke is his real name. You know him by his alias. He's been going by another name at GrandAire."

Larry frowned. "Another name?" Fear laced his voice. "You mean I know the killer?"

"Know him? You more than know him, Larry. He works among you!"

CHAPTER THIRTY-NINE

The man summoned by Alan Cavanaugh took the stairs to the level of the parking garage reserved for vice presidents and stood undetected behind a cement support column. He watched Callan move slowly toward his car, carrying the office-supply box containing his personal belongings. It was dark, quiet, and essentially motionless in the garage. The usually prolific Callan Morrow seemed lethargic, dragging his feet across the cement floor to his car parked near another set of stairs on the opposite side of the garage.

This would be a much easier hit than the man anticipated.

He eyed Callan carefully as the cold wind blew through the open garage and whistled around the base of his neck. Deep in concentration, he didn't feel its frigid sting. He removed his right glove and placed his bare hand squarely on the cold steel handle of the revolver in his coat pocket.

The garage's lighting system illuminated automatically to compensate for the darkness. The light allowed the man to see Callan much clearer now. The sullenness in Callan's face and the inattentiveness he gave to his surroundings was to his advantage. He watched closely as Callan reached into his right coat pocket to retrieve his keys, climb behind the wheel of his car, put the car in reverse and back carefully from the space.

The man reached Callan before Callan had time to switch the car into drive and exit. He pounded rapidly three times on the driver's side window to get Callan's attention.

Callan turned toward the raps, looking frightened until he recognised the familiar face of someone he trusted. Callan rolled down the window and laughed. "Wow, Max! You startled me!"

"Did I? I'm very sorry, sir. I didn't mean to. I happened to be on the VIP level when I saw you lugging a box around. Looks like I'm too late to help you with it."

"It's okay. It wasn't heavy, just awkward."

"Say, I heard you resigned," the security guard said. "I wanted a chance to say goodbye. Do you mind pulling your car back into that space so we can talk? I don't want to block someone trying to drive through."

Callan looked into his rear-view mirror. "I think we're fine here, Max. There's no one behind me." He turned to face the guard and added, "I can't believe how fast word travels. When did you hear I was leaving? Who told you?"

"I ran into your buddy, Larry," Max explained.

Callan nodded and gave a weak smile. "Ah, I see."

He didn't sound as if he believed Max, and fear returned to his eyes.

Max pulled the gun out of his pocket and pointed it at Callan's head. "Pull the car in the space, Callan. Now!"

Callan froze and didn't move the car. Instead, he stared down the barrel of the .38 Magnum like a rabbit in headlights.

"No!" a haunting bellow suddenly came from the stairs and echoed throughout the caverns of the garage.

Max turned and fired at the intruder. The bullet ricocheted off the back of the concrete wall inches from Larry Southard's head. Callan used the distraction to his advantage; he sped off, and peeled around the corner of the garage down to the next level.

Forgetting Southard, Max ran to the closest stairway to intercept Callan. He quickly assessed his options as the wheels of Callan's car squealed in his hurry to get away. If he cut through one row of cars as Callan passed, he'd have a clear, clean shot at his target as he drove by. On cue, Callan screeched around the corner. Max crouched between two cars, hoping to go undetected.

Callan must have seen him, however, because he accelerated as he turned the corner, cut the steering wheel sharply, and rammed his car into the row of expensive autos owned by gala attendees. The force of the impact butted one car into the next, catching an unsuspecting Max in a crouched position between two of the vehicles.

~

Larry heard the squealing tires, the horsepower of an accelerating engine, and the crunching of metal against metal. Although he was on the same floor of the garage as the accident, he didn't see it happen. He ran toward the direction of the noise and saw the carnage of twisted metal. Three automobiles with considerable damage were locked side to side against each other.

The car with the most damage belonged to Callan. The engine was pushed almost a quarter of the way into the front of the vehicle. He couldn't see Max Dennison anywhere.

Larry reached the driver's side of Callan's car and saw his friend slumped over the steering wheel, blood pouring profusely from his head. Larry's heart raced as he struggled to open the door to reach him. Unable to do so, he ran to the other side of the car and pried open the passenger side just enough to reach Callan.

"Cal," he called grimly. "Can you hear me? Come on, buddy."

Larry didn't know what death looked like. He'd never seen it in this way and refused to believe it could happen after all they'd been through. The bullet wound to the side of his head didn't lie, though. It had to be a bullet to cause the blood that saturated Cal's shirt from his forehead. Tears began to form as he fought back the pangs of sadness and panic that permeated him. He leaned against the back of the front seat for support and began to shake Callan.

It was no use. Larry lowered his head.

"Stop it," a small voice said from within the car.

"Cal?" Larry put his hand on Callan's forearm.

"Don't touch me."

Larry gulped and sucked a blast of cold air into his lungs. He climbed into the car toward his friend. "Cal, it's me. Don't worry, buddy. Hang in there."

"Don't touch me," Callan warned louder. "Just get me out of here."

Callan was able to tell him the pain was in his left arm and leg, mostly the arm. As they talked, Callan became more alert and anxious to emerge from the wreckage.

"What about your head?"

"My head is fine."

The blood streaming down the side of his face told a different story.

"You sure?"

"I said my head is fine. It just feels like a cut somewhere. Are you going to get me out of here or do I have to grab your neck and pull myself out?"

Larry did as he was told, still in shock over the series of events. His worst fear was that Max was watching, would find that his target wasn't dead, and would return to kill them both.

Callan grimaced with pain as he writhed from under the steering wheel. "It's my arm that hurts the worst. I think it's broken."

They continued to inch their way to the passenger side.

Larry looked to see if anyone was coming to help, but despite the sound of the tires screeching and the crunch of the impacts, no one came.

Eventually Callan stepped onto the pavement and assessed his aches and pains. "I'm fine. Let's go."

"Go?" Larry asked, stunned. "Go where? We're not going anywhere."

"Yes, I am," he said, limping toward the closest stairwell.

Larry jogged over and stepped in front of Callan, placing his hand upon his friend's chest, pressing him to stop. "Cal, somewhere out there Dennison is going to hunt you down when he finds out you're alive. He probably looked into the car as I did and considered you dead."

Callan shook his head. "Look between two of the cars. I nailed him pretty good. If I'm alive, Larry, it means Max is dead."

Larry stared at Callan, having difficulty comprehending what he'd just heard. He did as Callan suggested, however. He walked to the closest two cars near Callan's wreckage. He couldn't see anything between the first two cars, but between the next set, he crouched onto the cold pavement and peered under the wheel bases. Now he was sure. The mangled remains of the once-solid security guard were sandwiched tightly between a black Jeep Cherokee and a cream Lexus coupe. Two legs and blood from an arm that protruded unnaturally toward the cement were visible.

Larry rose to affirm that Max was, indeed, dead. His friend was already gone, however. Larry saw him making his way to the stairwell. At least his limp appeared to improve the more he walked.

Larry raced to catch him. "We're going to a hospital, pal."

"No, I'm going to Navy Pier. I'm going to make sure those damn planes come in. I want to see it for myself."

"That's not a good idea."

Callan gave him an evil eye and resumed his ragged walk toward the stairwell.

"Okay," Larry relented, "but after that, you're getting patched up."

CHAPTER FORTY

Terese sat her drink in the cup holder beside her. She was beginning to feel the wine. Was she talking too much? Was she too loud? Was she laughing at everything, funny or not? Was she slurring? She hoped she wasn't slurring.

"Are you all right?" Carolyn Snider asked.

"Oh, yes. Yes, thank you, Carolyn, how kind." Terese didn't want to admit she was tipsy.

"Aren't you well, darling?" June Elliott asked, eavesdropping on the conversation.

Terese smiled.

"You look fine. Nothing that more wine can't fix."

"No," Terese pleaded. "Please, June."

"Oh, Terese, darling, don't tell me you're finished. Surely you're not. Perhaps you're saving room for the extravaganza?"

"Yes, she is, as we all should," Carolyn responded, seemingly displeased with her impertinence.

"Good evening, ladies and gentlemen," Captain Lauder announced over the intercom system. "I trust this historic flight with GrandAire *Elite* is not only enjoyable, but memorable. If you're interested in knowing our location, we'll be joining the entourage of other planes shortly after crossing the southern shore of Lake Michigan. We'll be landing at Chicago Midway Airport very shortly where the temperature has climbed to a balmy thirty-six degrees under a clear, moonlit sky. Limousine buses will be waiting to take us downtown to the GrandAire building in celebrity style. So, please, sit back and enjoy the rest of the flight. If there is anything that Laurie and I can do to make the trip more enjoyable, please do not hesitate to ask."

"Mrs. Morrow, have you ever stopped to think about flying?" young A.J. Risen asked out of the blue.

Terese studied him closely. "I can't say that I have, A.J. When my boys were young, they were enthralled, but I haven't given it much thought since."

"It's marvelous!" Tom Elliott interrupted. "I don't mean marvelous as in glitter and gold or a Las Vegas show, mind you. I mean it's divine. It's a miracle."

"It is," A.J. agreed. "It's like a miracle, isn't it?"

"When I was a pilot in the Air Force, each mission was an exhilarating exhibition of not only my own talents and the skills of our military forces, but an exhibition of knowledge and the use of knowledge to do great things. It was as close to a divine experience as I have ever had or ever will."

"Oh, that's a shame, Mr. Elliott," Terese exclaimed.

Tom Elliott appeared taken aback.

"I'm sorry it came out like that. You are such a gifted individual. You're a successful attorney and business entrepreneur. I'm sure you've also been an inspiring mentor to many young people over the years. The experiences in your life have been extraordinary. Why, I believe it's a tribute to the kind of man you are, and now I'm blown away to find you were a pilot, too, no less. Forgive me if I find it odd that with all that surrounds you in wealth and knowledge that you've not found spiritual solace in the source of your gifts."

"Source?" he asked inquisitively as he sipped his highball.

"Divine source," Terese responded.

Tom Elliott laughed. "Oh, you mean God? Oh, dear lady, I used the word divine very loosely a minute ago. I rarely give it any thought that God had anything to do with the talents I've developed for myself."

"All things are from God," A.J. tried to explain. "'Every good gift comes down from the Father of light,'" he recited from *James.*

Tom Elliott scoffed. "I see what you're saying because that's what you believe. I respect that, but I ask you; what can your God give to me that I don't already have? What more do I need? All you say is true, Terese, and you are very kind to say all those good things about my life, but they weren't gifts, mind you. I worked for them. I earned every one of them, and I earned them myself. Nobody gave me a damn thing."

"I don't believe life is that finite, sir. It has more dimensions than what you describe."

"From my perspective, Mrs. Morrow, what you call a higher power I call human tenacity."

"No disrespect, sir," A.J. said, "but from my perspective, the name I give human tenacity in that sense is arrogance. It's arrogant for humans to believe that knowledge, wisdom, and talent have nothing to do with something greater."

Terese admired the young man's confidence to contradict such a powerful icon as Tom Elliott.

Tom Elliott, though, burst into laughter and slapped his knee. "What did you say you were studying in school?" he asked, laughing even harder.

"Business, sir."

"Change that to law, young man, and I'll hire you! I'd like another drink. May I get you fine people anything?"

Terese and A.J. refused politely as the lawyer walked toward the galley.

"Maybe I shouldn't have said what I said to him, but that's how I feel," A.J. told Terese. "Being in this plane above the clouds on a moonlit night is truly amazing to me. We watched the birds and learned how to fly. We have the capacity to develop future modes of flying that are beyond our comprehension, but I'm telling you, Mrs. Morrow, I can't help but feel—right now as we sit here—as if I'm a little closer to God because of it."

Terese smiled and reassured him. "I am, too, A.J."

Captain Lauder interrupted the festivities in the cabin to make an announcement: "Ladies and gentlemen, on both sides of the plane, you'll see the lights of the other GrandAire planes that will be accompanying us into Chicago Midway. If you're into the natural wonder and beauty of the flight, below is the majestic Lake Michigan with the moonlight reflecting off bergs of ice along the southern lakeshore of the Indiana Dunes. On behalf of Laurie, your attendant, and me, please enjoy and celebrate safely."

A.J. Risen stared wide-eyed in wonder out the windows of the jet upon the lights of Michigan City and the many towns on the lake's eastern coast.

On the right wing, the engine cylinder gently rocked back and forth as it had since takeoff. Ten minutes into the flight, the nuts from the two-cylinder studs had rocked loose. Now, by the southern shores of Lake Michigan, the gyrations increased. The cylinder rocked on the right engine's crank case, pivoting around the through bolt on the forward side of the base flange.

Even as this happened, A.J. gawked through the window and marveled at the light of the winter moon dancing off the lake's icy waves.

CHAPTER FORTY-ONE

Larry called Callan's attention to the amount of blood Callan had lost from the cut on his forehead and told him he needed to clean the wound before people on the street suspected violence and called authorities.

Callan tried to laugh through the pain, knowing full well there *was* violence, and the authorities really should have been called. The pain was getting worse.

Off the Navy Pier, Larry snuck Cal into a small bathroom of a fast-food restaurant. "I want to see how bad this is," he said as Cal fought to keep the paper towel Larry ran under water from being wiped across his forehead. "Hold still."

Cal looked into the mirror and accepted that his face didn't look quite as frightening once it was cleaned, though other bumps and bruises were beginning to appear.

"C'mon," Larry said. "How's the leg?"

"Fine. It'll be better tomorrow."

Larry laughed as they walked on the pier in the chilling air. "Oh, I don't think so, buddy. I'm here to tell you there ain't nothin' that's gonna feel better on your body tomorrow. I've put this carcass of mine through hell and back over the years. Trust me. By tomorrow morning, you're going to feel like ol' Max back there when your body realizes what the hell you did to it."

Callan ignored Larry and walked to the edge of the pier. The wind whipped off the lake and hit the side of his face. The pain in his arm and leg combined with the cold simply accompanied the rest of his agony associated with the evening. The only solace to be salvaged from the paralyzing events was the satisfaction of seeing Terese's plane fly across the winter sky and land safely at the nearby airport.

"Is that them?" Callan asked, pointing to the sky with a flick of his hand.

Larry pulled his coat up around his neck and squinted. "Should be."

Little white dots of light became larger and clearer with each second. Although the wind and cold made Callan's observation almost unbearable, the pier was the perfect venue for Callan to watch the planes come in, pass impressively by, and move on so he could, too.

"Who organized this?" Callan asked. He'd been so busy and concerned about the planes being in the air that he hadn't stopped to think who choreographed the formation. "Did you do this?"

Larry nodded, downplaying his role. "Yeah, I coordinated. Mark Reasoner executed."

"So tell me about that guy, Larry. What's his story?"

Larry stood at the edge of the water and looked into the blackness, eyes fixed upon the sky. "He doesn't have a story."

"Okay, then, let me ask it a different way. What's *your* story with *him*?"

Larry shook his head as if he didn't have a story, either.

"I was thinking that you rarely talk about him even though you work side by side."

"Why should I?"

"I don't know. I guess I thought it was Mark and not Max who was behind all the killings. I thought he might have been our mystery guy."

Larry inhaled some frigid air and allowed the condensation to roll freely from his face when he exhaled. He turned to his ailing friend and presented a look of disgust and irritation. "Hey, we came to watch the air show, not gab like two school girls. Let's watch the show and then get our frozen butts into the car so I can get you to a hospital."

Callan let the question go for now.

~

The descent of GrandAire Flight Two-Zero-Eight was uneventful except for the sudden gasp of A.J. Risen as he looked out of the right-side window of the plane. In the lights blinking on the wing, A.J. caught glimpses of something he hadn't noticed before. Streams of black liquid, like oil, flowed from the right engine, followed by a thin trail of murky white smoke—enough to cause the young man some concern.

A.J. didn't realize that as he tried to get the attention of Tom Elliott, believing he'd know what he was seeing, the cylinder hold-down nuts became separated from the studs, and the engine's load transferred to the remaining studs and through bolts. The contact gyration, speed and energy produced by the flight in motion began to fracture the remaining studs and bolts.

Tom Elliot didn't respond to A.J.'s gesticulations, and A.J. didn't want to upset anyone by shouting. Besides, the plane continued to glide above the blackness of the lake without incident.

Unbeknown to him, though, the hold-down nuts became loose and the bolts and studs eventually sheered from high-stress fatigue, allowing the cylinder to separate from the engine. In synchronous chronology, the piston fragmented, causing the connecting rod, wrist pin, and piston fragments to separate from the engine as well.

Kaboom!

"My, God!" Tom Elliott yelled. He pulled himself recklessly from his seat and turned to his wife. "Fasten your seat belt!" he exclaimed through the chaos of shrilled screams and exclamations.

June didn't hear the words, but understood the command and obeyed her instinct.

Elliott rushed to A.J. Risen's side. "What the hell is going on, son?"

"There's smoke. It's gotta be oil, Mr. Elliott."

"You keep watch, A.J. I'm going to talk with Captain Lauder."

Elliott staggered to the front of the plane, but a sudden loss of power and Lauder's inability to control the aircraft whipped him back violently. As he passed the guests, each one called out to him wanting to know what was happening.

"I don't know!" he responded. "Please be calm. I'll find out. Please be calm."

Laurie Banes called to the passengers to pay attention and began to brief them on emergency procedures and the use of their personal flotation device.

Tom Elliott entered the cockpit and saw Captain Lauder wrestling with the controls, holding the craft steadily in the air.

"What the hell is happening, Lauder?"

"I don't know, Mr. Elliott. Sit down. Please, sit down."

Elliott awkwardly made his way into the first-officer chair. "Reduce power, man," he said with authority.

"I am," Lauder replied, trying unsuccessfully to secure his shoulder harness while focusing on the instrument panels. "I can't see any damage from my vantage. Have you been able to see anything from the cabin?"

"Young Risen said he saw oil streaming from the right engine and a trail of white smoke. I can see through the lights on the wing there's some damage, perhaps the magnetos hanging down."

Captain Lauder turned his head sharply toward the former Vietnam pilot. "Are you sure?"

"Just observation."

"Okay, this isn't going to be easy."

Although the instrument panel revealed that oil pressure was decreasing rapidly, the fuel selector indicated that each engine was continuing to properly feed fuel from their respective fuel tanks to the engines.

"Better shut it down!" Elliott exclaimed.

"I am. I'm cutting the power, but it's still wind-milling. I can't get the propeller to stop."

"Two-Zero-Eight, what is your altitude and descent rate?" Air Control asked.

"We are, what, twenty, twenty-five, thirty, no, we're at two thousand feet with a descent rate of about two hundred feet per minute," Lauder replied.

The two men in the cockpit looked at each other when nothing came from the radio following their last response.

"Two-Zero-Eight, we've called authorities regarding your emergency situation," the controller finally replied. "There'll be crews on hand at Midway for your descent and landing. We've also called the Coast Guard. They'll be dispatched immediately into the lake."

Lauder watched the instrument panel. Fifteen hundred feet. Thirteen hundred feet. They were descending rapidly, too rapidly for the good engine to maintain proper altitude even at full power. He looked squarely at Elliott. Without a word being spoken, both knew what was in store.

~

Hamilton Perry invited guests and employees to make their way to the atrium window to see the spectacle of the entourage over the water.

Aysha wanted to spend the moment the planes flew over the GrandAire building alone with her boyfriend. She'd had enough pomp and circumstance for one evening. This was her moment now, and she wanted to spend it with the one person who'd supported her through it all. She caught Paeng walking alone, slowly toward the atrium window. She called to him, but he didn't hear her.

The band played louder, and Perry called the guests' attention to the windows.

"Ralph!" she screamed, hoping he'd stop or turn around for her.

He didn't. He continued to walk, almost mesmerized by the sight outside the window.

"Ralph, I've been calling you!" Aysha scolded when she finally reached him. She hesitated. Something wasn't right about his gaze out the window. "What's wrong?" She looked out of the window, too. The dotted points of light appeared like a string of extraterrestrial starships, forming to destroy the planet, a scene from a science fiction movie. She was awestruck by the sight.

Paeng surprised her; coming out of his trance, he looked at her and asked, "It's not supposed to be like this, is it?"

"Like what? I don't see what you mean. The planes are just coming together."

A woman screamed, "My God! What's going on?"

Aysha looked again. Suddenly she saw it, too. One of the planes was lowering closer and closer to the horizon.

"It's going to hit the water!" another cried.

A panic among the guests created a rush to the window while others stood in horror, face in hands, and waited.

Aysha stared through the glass. Her eyes fixated on one set of lights sinking lower and lower toward the water's surface.

Paeng called for her to step back, not to look. "You've worked too hard for it to end like this ... Aysha!" he called again, this time louder, as people screamed and began to move about, unsure of what they should do or where they should go.

Aysha moved forward rather than stepping back. She couldn't help but watch the horror unfold. All she'd worked for was contingent on the plane that was separating from the entourage. She pressed her hands against the glass to no avail, hoping to somehow push the aircraft back into the sky in line with the others.

~

Callan noticed the unaligned stream of lights caused by the gradual loss of altitude as one of the planes glided closer and closer to the watery darkness.

"What's going on?" he asked.

"I don't know," Larry replied.

"It looks like one is going down. Isn't that what it looks like to you?"

"I can't believe it, and I don't know why, but that's exactly what it looks like."

Callan stepped closer to the edge. "Which one is it, Larry?"

"I don't know."

Callan turned and limped to where his friend continued to focus on the plane's demise. "Don't give me that! You just said you organized the damn formation. It's the fourth plane. What plane is it? What flight is fourth in line?"

Larry stood frozen, fear glistening his eyes.

"Is it Indy?" Callan reached with his good arm and grabbed Larry's coat collar. "Tell me! Is it Indy?" In shock and grief, Callan yelled for Larry to respond, pounding on his chest through his coat. The color drained from his expression with each punch. Tears welled in his eyes.

Larry grabbed his friend by wrapping an arm around his back.

Callan slumped slowly to the ground. Tears streamed down his face, hitting the cold pavement of the pier like tiny hailstones.

CHAPTER FORTY-TWO

Captain Lauder turned the plane ninety degrees so it would land parallel to the icy waves that slapped against the frozen shore. He retracted the wing flaps and watched the blackness rise quickly to confront him. The craft landed flat as he'd hoped, but hard. The plane bounced and slapped hard against the waves a second time. He lunged violently forward against the dash, restrained only by his lap belt.

Tom wasted no time getting out of his five-point harness. One look at the pilot indicated the man was past help, but after a quick check to make sure, he staggered back to the body of the plane. He noticed Laurie Banes leaving her seat, where she must have assumed crash-landing position, to resume instructing and assisting guests who'd not finished donning their flotation vests.

The plane was equipped with enough personal flotation vests and devices for everyone, the kind in which each person was required to put their head through a hole and fasten the retention strap around their waist. When in the water, the user either pulled a ring that discharged carbon dioxide into the vest's chambers or blew their own air into two tubes, one tube for each chamber.

Some of the guests struggled to dislodge their vest from the fabric pouch under the seat. Others, in the confusion and because of lack of time to prepare, fiddled with the retention strap and left it dangling to their side rather than fastening it securely around their waist.

Terese Morrow was one—unable to pull her vest free. Tom saw her panic, grabbed a vest from another seat, and handed it to her. He then balanced his time between Terese and his wife, battling the alcohol-induced apprehension of his wife with professional indifference, separating the danger of the moment from the emotional attachment of the one he loved.

He helped Terese, who hadn't quite secured her vest to his satisfaction. "We're doing fine," he told Terese and June equally. "We're going to be okay."

"Please, everyone, remain calm," Laurie Banes requested repeatedly. "Remaining calm will keep us alive. We're all safe. Do not inflate your vest now. Inflate the life vests once you're in the water. Young man, I need you to put on a vest."

A.J. was assisting the Snider twins into their vests, securing their retention straps tightly.

"We're going to get into the water," Tom told the young women. "It's going to be cold, a shocking cold. Stay close together and try not to tread or swim around very much. Understand? Movement won't keep you warm in this cold water. Conserving heat by staying close together is the best thing we can do. Don't kick hard. Your vests will keep you afloat. How are you doing, Mrs. Holloway?"

Ellen shook nervously, tension clamping the muscles in her arms and legs into hardened masses.

"Ellen!" Terese screamed when she didn't respond. "Ellen!"

Ellen turned her head slowly toward the voice.

"We'll jump into the water together. Okay? I'll stay with you," Terese promised.

She shook her head. "I'm not going in. I can't."

A.J., still not in his life vest, struggled with the rocking and teetering of the craft in the choppy waters to rush to her side. "Mrs. Holloway, listen to me. You can't stay in here. We have to get into the water. It's our only hope."

Ellen's mouth opened and her lips moved, but no words were emitted.

"I don't think she can swim," Urban Snider said, watching the scenario unfold. "I think she's trying to say she can't swim."

"Young man! A.J.! You must put on a life vest now!" ordered Ms. Banes.

Tom rushed clumsily to A.J.'s aid.

"Ellen, please," Tom pleaded. "You don't have to swim. That's the beauty of this vest. Your vest will do the work for you, but you have to put it on because the plane is not going to float. The captain has called for help. Help is on the way, but they can only find us if we're in the water."

While Tom helped A.J. with his vest, Laurie opened the emergency door near the cockpit and then ducked into the cockpit. She emerged a moment later with a pasty expression and yelled for someone to open the other emergency exit.

"I'm on it," Tom yelled and rushed to do as she asked, urging the others close by to follow. "We'll go out this door and stay together."

Chilling water entered the plane and swirled rapidly around their ankles. "Stay together!" Laurie yelled. "Mr. Snider, you first, then help your family into the water. Stay together. Huddle close. Don't swim about."

Urban Snider did as he was instructed. Tom heard him gasp as the cold took his breath away and his vest inflated without incident. As his daughters slipped into the blackness, the sounds of their vests inflating merged with the fluttering propellers of rescue helicopters from the Coast Guard Station.

Rescue personnel illuminated the area and threw additional personal flotation devices from a helicopter into the water near the family in the event that any on board the plane did not inflate.

Mrs. Snider gasped as she entered the water. Her evening gown floated around her like a large jellyfish. Fear and the intense shock of the frigid water took her breath away, and she began to hyperventilate almost immediately.

"Mom!" Chelsea called. "Dad, help her!"

But buffeted by the waves created by the chopper, Urban Snider had strayed away from the sinking plane. His wife continued to gasp.

From inside the plane, Tom saw that Mrs. Snider hadn't inflated her device and was taking in water.

"Mrs. Snider, pull the ring!" Laurie called. "Pull the ring! Girls, help her!"

The panicked young women thrashed in the water toward their mother, screaming for her to inflate her vest, but Carolyn Snider was unable to do it on her own.

Her husband painstakingly tried to maneuver close enough to do what his wife was unable. He made progress, but Carolyn sucked more water into her mouth, and each time she did, she gasped. She flung back her head in a desperate attempt to create a natural levee with her chin to prevent water from entering, but it didn't succeed. She fledged and splashed as her larynx began to spasm, gurgling lake water from between her blue lips.

Tom knew that the woman was suffocating as a result of the spasms, even though no water was entering her lungs. They weren't taking in oxygen, either. Tom considered abandoning his charges to help, but Laurie slipped into the water, inflated her own vest, and reached for the helpless mother in time to pull the ring. The vest inflated. Laurie grabbed for Urban, who was now safely near his wife and urged him to stay with her, close to her, and above all else, to try to keep her head above the water. She then extended her arm as far as possible and seized the daughters, who by now had reached a mild panic. Once in hand, she drew them near to their parents.

June was next. She stood at the edge of the door, contemplating the entry, water now up to her knees. Laurie encouraged her to enter. After a secondary vote of confidence from Jack and Deanna McClintock, June made the plunge.

Laurie pulled the ring for her. One side of June's vest inflated, but the other did not. Tom grit his teeth, but trusted that Laurie had the situation in hand. Given the closeness of the rescue team above, his wife should be all right, but he was still concerned for her safety. The amount June had had to drink exacerbated the situation. The alcohol would make her a prime target for additional loss of body heat. He was glad he'd not overindulged.

One of the vests dropped by the Coast Guard from above floated nearby. Amy Snider moved it close to where June could hold onto it. Two rescue divers fitted for the cold water navigated a life raft towards them.

Jack and Deanna McClintock gave each other a kiss before Deanna entered the water.

Jack yelled over the noise of the helicopter. "Ms. Banes! I haven't seen Captain Lauder. He's still in the cockpit. Does he need help?"

Laurie shook her head solemnly.

Jack nodded in understanding and entered the water, reaching for his wife.

Tom turned his attention back to those on the other side of the plane. A.J. had taken charge and was already in the water to help the women out of the sinking tomb. Now in a fully inflated flotation vest, even he, with his youth and experience in the water, gasped from the freezing water.

"Mrs. Morrow, you next, okay?" he said. "Then, Mr. Elliott, help Mrs. Holloway into the water, then you slip in. Okay? We're going to be fine if we keep this orderly and we stay together."

~

Terese hesitated before making the plunge. She looked out across the lake. The moon danced with a macabre array of contrasting lights, reflecting from the water. She saw A.J., his eyes wide with the anticipation of her entry— youthful encouragement, naïve of mortality.

"C'mon, Mrs. Morrow, it's okay," he called, outstretching his arms.

She made sure her thumb was securely positioned within the ring, ready to pull the moment she hit the water. She didn't know why she closed her eyes, but she did and made the plunge. The gut-wrenching pain of the icy water against her skin took her breath away and her thumb slipped through the ring.

The ring!

313

Not only that, but her entire vest wrestled itself free from around her head as she dipped below the surface of the water. The importance of the retention strap around her waist, the strap she didn't manage to tighten, became clear too late. As her head bobbled above the surface, she slapped against the waves hoping to feel A.J.'s forearm or the vest that was slipping from her grasp.

She swallowed hard.

One gulp.

Two.

Her lips froze as she gagged, her left hand tackling the vest, but unable to take hold securely. She heard someone yell, but couldn't tell where they were or what they were saying.

She went under again. Suddenly, a tight grip under her arm lifted her far enough above the water line for her to see flashes of the moon against the side of the plane.

Ellen crouched in the exit then suddenly disappeared into the water.

"Don't thrash!" a male voice cried.

Terese heard the voice, but didn't know if the command was for her. She obeyed, but nothing was clear to her anymore—not sounds, not sights, not even the numbing sting from the icy water. It was all blurry and confusing. She tried to look around to find Ellen, but couldn't. Where did she go? Oh, God. The cold penetrated deep into her body along the nerves of her spine and into her brain. Who has me, she wondered? Who is lifting me? She didn't know, but she was sure she was still afloat.

Suddenly, she felt the presence of others. Her lips were too blue and too large and frozen to speak. She couldn't ask if they were all okay or if their attempts to survive were going to be futile. All around her was darkness. Even the muffled sounds of the men talking between themselves seemed distant and dark.

Terese felt someone hit her on top of her head, a dull thud that created no pain. Again, it happened—then again. The water around her churned and she realized it was a hand swinging wildly from someone nearby. Terese blinked water from her eyes and peered at the person. It must be Ellen! She was sinking and gasping. Her vest didn't seem to have inflated at all.

"Hold her!" she heard someone say.

Ellen choked and flung her arms in a drastic attempt to find something, anything to keep herself afloat.

The plane sank a little lower, the water level nearly to the top of the cabin windows.

"Here!" the same voice called. "Here!"

A vest passed in front of Terese to Ellen, but her friend didn't take hold.

"Grab it! Here it is!"

"She can't," the person holding Terese said. She realised it was Tom Elliot.

Ellen flung again, this time striking across Terese's face with such force that even though her skin was paralyzed by numbness, Terese knew she'd been struck hard. She opened her mouth and water took immediate advantage of the gap.

Tom lost his grip on her, but regained his stronghold quickly.

Terese looked in his direction. His face was blurry, hidden behind icicles forming on her eyelids. She could see shadows, two watery shadows in front of her as the waves splashed around her. She couldn't make out what they were yelling, but they quieted when the waves subsided suddenly. She strained to look and hear. When she moved, the man holding her lost his grip once again. Cognizant enough to reach, she did so and felt his hand upon her arm pull her upward.

She turned her head in time to see one of the shadowy figures close to her, but only for a moment. Without warning, it drifted away. It left slowly, outstretched as if going somewhere, leaving the flickering moonlight as the only reminder that it had even been there at all.

"Don't!" Tom yelled, his voice rasping as the second shadow dove to follow. "Don't, A.J."

Cold shrouded Terese from above.

Tom's grip failed.

She heard a voice, this time very clear, very pronounced. She couldn't discern where it was or where it came from, she just knew it was there, and she wasn't afraid.

She felt Tom reach one last time.

CHAPTER FORTY-THREE

The headlines of the *Illinois Chronicle* remained face up on a small table in the third-floor lobby of the Lakeshore-Cushing Professional Medical Center.

Tragic Celebration, Lives Lost in Airline Promotion

Callan leaned forward. He turned the paper over with his good hand so its front page wouldn't stare him in the face. He leaned back and closed his eyes, content to let the world write its headlines without him. He sighed—apathetic about the physician who'd set his arm calling him back to the examination room to look at it again. He wouldn't have come if Larry and Marlene hadn't prodded him to do so.

Callan opened his eyes long enough for Aysha to hand him a fresh cup of coffee that'd she made from supplies in the corner of the room.

He accepted it gratefully, watching the steam swirl above the cup as if it had taken a spirit of its own. "Thanks. You don't have to go through all this trouble for me."

"Oh, I think I do," she replied. "If I remember correctly, you're not that good with coffee makers. That's even when you have two good arms."

A grin slid across his face. He held the coffee securely and leaned back, closing his eyes once again. His head began to pound. He didn't know why it pounded, but a number of reasons came to mind: the cut on his forehead, caffeine deprivation, anxiety, guilt, abounding grief.

He heard Aysha say, "Coffee."

He opened his eyes. "What?"

Aysha smiled. "I said coffee. I can't think about you and coffee in the same breath without looking back on that day when you said I didn't drink coffee."

"Oh, don't tell me you're bringing that up again."

"I can't help it. It's when you told me about my potential as an investigator."

Callan returned to his former posture. "It was true. You were a big part of uncovering evidence for the authorities in this case. If you hadn't probed when you didn't have to, the arrests may not have been made, and we who survived may not have done so."

"I've never said thank you."

"For what? I didn't do anything."

"Yes, you did. You gave me awareness. You gave us all awareness."

Callan grinned as he rested against the hard cushion of the chair, allowing his legs to stretch outward in front of him. He drew in a large breath of fresh air and exhaled as he thought about what he'd lost. "Awareness sucks."

"No," Aysha countered. "Don't say that."

"Yes, it does. With awareness comes a realization that we have to do something if something needs to be done. I believed that at one time, Aysha, but I've changed my mind. I don't want to be aware of anything anymore. I can't. I'm tired. Awareness cost me everything—my wife, my family, my job, my confidence—everything."

Aysha hesitated, then tapped him on the leg and changed the subject. "Marlene took your sons across the skywalk to the hospital cafeteria. Are you getting hungry?"

"Hospital cafeteria, did you say?"

"Yeah. You hungry?"

"That would be a *big* no."

"The food's not that bad here," she said encouragingly.

This time, Callan couldn't help but laugh. "Aysha, awareness isn't the only thing that sucks around here. Where is Mrs. Argos with her tiropita and baklava?"

"Actually, she stopped by this morning."

"I missed her?"

"Apparently."

"Mrs. Powers?"

"Came along for the ride. You're late on your rent, by the way."

The comment brought a genuine laugh from him. "Evict my ass," he teased. The jostling from his laughter made his arm hurt even worse. He heard the lobby door open.

Paeng entered and walked casually across the room. Callan sat up to greet him.

"You doing okay?" Paeng asked, his gaze assessing.

"He's pathetic," Aysha answered as she rose so her boyfriend could sit next to Callan. "Wallowing in self-pity."

Callan agreed. He'd earned his self-pity.

Aysha bent down and gave her former supervisor a kiss on the part of his head that didn't hurt. Before she left for the cafeteria, she stood near the doorway and asked, "Are you going upstairs after you see the doctor?"

Callan nodded reluctantly. He then turned to Paeng and said, "Give me some good news, buddy."

Paeng pulled out a small, spiral flip pad that contained his notes. "Alan Cavanaugh and Carol Chambers were arraigned today with charges all the way from first degree murder to bribery, extortion, you name it. They were remanded until trial. Tony Burris hasn't been charged with anything; not enough evidence to suspect he knew or participated in the crimes they committed."

"You're kidding. Tony had to suspect," Callan said. "How can a guy in his position not suspect something of this magnitude?"

"Prove it," he challenged. "How could Hamilton Perry not know as well? Or Ken Holloway for that matter?"

Callan believed he knew the answers to those questions. Hamilton Perry and Kenneth Holloway chose not to know.

"We're still working on this Michael Benning guy in D.C. He works for the FAA. He accepted bribes to cover up improper maintenance, inadequate testing, and the lack of authority to approve a flight plan over downtown Chicago, to name a few. He's been making a good living doing this sort of thing with several other small airlines, too. He'll probably be arrested tomorrow or at least by the end of the week."

"Is he the person who received all that money Carol expensed and requisitioned?"

"He and others. There were others, Cal, but I'm not involved with that investigation or privy to the information. It's still ongoing."

"Anything else?"

"Three other GrandAire employees were arrested. They were from operations on the maintenance side. Mechanics."

"The name of Mark Reasoner one of them?"

Paeng flipped a couple of pages in his spiral note pad and read his notes. He shook his head. "He's not one of the names listed."

"I'm surprised."

"Something I should check into?"

Callan thought for a moment before shaking his head. "No, probably not. If his name hasn't come up by now, I doubt there's anything there."

"If it makes you feel any better, this Murray Thompson guy was already on top of what was going on at GrandAire. He had investigators from our office involved. It's why the arrests came together so quickly after the accident. It's also why the hits on both Thompson and Pierceman were accelerated by Cavanaugh. Cavanaugh found out that both of the men were gathering evidence independently and could be key witnesses."

Callan nodded, indicating that he suspected as much.

"I don't think you did," Paeng said. "You were very close to being killed yourself. Too close. Do you realize that?"

"The parking garage incident was a quick lesson in reality. I'm still in shock over Max Dennison. I trusted that guy. I believed he was our ally."

"Not Dennison, Cal, Warmke. His name was Tom Warmke. Cavanaugh was passing the guy big bucks to do a lot of dirty work, including stalking, surveillance, and murder."

"Can he be traced to Thompson and Pierceman?"

Paeng nodded.

"What about the Mendoza girl?"

The nodding stopped.

"We're coming up short there. Nothing but dead ends, but we do believe there was a connection between her and Warmke. Right now, we believe it was as simple as him bugging that table at Centro Margarita and Mendoza being paid to make sure we were escorted to that table. That's why the disturbance at the restaurant that one night was so significant. Aysha wanted to change tables. Carlotta knew she'd be in trouble if we didn't sit by the window. She'd already been paid to ensure that. A commotion developed, and Warmke needed to shut Mendoza up before she talked to authorities. That's what we think so far. We haven't been able to substantiate it fully."

"How's Cecilia, her sister?"

"She's fine."

"That's it? She's fine?"

"That's all I can say. Who knows but Cecilia herself?"

Paeng stood to leave. He shook Callan's hand and told him he was glad he was doing better.

"Will you be up on the fifth floor when I'm finished here?" Callan asked.

The young Filipino shook his head thoughtfully. "No. This is your time with your family. You have our blessings and good wishes, though."

CHAPTER FORTY-FOUR

Callan thanked Paeng and trudged to the fifth floor, but not before an anti-inflammatory shot in the hip and a stiff lecture by the orthopaedic specialist who set his arm. He waddled to where Marlene leaned against the opposite wall of a room shrouded with tension, but hope.

Marlene stood upright and gave him a welcomed hug when he approached.

"Is she awake?"

"Not yet, but don't worry. The doc says it's not going to be long."

He sighed heavily. "Larry in there?"

Marlene shook her head. "Aaron Lauder's wife was downstairs. He went to talk with her. She was in the professional center seeing a doctor for some medication. She's taking her husband's death very badly."

"I bet Larry is, too."

"Larry hired him, you know. Larry is a perfectionist as a pilot, and when things aren't right, he takes it hard. If only—"

"Don't. I know what you're going to say. If only he had his complete harness fastened and not just his lap belt, he wouldn't have hit his head like he did. It doesn't help to think that way. I have to believe that he didn't have time or was too busy trying to save the plane and the passengers to worry about himself."

"I don't care. It doesn't make it any easier."

"How's Tom Elliott?"

"He's better. They say he had a mild heart attack once he was pulled into the Coast Guard rescue boat from the raft. Fortunately, medical personnel were quick to respond. It could have been bad, also."

"I know, and I owe him," Callan said. "I owe him everything for reaching down one more time to get her."

"I'm not a spiritual person, Cal, but I have to tell you that I've been doing a lot of thinking upon hearing that story."

"Yeah, me, too," he answered reflectively. "How's his wife?"

"June was released. She came through it okay. She's still in shock, though, Larry said. It's all been too surreal for her. Carolyn Snider is still in bad shape, though. She's doing worse than Terese. She's going to make it, but they're concerned about the oxygen deprivation she suffered in the water and whether or not it'll have any long-term effects in her speech. I guess she was experiencing what they call a dry drowning. I'm not sure what that is, but it has something to do with the larynx. Her husband was released yesterday afternoon. Their daughters made it fine, of course. They were young and strong."

"There was one other couple, wasn't there?"

"Yes. They came out okay, too. The McClintocks spent the least amount of time in the water. Of course, they had some hypothermia, but it was managed by the Coast Guard rescue team that arrived on the scene."

"And the flight attendant?"

"Larry said she's doing well. She didn't require hospitalization for very long. She performed exactly as she was trained, and Larry credited her for the minimal loss of life. It's amazing there were only three lives lost—the pilot, that young man and, of course—"

Callan lifted his hand to stop her before she mentioned the name. He found it hard to think about Ellen and even more difficult to recall the final words he and Kenneth had spoken to each other. Callan didn't mean for the accident to come true. He'd just been trying to make a point.

"Go in and be with Terese," Marlene insisted. "Your sons are in there, as are her parents."

Callan blew her a kiss as he walked to the doorway. Gil was the first to spot him as he walked through. He grabbed him around the waist and squeezed him tightly. Brandon, standing near the window ledge, walked toward his father and gave him a quick, genuine hug, but said nothing.

Terese's mother sat in a chair between the bed and the window close to her daughter. Her father stood directly behind her mother.

Callan acknowledged them and reached for Artie Beckman's hand. Callan noticed the once firm handshake of the solid Crystal Valley farmer was weaker, less confident.

Marie Beckman's hug was the same as he remembered, warm, sincere, and gentle with the familiar smell of Jergen's lotion.

Callan turned to Terese after the greetings. He was getting used to the pale murkiness of her skin and the endotracheal tube inserted into her throat, allowing small amounts of spittle to escape past her lips.

He walked around the bed and took a seat next to his wife, adjusting the covers mindlessly and straightening the sleeve of her gown as if it made her more comfortable or, somehow, what she would've done herself if she was awake.

The footsteps of someone entering interrupted the silence in the room.

"Good morning," a voice said lightheartedly. "How are we doing here? Let me take a look."

The voice belonged to Dr. Emile Andres, a pulmonary specialist. Callan stood and shook his hand, then allowed Dr. Andres to move around him so he could check Terese's pupils and listen to her heartbeat. He smiled kindly to Mr. and Mrs. Beckman, acknowledging their presence, before turning to Callan. "She should be waking soon," he reassured him. "We're going to be removing the intubation equipment. She's keeping a sufficient oxygen level with the high-flow oxygen mask. That's a positive sign. We'll continue the IV's, however. I'd like the nurse to come in and draw some more blood for us to check her electrolytes, platelets, arterial gas, BUN, PT and PTT levels."

Seeing the non-reaction on the family's faces, Dr. Andres turned specifically to the boys and Terese's parents. "She's doing well. She's strong and coming out of this very well." The specialist turned back toward Callan. "As I mentioned earlier, we were more concerned about the secondary effects of hypothermia than the pulmonary edema or water in her lungs from the submersion. Once on the boat, the Coast Guard did exactly what was needed to keep her alive and prevent further effects from the cold and re-warming shock. Too often, people will attempt to re-warm a hypothermia victim too rapidly, causing what we call a re-warming shock, but in Terese's case, rescuers used a medical device that slowly delivered warm, moist oxygen into her lungs. The treatment prevented further respiratory heat loss and stabilized her heart, lung, and brain temperatures, temperatures of the most critical organs for the body. It was done in such a way as to prevent any fatal heart arrhythmia as well."

"Is that what happened to that man?" Mrs. Beckman asked her husband as if he would know the answer.

Artie Beckman directed Marie's question to Callan. "She's referring to Mr. Elliott, the man who saved Terese's life. He suffered a heart attack or something."

Callan looked to Dr. Andres for input on Tom Elliott's condition.

"Without violating Mr. Elliott's confidentiality, I can't go into details, but I can say that as the blood warms and returns from the cold extremities of the body such as arms and legs, it can carry back to the heart certain metabolic wastes that can cause an arrhythmia. As a profession, we're becoming more knowledgeable about hypothermia and how to treat it to save lives. Mr. Elliott and your daughter were rescued by the best, I can assure you that."

The family knew exactly how fortunate they were to have Terese with them—for many reasons.

Callan walked Dr. Andres to the door and saw his friend, Larry, standing patiently in the hall, talking to Marlene. Larry looked drawn, older, and paler than Callan had ever seen him. Callan approached Larry and shook his hand. "How are you doing?"

Larry didn't answer the question. He responded by asking the same. "You?"

Callan didn't answer, either.

"I just came from seeing Aaron Lauder's wife."

"That's what I heard."

"How do you explain what happened to a spouse when you don't understand it yourself?"

"You can't, and it is better you don't. Trust me."

Larry shook his head in disbelief. "I also wanted to make sure she didn't read the paper," he said solemnly. "That wouldn't give her any comfort."

Callan recommended the two of them walk to the waiting area at the end of the hall.

"Being in the air all these years," Larry began, "I know that any incidents that happen make your records, skills, and qualifications open to scrutiny, but, my God, Cal, the media has been scouring Aaron's records and rummaging through years of flight plans and incident reports to find anything they can use against the guy."

"What have they said?"

Larry found a newspaper crumpled slightly in a nearby chair. He handed it to Callan and pointed to a paragraph:

Although it will be months before the probable cause of the accident is identified conclusively, a spokeswoman from the National Transportation Safety Board says that it appears the fatal crash into Lake Michigan was due to the inflight failure of the right engine and the pilot's inability to adequately manage the plane's performance after the failure.

"But you know differently?"

Larry flung the paper down onto the chair. "Pilot failure, my ass," he blurted.

Callan prompted him to explain.

328

"From what I've learned so far, differential compression checks are done to identify leaks in the engine cylinders. The leaks are usually symptomatic of excessive wear and tear inside the cylinders or other problems like a crack in the cylinder or valves. The mechanics are supposed to record the checks into a log by engine. This was done, but Reasoner says he looked at the logs following the crash and thought that a couple of the readings looked questionable to him. The checks were done up here in Chicago before the plane went to Indy to pick up the Gala attendees."

"What did Reasoner do about it?"

"He asked his mechanic how he performed the check. He asked him if he was sure he got the piston reading at top dead center of its compression stroke when he performed the check for each cylinder. The mechanic said he was sure the check was performed correctly for those cylinders he did himself."

"Who else would do them?"

"He said he let his assistant mechanic finish what he didn't do. Mark told the mechanic that if he'd checked the log like he was supposed to, he would've seen that the compression checks yielded readings so low that he would've had no choice but to ground the plane before it left Chicago, let alone Indianapolis."

"Were the checks performed again in Indy?"

"No, not at all. Reasoner said someone in senior management didn't think it was necessary for the normal routine to be conducted down there. He said it was a time and cost-saving measure to get the show on the road."

"Who in senior management?"

Larry shrugged his shoulders. "I presume the only person with authority and expertise to make such a decision."

"Alan Cavanaugh."

"Authorities are questioning why the plane didn't have a secure door leading into the cockpit. They don't like the fact that Tom Elliott got into the cockpit during an emergency."

"Wasn't there a co-pilot?"

Larry lowered his head.

"What's the matter?" Callan asked. "Was there supposed to be a co-pilot?"

"I swear I scheduled one, but Cavanaugh dismissed some of them to save money. He told Reasoner that if any of the captains had experience or training for single pilot operation to let them fly as such. Reasoner followed his orders."

"Why did Reasoner give a shit? What about you? The pilots are your responsibility. Didn't Cavanaugh talk to you first?"

"No, he didn't bother. He knew I would refuse."

"Of course he knew. That's why he went to Reasoner."

"From there it gets worse," Larry said. "The maintenance company we have a contract with removed and replaced the engine cylinder in this plane several times in the last couple of years. Before applying torque to the cylinder studs, they'd coat them with this aluminum copper graphite, I don't know, lithium compound shit instead of clean aviation grade engine oil. The manufacturer doesn't recommend using this compound in engines that vibrate a great deal because it could contribute to a loss of torque. Needless to say, that's what happened to this plane. Reasoner spent half the night looking into their maintenance records and their maintenance routines."

"But aren't these records checked by the government periodically, too?"

"All the time."

"Then what happened?"

"GrandAire's money didn't go for maintenance or to hire third-party contractors to perform maintenance. Their money went to pay inspectors to overlook all that."

"Who found this out?"

"Reasoner. I could go on and on."

"Save your breath," Callan said. "I bet the FBI and other authorities already know about much of that. Paeng said that three employees on Reasoner's side of the shop were recently arrested. I don't get it."

"Get what?"

"Reasoner. It seems rather peculiar to me that Reasoner finds out all these facts that were supposed to be his job to find out in the first place. Did he have anything to do with these corrupt practices?"

"As far as we can tell, he wasn't involved."

"As far as you can tell."

"Hey. I know you don't like the guy, Cal, but he wasn't involved."

"You seem pretty sure. What can I say? I had him pegged wrong. So tell me now. What is this about you and Reasoner? You wouldn't tell me at Navy Pier. I don't understand it."

"Not much of a story, Cal."

"Tell it."

"I was intimidated by Mark Reasoner at first. He was Cavanaugh's pet. He never got his ass chewed out like I did. He had a swanky education. He talked good and clean.

He didn't have a twang or say stupid things at fancy parties. I was out of my league coming up here to work at GrandAire."

"But you made something of yourself."

"Yeah," he laughed. "I made a mess out of our lives, of yours, of Marlene's, of Terese's."

"We learn from our mistakes, Lare. That's what counts."

"You know what I've learned? Even though Reasoner had all that going for him, he was just a pansy, and Cavanaugh knew it and played on it. Mark was so afraid that he'd mess up his perfect suburban world that he didn't challenge what he knew wasn't right."

"He wasn't the only person at GrandAire guilty of that."

"Are you talking about Ken Holloway?"

"No, I'm guilty, too."

"Now you're talking nonsense," Larry scolded. "What do you mean? Hell, you were the one that kept it in front of all of us until the truth was discovered."

"I don't care, Larry. It wasn't enough." Callan lifted his head and walked toward the window where the sun was trying to sneak through the cold February snow clouds. His dispirited spiel didn't last long, though. From down the hall came the sound of running footsteps. The men turned to see Gil sprinting toward them.

"Dad! Dad!"

Callan stepped anxiously toward his son, worried that something critical had happened to Terese.

"Dad! They took that tube out! Mom woke up! She's awake!"

Callan felt relieved, and his heart raced with elation at the news, but his conscience and guilt made him hesitate.

Larry noticed the hesitation and pointed toward Terese's room. "This is a chance to pick up on the future," he said confidently.

Callan thanked him and walked to the room. Standing in the hall out of eyesight, he strained to hear her voice and determine for himself that she was okay. He couldn't hear anything except Mrs. Beckman talking, asking her daughter several times how she was and if she needed anything. The only thing he could see were Gil and Brandon standing at the foot of the bed in eager anticipation to having their mother back to full health.

"Want to see the boys?" Callan heard Marie Beckman say.

Terese must have nodded or whispered a yes because in an instant, both boys disappeared from the foot of the bed.

Callan stepped closer to see as much as he could without allowing Terese to see him, but he couldn't see what he wanted. He couldn't see her smile, hear her voice, or know how she was responding. A low, reserved mood of laughter from inside the room comforted him. It was good to hear the levity. It must have meant that all was well after all. Content, Callan turned to walk toward the elevators.

"Psst, Cal," he heard quietly from behind.

Callan turned around to see Artie Beckman in the doorway, urging him to come back. "Come on in," he encouraged. "I think it would be fine."

"Thank you, Artie, but I think it would be too soon for her to see me right now."

"How can you say that? She needs you now more than ever."

"No, I know my wife. There are some things she needs to process before she can accept. I don't know if this accident is going to make her angry or grateful, and there are no guarantees how she'll feel about our relationship now. I want her to be ready to decide on her own time."

"I wish you'd reconsider."

When Artie saw that Callan's mind wasn't going to change, he added reluctantly, "Take care of yourself; take care of that arm; and if you change your mind or need anything, you know where to find us."

"Dad?"

Gil's voice called from the doorway, panic in his eyes at the thought of his father leaving.

Callan tried to explain why he had to go.

"But Mom just woke up. She's talking to us. Here's your chance."

"It's not about *my* chance, Gil. Trust me on this."

Although Gil didn't understand, he hugged his father and took his words by faith. The two walked in unison to the elevator. As the door opened, Callan was surprised to see a familiar face—Candice Reid.

Like Callan, Candice said she debated whether or not it was too soon to visit Terese. Unlike Callan, she had nothing to lose by visiting. She wasn't there to tell Terese, "I told you so." She wasn't there to hear about the details of the plane crash. She said she was simply there to let her friend know that she could be counted on for support in whatever she needed during her recovery. Candice also wanted to be there to help break the news of Ellen's death and to support Terese through the grief as best friends do—disagreements or not. The most important issue she believed Terese had to consider, though, was the one she couldn't help her with.

"And what issue is that?" Callan asked.

Candice touched his arm and answered his question by saying, "Give me some time with her first. I'd rather she tells you herself."

CHAPTER FORTY-FIVE

Packing wasn't one of Callan Morrow's strong suits, but he was resilient in his resolve to get it done. He had much to look forward to with the acceptance of a new job in west central Indiana; not only a new job, but a new career and a new outlook. The only thing that stood in his way was packing.

He took a break to look out the window toward the long row of houses along Putnam Street. As always, the street was quiet and unpretentious. He opened the window to get closer to the feel of the city and the smell of spring, took a deep breath and exhaled slowly, pleased that he had a new beginning.

Peripheral movement on the street caught his eye. He strained to see what or who it was. Two people, a man and a woman, walked casually to the entrance of the Wingate-Powers below. He couldn't hear well, but he could hear enough to know the woman was arguing. Her partner had parked too far away when there were plenty of places near the entrance. She pointed to one such space.

"It's not cold. The walk did us good," he said as they entered the foyer.

Callan laughed. He waited to hear the foyer buzzer, beckoning him to grant them access to the building, but none came. Instead, he heard the clomping of footsteps and the *rat tat tat* of a familiar knock at his door. It would be Mrs. Powers, he guessed, and he was right. He greeted his landlady, unable to hide a smirk.

"Mr. Morrow, I'm sorry to disturb you, but I caught a couple of suspicious prowlers outside my door. The only tenant in my building that seems to attract such unsavory individuals is you, so I brought them to you straight away."

Callan laughed at Mrs. Powers' well-played role. "How kind of you," he said. "Would you all like to come in?"

"No, the sight of you packing breaks my heart. I can't accept your invitation."

The old woman turned to address Aysha and Paeng. "But I will accept yours," she said gleefully.

Aysha smiled. "I'm so pleased."

Callan ushered the couple in.

Aysha wasted no time entering and looking at each pile of objects. "I don't know why you're even bothering, Cal," she said, lifting a towel that covered a half-dozen plastic margarine containers. "I'd throw out most of this stuff. How can you pack with a broken arm and poor taste?"

"Hey! Those little containers hold scoops of leftover gravy or bolts that came off things that I can't remember what I took apart. Besides, they're the only containers from the kitchen that have lids."

"I'm not even going into the kitchen. How's your arm, by the way?" She picked up a small sack and looked inside.

"My arm's better, thanks for asking, and stop looking through my things." Callan grabbed the sack from her

337

hands and tossed it on top of a pile with the margarine cups. "Is this why you drove all the way out to Oak Park? To torture me in my last days? And what was that dialogue with Mrs. Powers?"

"I invited her to your farewell party. We'd like to invite you, too, if you'd be nice long enough for me to do so. After all, you are the guest of honor."

Callan grinned. "So I take it you invited all my friends to this little shindig?"

"Cal, the only friends you've made in Chicago these past few months have been either arrested or will be indicted soon. You have that special way with people. Nevertheless, being the city's greatest party planner that I am, I managed to pull a few rabbits out of my hat. Your entry into the academic rankings as a college professor is worth celebrating, it appears."

Paeng asked how Callan made the transition to academics. "I thought you'd return to banking, since you know that industry well."

Callan explained that the events of the GrandAire investigation gained national attention quickly. As a result, two employment opportunities followed. One was with a consulting firm specializing in forensic accounting. The other was from Vermillion College, a liberal arts school in west central Indiana. Not only did the position include teaching a forensic accounting and auditing class, but administration was eager to establish a forensic accounting curriculum to attract new, young students and to address a growing national problem related to financial fraud. The idea behind the school's thought was to provide a pool of well-educated individuals to meet the concerning trend.

Callan talked about the opportunity, then asked Aysha, "What happened to the director of marketing promotion you got at GrandAire? Didn't it work out?"

"Are you kidding? There wasn't any promotion, Callan. It wasn't real. Carol announced it just to throw me off so I wouldn't suspect the demise she and Alan had planned for me."

"I'm sorry, Aysha."

She shrugged it off. "Forget it. GrandAire wasn't me. I thought it was, but it wasn't. I've landed on my feet in much better shape than I ever dreamed. I've accepted a position with a large marketing firm downtown. I'll be starting at an entry level, but the experience will be worth it."

"She's going to be tough to live with now, Paeng," Callan said, giving him a lighthearted look of sympathy.

"Don't feel sorry for him," she said scornfully.

Paeng nodded proudly. "I was accepted into the Academy at Quantico."

Aysha gave the context: "The exposure of the GrandAire examination brought him some attention. The FBI realised he was a good candidate for their Criminal Investigative Division. They were impressed by his solid research: his ability to accumulate comprehensive facts and evidence, and accept constructive criticism from his colleagues. And his computer technology skills and foreign language proficiency are skills they're actively recruiting to fill a void in their program."

"We do have reason to celebrate, don't we?" Callan exclaimed. "Too bad we don't have anything to toast with!"

"We'll have plenty at your party, Cal. We'll celebrate there."

CHAPTER FORTY-SIX

Larry and Marlene arrived promptly at the Wingate-Powers to walk with Callan to Argos' for his farewell party. Marlene tucked her hand under Larry's arm as they strolled the few blocks down Oak Park Boulevard, her hair flying back across her shoulders.

Callan glanced at the alcove across the street from the restaurant and wondered how long it would be before any of them would be able to walk down a street, work late in an office, or enjoy a cool drink at a café table without thinking of impending danger. He tried to shrug the eeriness from his mind, but two unresolved issues plagued him: the disappearance of Carlotta Mendoza and the identity of the informant within GrandAire to the advocates at Kerlin Bender.

Larry was even more interested than Callan in determining the identity of the informant. "Mark Reasoner and Mary DeFrantz are both plausible," he said.

"Even Downing herself," Callan offered.

"Marcia Downing?"

"Certainly! Wasn't she a stickler about access to files, systems, and the physical layout of her department? Was she like that because she was internal-control conscious, or was she trying to preserve uncorrupted data that she knew would be helpful to authorities? Wasn't she the one who had access to all the critical data that we eventually uncovered?"

Larry frowned thoughtfully. "I just thought she was obsessed with following policies. It didn't occur to me there might be a reason why she was so diligent."

"Precisely," Callan said, "making her a perfect informant."

Larry nodded, appearing pleased at the hypothesis.

Callan looked through the windows of Argos' to see who had gathered in his honor. The familiar faces of the friends and acquaintances he'd gotten to know over the past few months were animated with a jovial spirit.

Aysha and Paeng met them at the door.

The crowd turned to applaud as Callan walked toward them.

Brandon poked his younger brother in the back. "Hey, runt, it's Dad."

The poke was the only enticement Gil needed to nudge his way through the gathering to his father. Callan gave him a long, zealous hug and asked him how he made it to Chicago. Callan secretly hoped Terese had accompanied the boys to the party and was hiding somewhere nearby.

Gil's disposition turned sour. "Brandon drove."

"That's not so bad, is it?" Callan asked.

He watched as his youngest left to join two boys whom Cal didn't recognize. The boys inhaled a plate of loukamathas, a sweet, round doughnut pastry that was placed before them with promises of more. After serving the plate, the waitress approached Cal, who stood alone surrounded by conversation and laughter.

"I'm going to miss seeing you here at Argos'," she said. "I expect my income is going to be cut in half now that you won't be coming in anymore."

Callan assured her that Larry would still need his barstool therapy sessions.

Suddenly, a familiar voice called from behind the waitress. "I'm sure you'll miss him, dear, but not as much as me."

"Who's that?" Callan teased, knowing full well who it was.

Bernadette Powers emerged, arms outstretched. Callan received her hug, catching a whiff of *Forever Krystle*, the familiar fragrance that reminded him of her. The lines on the woman's face were not as pronounced as they were in the darkness of her dreary parlor the night she'd spotted a prowler around her apartment building. Her eyes had life for the first time in many months. Callan was delighted to see that she no longer had the burden of worry.

No sooner did he express his relief when she broke into a monologue about the anxiety she'd suffer not knowing if he was going to be okay.

"But the point is not to worry at all, Mrs. Powers," he said, holding her dearly. "You have inside you what it takes to deal with your apprehension and concerns. You have a beautiful spirit and a wonderful compassion. I wish you could allow yourself to be comforted by a Spirit that cares for *you* in the same way."

Mrs. Powers looked quizzically at Cal as he took both of her hands in his and recited one of his favorite verses from *Philippians* that expressed the sentiment he wanted her to hear. She smiled respectfully and took a step back. She promised nothing, just lifted her arms and placed her hands around the back of Callan's neck to draw him down so she could kiss the side of his face one more time.

As she quietly walked away, Wynetta Argos took Callan's hand. "She needed to hear that, Callan, whether she'll follow it or not. I know you feel bad, perhaps even guilty about the chain of events that happened and how they affected everyone in this room, but you brought new life for many of us—especially two old women."

"You've always had life, Mrs. Argos. I did nothing new."

"You brought a new spirit to me, though. I'm determined not to be content with the unacceptable any longer. These events helped me look at my friendship with Bernadette differently, too. I didn't realize how lonely she is. She fills her life with worry and anxiety to fill the void. I'm going to be a better friend and visit her more often."

Callan embraced her. "Mrs. Argos, I feel like Dorothy to the scarecrow in *The Wizard of Oz* when I say I'm going to miss you most of all."

"No, you'll be too busy to miss me. Besides, you'll be back to see me, I'm sure. Unlike Bernadette, I hunt down those who neglect me." Her son passed behind her with two plates of appetizers, and she called out, "Isn't that right, Georgie?"

"You, Mama? Hell, that Ted Warmke was a pipsqueak at hunting people down compared to you." George returned to the bar and called through the door to the kitchen, "Cecilia, bring out another plate of chicken and some more of the spanakopita and tiropita, will you?"

Callan looked at Mrs. Argos with a surprised look on his face. "Did I hear George call Cecilia's name?"

Just then, Cecilia Mendoza came through the double swinging doors of the kitchen with two plates brimming with Mediterranean cuisine.

Wynetta smiled broadly. "Yes. I did a little meddling. I looked her up, and I said to her that I needed some help for today."

"Did you now?"

"Well, maybe not so much that I needed the help, but I figured you needed to have a word with her, so I did it anyway."

"Mrs. Argos, the FBI is doing just fine in their investigation of Carlotta's disappearance. There's no need for you to meddle."

The old woman lifted her finger in the air to interrupt. "Aw, but just in case."

Cecilia recognized Callan immediately and shook his hand.

Callan looked into the young woman's eyes and saw innocence and peace beaming back as if she was pleased and contented with the events of her life. Of all the people in the room, Cecilia should have been the one person who was disheartened and frustrated by an issue left unresolved—the disappearance of her sister.

"If I regret anything, it's that we haven't yet located Carlotta," he said sincerely.

Cecilia closed her eyes. For a moment, it appeared that she had something she wanted to say.

"What is it?" he asked. "Cecilia, if you know something, you have to tell us."

She opened her eyes.

This time, Callan saw fear and defiance. He reached into his pocket and pulled out a piece of scrap paper. She handed him a pen from her waitress cloak and watched him jot down his phone number. He added Aysha's number, too. "Here," he said, handing her the piece of paper and her pen.

She didn't want to take it. "No; no more questions; no more prodding into the past." She looked at Callan pleadingly.

"Take it, Cecilia. You're not fooling anyone, especially not me. You may be afraid to have Carlotta come back to Chicago because you don't believe she's completely out of danger. I understand that, but you have to understand that valuable time and resources are being used to search for someone who may not be missing. I want you to think about that. When you do, I want you to picture the countless number of other women who have sisters who are missing out there that we're unable to find because we're devoting our efforts on your wild goose chase. When you dig deep enough into your heart to tell us the truth, give us a call." He repeated the instructions and waited for her to tell him that she understood.

"May I go?" she whispered. "I need to help Mr. Argos."

Callan nodded and watched her move around the back of the bar to the kitchen. He looked at the floor, hoping to find answers. Instead, all he found was a balled-up napkin Cecilia had wadded in her hand and dropped between his feet. He kicked it around a few times to make sense out of what Cecilia Mendoza was hiding, what the truth really was.

"That's tough," a female voice said softly.

He looked up. It was Mary DeFrantz.

"I'm not sure I'm buying her silence," she said. "Do you?"

"No, but at least I'm glad to know Carlotta's okay, that she wasn't murdered. I'm content with that for now."

345

"Is that what she confessed?"

"No, but she doesn't have to tell me. I can read it in her." Callan turned to his colleague and took her hand. "You were a trooper through all this, Mary. Thanks for putting up with all my antics."

"No," she laughed, accepting a Cabernet from a waitress. "I can honestly tell you that I was not a trooper. I was more like a pooper, let the truth be known. What you do for a living is not my bag. Give me a general ledger and a hot cup of coffee. That's all the excitement I need for the day."

"You don't really mean that."

"Oh, yes, I really do. It's comforting to know that Tony will be more diligent in his responsibilities because of what happened. Hopefully, he'll hold us all more accountable for the checks and balances in the system. That part I don't mind doing."

"Take good care, Mary," he said as they embraced. "Always believe good things will come."

She nodded and let him go, indicating a woman standing beside them.

The woman was Candice Reid. He gave her a hug that she ardently returned.

"I have a surprise," she said. "I want you to meet someone, a stranger of sorts."

CHAPTER FORTY-SEVEN

Callan looked ahead to where Candice directed him. Sometime during the conversations with the many guests who'd come to bid him farewell, Terese had slipped into a seat by the windows, her back facing them. Halfway to the table, Candice stepped away so Callan could make his approach alone.

"Candice said you're a stranger in these parts," he said, approaching cautiously.

Terese smiled and gestured for him to have a seat.

"You look nice," he said.

"Is that your best pickup line to strangers?"

"It's better to be conservative, I've learned. Listen first, talk later."

"I believe you're entirely right. I've learned that, too, recently."

"I can't believe there was anything for you to learn. You look like the type of woman to have been right all along."

"I am," she said teasingly, "but I have this friend who learns the hard way, and I'm taking some lessons from her."

"A friend?"

She smiled.

"That's interesting, because I have this buddy—professional, nice family, fairly intelligent, *very* good looking."

"Really?" she asked.

"Oh, yeah," Callan said confidently. "Just ask any one of the people in this restaurant. They'll tell you that he's been stalked and hunted in recent months. It couldn't be for anything but his good looks."

Terese laughed at the insanity of Callan's humor.

"Sounds intriguing," she replied, regaining composure. "I bet my friend would like this guy."

"Yes, I believe she would, but I have to admit, he's a bit arrogant. He lets his arrogance get in the way of his true passion."

"I can't imagine any man doing that."

"Sometimes it happens," he said. "His true passion is the love of his life, but the fool let her slip away."

Terese reached out and touched his hand. "Not to worry. My friend's a bit arrogant, too. She thought her man should be totally at her beck and call. She asked him to choose between her and his greater passion."

"Oh, but there should be no greater passion," Callan challenged, "and it shouldn't have consumed him."

"How I wish life was that simple for our friends. As much as my friend wishes life had clearer answers of yes or no, right or wrong, it isn't that way. In fact, I think my friend was a hypocrite in many ways."

"Whatever are you talking about?"

"My father said to me in the hospital that you came to see me. You were there everyday until I woke up. He said he urged you to stay to be with me, but you wouldn't. He said you wanted to give me time and space to sort things out first."

"Yes, that's true."

"I was surprised that he asked you to come in."

"I don't understand."

"All I kept thinking was about that money he gave to you—no, to both of us—that we lost in a business venture that went sour. I wondered why he wasn't still angry with us—especially to you—for what happened."

"What did he say?"

"He said, 'It was a gift, sweetheart.' He said he loved us so much that he wanted us to see our dreams succeed. He said he knew you didn't squander the money. He'd lived long enough to know that some business ventures fail despite a person's best efforts."

Callan didn't say anything. He was humbled by what he heard.

"I remember telling you when you started looking into the source of the Monon crash that sometimes things happen without reason and you can drive yourself crazy trying to find the answers. Things happen. Sometimes there's a reason that's obvious, sometimes there's not, but there's always a reason. I'm so grateful you stuck with the Monon investigation, Callan. Getting to the source of the crash made a difference."

"But what about your father's money?"

"It doesn't matter. We tried. We failed, but we didn't go bankrupt or lose our house or anything. Father was happy to lend us the money unconditionally. There are instances when finding fault doesn't make a difference. What happened to Father's money and the business venture doesn't matter to me anymore."

Callan looked into her eyes and understood more of what she wanted him to see. "So what do you think we should tell these friends of ours?" he asked. "Do they deserve a second chance?"

"They may," Terese replied. "Yes, I think we should recommend it. Perhaps they can talk about it later, someplace quieter."

"A place where there are not so many people looking at them?" he asked, noticing that practically everyone was trying not to look in their direction, yet couldn't help but do so.

Terese laughed. "Are they really?"

Callan smiled.

She squeezed his hand tighter. "Red would be proud of you ... and very pleased," she said. "He'd thank you, too. I know he would."

Callan nodded and thanked her for saying so, then someone entering the restaurant suddenly diverted his attention. "Will you excuse me, dear?"

Velma Hofmeyer stood inside the doorway, looking around as if wondering how to proceed into the party.

Callan gave Terese a gentle kiss and held her hand as far as her arm could stretch as he walked toward the executive assistant. He extended his hand to Velma and squeezed it gently to draw her near, delighted that Larry had the foresight to invite her to the gathering. He told him so when Larry joined the two of them.

"Nonsense," Larry said. "It would've been lunacy not to have her here. Why, Ms. Hofmeyer has been through as much as we have."

"And the challenges continue, don't they?" Callan asked her. "I hear that Hamilton Perry resigned recently."

"Yes," she said, "but he was asked to do so. I believe the board saw fit to have him replaced."

"I'm sorry," he said, remembering how close she and Mr. Perry had worked together.

"Oh, please, Mr. Morrow, don't pity me. The truth of the matter is that he often angered me because of his indifference. I don't believe people who are indifferent should be surprised when people who make a difference try to do so and succeed." Velma looked to the small group of women that included Candice Reid and Mary DeFrantz who were laughing and exchanging quips with Terese in the center of the room. She turned to Callan. "And that goes for spouses, too."

"What did you just say?"

"I said, that goes for spouses, too."

"No," Callan said, "before that. You said people who are indifferent shouldn't be surprised when people who make a difference try to do so and succeed."

"Excuse me?"

"You weren't talking about Larry or me, were you?"

She didn't respond.

"You were talking about yourself," Callan said. "You also made a difference."

Velma Hofmeyer bowed her head modestly.

"You were the one person who could forward information to Kirklin Bender in such a way that no one would ever suspect."

Larry looked taken off guard by Callan's comments. "I don't understand," he said. "Cal, I thought you said the informant was Marcia Downing?"

"Obviously not."

Velma lowered her voice. "Until the trials are over and all who are guilty are sentenced, I'll limit my comments and use discretion in what I say."

"Then it is true."

"It was a difficult task to pull off at times. I'm surprised someone from within GrandAire didn't suspect me before now. I always believed Carol Chambers thought I was up to something."

"How did your relationship with Kirklin Bender come about?"

"I knew Murray Thompson quite well when he worked for Mr. Cavanaugh, much in the same way as I know you two. I retained our friendship after his departure and sent packages to him periodically. You saw me one day in the lobby, Mr. Morrow, carrying a package that I was sending to Mr. Thompson. I thought for sure you thought it odd and suspected something."

"No, Velma, you play all of your roles very well."

"Then I believe Carol was the only individual within the company who knew my story."

"Your story?"

"Yes, she was close to a discovery of my role, but you provided the necessary diversion to keep my identity secret, Mr. Southard."

"Me?" Larry asked. "What did I do?"

"Northwoods Aeronautics was a much more viable and believable informant candidate than me when you started that company. When they discovered your invoices and that some files were missing, Ms. Chambers and Mr. Cavanaugh switched their attention from me to your consulting business as the way information was being released from the airlines to the law firm in Austin. I'm very sorry the consequences of their inquiry ended the way it did with Mr. Pierceman's death. It just went to show what serious trouble we were all in from what was going on in GrandAire."

"I don't understand, Velma," Callan said. "What did Carol Chambers know about you that would make you such a plausible informant suspect? I always suspected something between you and Carol, but I could never put my finger on it."

Velma avoided looking at the men's eyes. She paused and swallowed before continuing, "Like you, Mr. Morrow, I followed the proceedings of the Monon litigation after the accident. I followed all of it. I was an advocate for change in the way testing was performed by aircraft manufacturers. I believe Ms. Chambers became curious as to why a person in my position would be interested in such technical operational activities as proper aircraft maintenance, testing, and inspections. She became curious as to why I even cared. Perhaps I was imprudent or arrogant at being so well versed that I gave myself away to her."

"I don't see how that connects the dots."

"She also knew I was a widow."

"A widow?"

"Through her own investigation, she discovered that my husband, who often commuted between Chicago and Indianapolis for his job, was on the Midland flight."

"No," Callan exclaimed.

"Yes, he lost his life at Monon." Velma closed her eyes and took a deep breath. "She never trusted me, I'm afraid. She was fearful that in my capacity as Mr. Perry's executive assistant I was not an objective employee of the company. Though she had many illegal and misguided thoughts, her distrust of me was well-founded. Her biggest mistake, though, was that she underestimated me."

Larry nodded. "You've done some great things, Velma, and you've done GrandAire passengers a great service by not letting your spirit wane, but we have a lot of work ahead of us in the company to regain our customers' confidence."

"I'm ready for it, Mr. Southard." At that, she turned to Callan solemnly. "Mr. Morrow, I regret that I won't be seeing you Monday morning. It would be so nice to have you back, but I understand that you have a new and exciting venture of your own in academia. I do hope it won't keep you away from Chicago for too long. I presume I'll see you again sometime, somewhere in the future?"

Cal laughed at the question posed to him more as an ominous forecast than as an invitation. "Yes, Velma, you may presume it," he said. "In fact, as we accountants and auditors say, you can count on it."

A Note from the Author

Did you enjoy my book?

If so, I would be very grateful if you could write a review and publish it at your point of purchase. Your review, even a brief one, will help other readers to decide whether or not they'll enjoy my work.

Do you want to be notified of new releases?

If so, please sign up to the AIA Publishing email list. You'll find the sign-up button on the right-hand side under the photo at **www.aiapublishing.com**. Of course, your information will never be shared, and the publisher won't inundate you with emails, just let you know of new releases.

Acknowledgements

You only live once, but if you do it right, once is enough.
Mae West is credited for that quote. It's one of my favorites. I've been fortunate in my life to not only live by that mantra but also surround myself with individuals who live physically, intellectually and spiritually by that mantra as well.

I've waited a long time for this book to be finished so that I could thank my good friend Valita Fredland for the inspirational discussions we used to have about finding our true passion in life. This book touches on the human passion inside each of us—with all of its virtues and conflicts. Valita is an individual who squeezes as much life as she can out of each day. Her professional strength and integrity balanced by her personal love for life are virtues I've admired and remembered as I wrote this book.

Mikel May is another one of those individuals. I would be remiss in not thanking him for his technical expertise in reviewing excerpts of my manuscript. Mikel was a former crew chief with the U.S. Air Force, a former pilot for ATA Airlines, and is now a captain for the world's largest operator of private jets. What I appreciate the most about Mikel is his technical proficiency and knowledge of piloting balanced with his love for a great story. I owe the air crash scene into Lake Michigan toward the end of the novel to Mikel for making it more realistic and exciting. I couldn't be happier with it.

Other than my family, no one has inspired me more to keep writing through the years and to publish my works than my good friend Marcia Gonzales. The character Rafael "Paeng" Ramirez came from discussions with Marcia. We would laugh for hours over the absurdities of corporate life. Our work as compliance officers was often filled with tense and complex cases, but we never failed to balance gravity with levity in everything we did.

Finally, I must give tremendous credit to Tahlia Newland of New South Wales, Australia, Charles Ray of the USA, and Kevin Berry of Christchurch, New Zealand, for their expertise in perfecting the manuscript and for giving me insight to make future manuscripts worth reading.

Although I started writing the story in McCordsville, Indiana, near Indianapolis, I wrote the majority of the novel at my home in Old Metairie, Lousiana. Indianapolis was the catalyst for developing my characters and capturing their individual passion in their roles, but New Orleans brought the characters to life for me. I sat many an evening at The Chartres House in the French Quarter, eating great food, drinking Abita brew, and watching a multitude of individuals pass by the open doors of the restaurant as I wrote, allowing the conversations and actions of the characters to develop.

When I needed or wanted to get away, I found other sources of inspiration. The waves near my beach home in Gulf Shores cleared the clutter in my mind so that I could think more clearly about the plot or make revisions as necessary to improve the manuscript. I wrote in Pensacola, Palm Beach, St. Petersburg, and Jacksonville in

Florida, but I also created scenes in Chicago, Charlotte, San Antonio, Austin, New York City, Washington, D.C., Nashville, Louisville, and St. Louis; whenever I had a moment wherever I was. A long weekend alone in a remote neck of the woods near Belfast, Maine, was the perfect setting for writing the winter scenes.

It was Pearl, Mississippi, however, where I met a young waitress of color who asked to read a sample of what I had written as I sat at the counter with a cold drink in my hand. I was her only patron. It was hot, sunny, and lethargic outside; stuffy and close inside. Beads of perspiration slid effortlessly from her temples as she read. When she finished, she returned the pages to me with a far away look in her eyes. I asked her what she was thinking.

"I hope you finish this," she said. I promised her I would. She smiled and with conviction replied, "Good, because it makes me want to write something, too; a story inside of me that needs to be told."

That was the best inspiration of all.

Gary Lee Edward Kreigh.
Gulf Shores, Alabama.

CPSIA information can be obtained
at www.ICGtesting.com
Printed in the USA
BVHW081613151219
566735BV00001B/26/P